Into the Fire

OTHER BOOKS AND BOOKS ON CASSETTE
BY JEFFREY S. SAVAGE:

Cutting Edge

Into the Fire

a novel

JEFFREY S. SAVAGE

Covenant Communications, Inc.

Covenant

Cover image © 2002 PhotoDisc, Inc.

Cover design copyrighted 2002 by Covenant Communications, Inc.

Published by Covenant Communications, Inc.
American Fork, Utah

Printed in Canada
First Printing: July 2002

09 08 07 06 05 04 03 02   10 9 8 7 6 5 4 3 2 1

ISBN 1-59156-042-X

Library of Congress Cataloging-in-Publication Data

Savage, Jeffrey S., 1963-
    Into the fire / Jeffrey S. Savage.
        p. cm.
    ISBN 1-59156-042-X
    1. Businessmen--Fiction. 2. Mormon families--Fiction. 3. Business failures--Fiction. 4. Cancer--
Patients--Fiction. 5. Missing children--Fiction. I. Title.

    PS3619.A83 I58 2002
    813'.6--dc21   2002067396

To everyone who struggles with adversity and has the courage and faith to trust in the will of God.

ACKNOWLEDGMENTS

Writing *Into the Fire* has been an experience both emotionally and physically draining. During the time I worked on it, I came to rely heavily on the support of my family and friends. It is with a deep sense of gratitude that I recall all of the support that so many individuals provided.

Special thanks to my parents Dick and Vicki Savage, and my brothers and sisters for their unwavering support and valuable insights. Kathy and Deanne, you are both awesome and your advice was always appreciated. Steve, thanks so much for the trip up to the cabin and the technical advice you provided. Next time, let's just make sure that the cabin is not occupied by a family with two killer dogs.

To the members of a truly fantastic critique group: Stephanni Hicken, LuAnn Staheli, Annette Lyon, and Michelle Holmes; as always your help is invaluable. Thanks to Angela Colvin for her great editing, and to Bill Sheehy of Santa Teresa High School for instilling the spark so many years ago.

Finally, as always, none of the stories would be possible without my wife and children. Erica, Scott, Jacob, and Nicholas, you guys really are the best. Jennifer, you are my inspiration, my first and last audience, and my reason for being. I love you forever.

PROLOGUE[1]

There was a man in the valley of microchips and disks, whose name was Joe; and that man, like most of us, was trying to do what was right.

He feared God and was honest and upright in his business dealings. He went to the temple, paid his tithing on time, and made it out to visit his home teaching families, albeit often on the last day of the month.

He married a wonderful woman who brought music and laughter into their home and made everyone who visited them feel welcome. They had three children—a lovely daughter, who had just been accepted to BYU on a scholarship; a son, who was hanging out with the wrong crowd in his high school (but didn't all kids go through a phase like that at one time or another in their lives?); and a blonde-haired, blue-eyed surprise of a daughter who had been born with what the world called a disability, but who had a spirit so strong and bright that on the day she left premortality to come to earth, the other sprits there mourned her loss, brief as it would be, and the earth rejoiced at her coming.

Joe's substance was significant, having founded one of the most successful networking hardware firms in the valley. He lived in a house that had graced the covers of several local architectural magazines, and drove a car with heated leather seats and a GPS navigation system that could instantly tell him how to get to anywhere in the continental U.S. and Canada. He regularly donated to the local charities, several of whose boards he served on, and was well respected by those both inside and outside of the Church.

Now there was a day when the sons of God came to present themselves before the Lord, and Satan came also among them.

And the Lord said unto Satan, "Whence comest thou?"

Then Satan answered the Lord and said, "From going to and fro in the earth, and from walking up and down in it."

And the Lord cast His eyes round about, and His gaze fell upon a certain man, a man who could be further purified and strengthened through the fires of adversity. And He said unto Satan, "Hast though considered my servant Joe? He is an upright man, one that feareth God and escheweth evil."

Then Satan answered the Lord and said, "Doth Joe fear God for nought?

"Hast not thou made an hedge about him, and about his house, and about all that he hath on every side? Thou hast blessed the work of his hands, and his substance is increased in the land.

"But put forth thine hand now, and touch all that he hath, and he will curse thee to thy face."

And the Lord, in His infinite wisdom, knew that Satan had underestimated Joe and He said unto Satan, "Behold all that he hath is in thy power."

So Satan went forth from the presence of the Lord, laughing evilly as he prepared to execute his plans. Dark mists roiled around him as he called forth his minions, and his voice rolled and crashed as thunder as he sent them to earth to do his bidding.

With a flick of his finger, as though shooing away a gnat, he watched with delight as Joe's worldly possessions were snatched from him. With an icy breath, he stripped Joe of his titles, and turned the respect of his peers into derision. Finally he reached forth his hand and closed it around Joe's wife and children, meaning to crush them in his powerful fist.

But then something unexpected happened. Joe pulled his family to him with the strength of iron bands, and in a voice so quiet that it was almost inaudible even to himself, he spoke four words. But the words carried with them a faith that had lain dormant inside him for years, a faith that only the very real possibility of losing his family could call forth. And the words which he spoke echoed off of the steel and glass walls of the valley's buildings and struck at the very ground upon which Satan and his servants stood.

And hearing them, Satan trembled.

NOTES

[1] See Job chapter one.

CHAPTER 1

The day the sky fell on Joe Stewart started out just like any other day, that is, pretty much perfect as far as he was concerned. At 6:30 A.M. the CD player on his alarm clock clicked on, and waves of violin music washed across the spacious bedroom that he and his wife, Heather, shared. He had loved classical music for as long as he could remember. One of his earliest recollections was of his mother lying on the living room floor beside him one afternoon, he could have been no more than three at the time, as they listened to an especially beautiful piece that he thought might have been Tchaikovsky.

"Close your eyes," she had whispered to him, "and imagine that you can fly. Let the music carry you anywhere you want." The two of them had lain side by side, silently lost in their own worlds. For him, the strings had been the energy, the source of all motion. The brass were powerful crosswinds that tossed him wildly across the sky, the woodwinds updrafts, rocketing him above the clouds and then plummeting him back toward the earth. To this day, when he closed his eyes and listened to the evocative strains of an especially good concerto, he could feel his spirits float skyward.

"Okay Superman, rise and shine." Heather rocked his shoulder, spoiling the imagery, and then padded into the bathroom where Joe could hear the spray of water against glass as she turned on the shower.

Groaning, he rubbed one palm across his stubbly cheek and rolled out of bed. Below, the metallic rattling of a whisk tapping against the side of a mixing bowl signaled that Tia Sanchez was down in the kitchen beginning to prepare breakfast. Joe's stomach growled, anticipating the aroma of sautéing onions and peppers and frying sausage that would begin wafting up the stairs over the next few minutes. It was Friday morning, which, in the Stewart household, meant Denver omelets.

He had just enough time, he thought, for a few laps in the pool before eating if he hurried. Quickly changing into a pair of swim trunks that sported yellow and blue dolphins swimming across them, he draped a towel over his shoulders and then stopped for a quick glance in the mirror. Not bad for a man in his midforties. His gut wasn't exactly washboard material, but on the other hand it wasn't hanging out over his trunks either, like a lot of the guys at the office. Other than a painful rash on his upper thigh, that he'd been trying to get rid of for the last week without success, he thought he looked pretty good. When he and Heather took their daughter Debbie to BYU this fall, he wouldn't even be surprised if some of the girls in the dorm mistook him for her older brother. But then, allowing his gaze to travel up to the wrinkles that had gathered around the corners of his eyes over the years, and the loose skin beginning to sag beneath his chin, he conceded that he would have to be a *much* older brother.

"Okay, so I may not look like an older brother. But hey, isn't there something to be said for being the totally hot-looking father?" he asked his reflection.

"Totally hot?" Heather stepped out of the shower and slipped up behind him. "I'm afraid that the kids would consider that a contradiction in terms. You can't be *totally hot* if you're old enough to say 'totally hot.' I think you have to be 'tight'." She grinned up at him in the mirror and patted him on the rear.

"I'm not sure I could ever think of *tight* as a compliment," he said, turning to face her. "How about 'rad'?"

"Way out of date." She gave a quick shake of her head. "Might as well try for 'groovy'."

Heather was four years younger than Joe. The kid sister of his best friend in high school, he'd barely noticed her until he returned from his mission—finding that the scrawny little thing who'd tagged along behind them at dances and youth activities had grown up in the two years that he'd been gone. *She was a knockout when I married her*, he thought, *and if anything the last twenty years have only made her more beautiful.*

Her reddish-blonde hair was wrapped turban-style in a dark blue towel, with only a few wisps escaping out from under the edges, and he could just make out the floral scent of the shampoo she had washed it with. Beneath the towel, her bright green eyes crinkled with good humor, something he hadn't seen much over the last eighteen months. It was good to see her smiling again.

When the doctors had first diagnosed her breast cancer, it had been a terrible shock to all of them. It felt as though they had gone through every emotion imaginable—from disbelief to terror, and finally to a kind of numb acceptance. But through it all, Heather had been the tough one, able to adapt, when it felt to Joe like the whole world had just crumbled around them. She had even managed to retain her sense of humor during the initial surgeries and the chemo, although it had made her so sick that she could barely get out of bed some days.

But when they learned that the tumors had returned—that she would need to undergo a double mastectomy, something inside of her had finally broken. It was as if the reserves of strength that had carried her for so long had finally run dry. The woman he had known and loved for more than half his life had disappeared, replaced by a shadow that stayed locked in the house, unwilling or unable to let him help her.

Joe had taken six months off of work, taking her to the best doctors money could buy and, with Tia's invaluable help, caring for the children. They had tried everything from counseling to acupuncture. But the services and medications the doctors provided had done nothing to keep her from sliding ever deeper into the abyss, and finally she refused to see them at all, positive that they were only making things worse. As the months passed, Joe became more and more desperately afraid that he was going to lose her forever to whatever darkness had claimed her.

He thought that it might have been little Angela who finally brought Heather around. Holding her mother's hands for hours at a time, talking to her in the breathy slurred syllables that Heather had always been the best at translating, and crooning songs whose melodies were sometimes recognizable, but just as often not, she was the only one who seemed able to get through. It was as if deep in her Down syndrome–clouded mind, Angela knew that it was her chance to repay her mother for all the time Heather had spent helping her over the first six years of her life. Heather's recovery had been a struggle, and while she still had her bad days, Joe thought that just as her body had beaten the cancer into remission, her spirit was fighting the depression too.

Wrapping his arms around her still-wet shoulders, he began to pull her toward him until he felt her body tense beneath her damp towel, turning in his embrace so that her shoulder butted up against his chest. *Stupid,* he thought. How could he have forgotten how sensitive she was about physical contact near the scars that marked where her breasts had once been? It was just seeing her so much like her old self, that for a moment he had let slip from his mind the pain that was still hidden so close to the surface.

"I'm sorry," he fumbled, raising his hands up from her shoulders to caress her face.

Shaking her head, she clasped his hands between fingers that still looked so thin and fragile to him, and pressed them to her lips. "It's not your fault. I'm really all right. It just that sometimes I feel so . . ." she struggled to articulate the thought, finally shrugging her shoulders and dropping her hands in frustration.

They had come so far, but sometimes it still seemed like there was a brick wall between them. Not a physical barrier. That was something they could deal with. Many times over the years Joe's work had forced them to be apart for a week or two at a time, and they had dealt with the separation, if not accepting it, then at least bearing it. But this was more insidious. It was a communication barrier—a connection barrier. Joe knew that his wife loved him and thought she knew as much about his love for her. But since her depression, sometimes all they could do was stare silently at each other, standing only inches away from one another, and yet they might as well have been on opposite sides of the universe for all the good it did them.

They were saved from the awkward silence by the sound of pounding feet coming up the stairs outside their bedroom. Heather smiled up at Joe, the tension now broken, and pushed him toward the bathroom door while she reached for her robe.

"I think you are about to be assailed," she said.

With a mock sigh, Joe turned and headed back into the bedroom, but they both knew that this was the highlight of his morning. He had scarcely stepped into the room before a towheaded missile dressed in red, footed pajamas launched herself at him with a shout that would have done a Comanche proud.

"Addy, addy!" Angela fearlessly plowed at full speed into Joe, and then whooped with glee as he took her in his arms and spun her up into the air. *No father*, he thought, *could ever hope for a better welcome.* Every morning it was the same. Angela was always overjoyed, as though it had been months instead of hours since she had last seen him. And no matter how difficult a day he might have had at work, he couldn't help smiling as he neared home, knowing that she would be waiting—her blue, almond-shaped eyes opened wide with excitement—to leap on him the moment he walked through the door.

Settling her back down to the floor, he brushed her curly blonde hair back out of her eyes and with a look of great seriousness he knelt in front of her and asked, "Did you sleep well last night?"

"Yes," she answered back, equally serious.

"You didn't get eaten by any monsters?" Joe continued earnestly, as though asking whether the temperature of her room had suited her. From the bathroom doorway Heather rolled her eyes, but it was a part of their morning routine that she'd learned to live with.

"No motaz." Angela shook her head.

"And no handsome princes sneaked in to kiss my little Sleeping Beauty?"

Again she shook her head, but with obvious impatience.

"Well then," he stood, "I guess that just about covers it. Let's head down for breakfast."

"Addy," she shouted, shaking a pudgy finger at him. Heather couldn't help laughing at the look of utter exasperation on Angela's small face, but Joe pretended complete bewilderment.

"Did I forget something?"

"Patafwy kiz. Patafwy kiz," she said, pulling his face toward hers.

"Oh of course, butterfly kisses." He slapped his forehead. "How could I have forgotten?" He could no more have forgotten their morning butterfly kisses than he could forget his own name, but it never failed to send her into a spasm of giggles when she had to remind him.

Leaning gently forward, he turned his cheek toward her until he could feel her eyelashes blinking open and closed against his skin. And then, taking her baby-soft face in his hands, he gave her his own butterfly kisses. He couldn't remember when they had first started this morning ritual, but after she'd given him the Bob Carlisle CD with the song about a father and daughter who shared "a hug every morning and butterfly kisses at night" as a Father's Day gift, it had become their special greeting.

"Duhkee, patafwy kiz." She smiled, snuggling against him.

"Thank *you*, for butterfly kisses," he said, hugging her tightly.

Heather's third pregnancy had been completely unexpected, both Joe and Heather accepting as fact that she had been unable to conceive again after giving birth to their second child. So when her obstetrician had confirmed that her "morning sickness" was actually *morning sickness*, it had been a shock to them both. But twelve-year-old Debbie and ten-year-old Richie had been delighted. Heather had been especially excited when the ultrasound showed that it was going to be a girl. Debbie had reached the age where she was willing to wear anything *but* what Heather suggested, so the thought of dressing up a little girl in frilly dresses and tiny patent leather shoes had tickled Heather.

When they received the call from the doctor's office requesting that they come in for a meeting there had been a mild sense of unease, but nothing more. Maybe, they hypothesized, the doctor had seen a second tiny body on the film. Twins ran in Heather's family. But when they had requested an explanation, the nurse's silence had spoken volumes, and when the obstetrician asked them to go through more tests, it was with a sense of grave seriousness.

"Down syndrome?" Joe had repeated, sure that he'd misunderstood. What had they done wrong? They'd asked. Was it because they were older this time?

The doctor had assured them that it was not their fault. Down syndrome was simply a case of the body having an extra chromosome. It didn't appear to be genetic, and to date no one had been able to determine a cause, no less a cure. She had calmly explained that there was no way to be sure, unless they performed further tests, and that if those tests came out positive, there were other alternatives they could consider. There was no need to force that kind of trial on either them or the child. Joe was still trying to understand what other *alternatives* she might be referring to when Heather answered unequivocally.

"No. Abortion is not an option."

The children had been just as shocked when they were told. "You mean she's retarded?" Richie had asked. And Debbie had worried about what her friends would think.

Joe and Heather had explained what they'd been able to glean from the pamphlets the doctors had given them, and the few books they had been able to get their hands on, but they still felt woefully unprepared for what was to come. Research had come a long way, but the things the doctors didn't understand still far outweighed the things they did. The weeks leading up to Angela's birth were filled with fear and late-night worry, but the biggest change she brought into their lives had been something that no medical journal could have predicted.

The past six years had come with many trials they had never expected, and until they had actually raised a child with severe mental disabilities they'd had no idea the amount of energy and commitment that it required. But it was the spirit of unconditional love, the sheer almost overwhelming happiness that she exuded from the day she was born, that had won over everyone she met.

Now, gently prying her arms from around his neck, Joe stood, and ruffling her baby-fine hair he started toward the door. "I've got to go get my swimming in or I'm going to get fat," he said.

"No, *phat* is good," Heather laughed behind him.

"Goot," Angela agreed.

* * *

The first sign of trouble that morning came just as Joe was toweling off after his swim. As he stood by the side of the pool, enjoying the late May sunshine, the French doors that connected the kitchen with the backyard swung open and Tia Sanchez stepped out onto the patio holding the white cordless telephone with one hand while she shaded her eyes with the other. Her neat black hair was pulled up in a bun on the top of her head, her dark eyes peering from an unlined face that could have been anywhere in age from thirty to fifty.

"Mr. Stewart. You have a phone call. He says it's Leon from the office." Joe had given up on trying to get Tia to just call him Joe like everyone else did, although after seven years together she might as well be family. Tia was Spanish for "aunt," and although he knew that she had a first name, Joe couldn't recall it for the life of him. The kids had started calling her Aunt Sanchez soon after she began working as their cook and housekeeper, and after she taught them how to say *aunt* in Spanish, they used it so regularly that eventually Heather and Joe adopted it as well. It suited the relationship that they had formed with her.

"Thanks Tia." As he took the phone from her, a small knot of concern formed in his stomach. It had been a tough year for tech companies, *his* being no exception. Stock prices at Infinity Networks had dropped from a high of seventy-five dollars down to seventeen dollars, and they would probably have dropped much lower if he hadn't leveraged his own options and mortgaged his house to the hilt to buy back more than a million shares. When the market saw that the CEO was willing to buy even more shares than he already owned, it seemed to recover some of its old confidence in Infinity's sound business practices. It had been a big risk, but it paid off well, and the stock had slowly risen back up to twenty-four dollars and settled there.

Still, it was unusual for anyone to call him on his home phone. His mobile was on the dresser in his bedroom where he wouldn't have been able to hear it ring from the pool. But normally, if he hadn't answered that number, they would have left a message and waited for him to get back to them. And he was doubly concerned that it was Leon Kensington on the phone. As Chief Technical Officer of Infinity, it was his job to oversee both the hardware and software engineering for the company's products. For the most part he was what the other engineers called a "lab rat," content to keep his nose buried in research, testing, and design, only surfacing when it was absolutely necessary. If he was calling, it was obviously about something he thought was pretty important.

"Leon, you're up early." Joe glanced at his watch, noting that it was not yet a quarter past seven.

"Joe, we've got a catastrophe on our hands down here." Leon sounded as though he had just run up a flight of stairs. Not a small task at his size.

"Calm down and tell me what's wrong." Joe took the words of his CTO in stride. Leon was also prone to overstatement. His idea of a catastrophe could include anything from an overtaxed server to the building being engulfed in flames. But he had to admit that from the tone of Leon's voice it sounded like something more than an overtaxed server.

"I don't think you're going to want to hear this over the phone," Leon puffed. "How soon can you get down here?"

"Well I need to get dressed and have breakfast—" Joe started before Leon cut him off.

"You're not going to want to eat anything this morning, Joe. You really need to get down here right away. I don't think the press has caught wind of this yet, but when they do, accusations are going to start flying."

"Okay, I'll be right in." Joe paused, wondering how hard he should push his CTO for an outright answer before deciding that, whatever the problem was, he should probably deal with it in person. He was still fairly sure that Leon was overreacting, like Chicken Little, interpreting a falling apple for something much worse. But whatever it was, if it had rattled him that badly, it needed to be dealt with before his fear carried to anyone else. In this kind of business climate, panic was contagious. That made him think of another question that he *did* need an immediate answer to.

"Have you talked to anyone else about this?"

Leon paused just long enough that Joe knew he wasn't being entirely truthful before answering almost coyly, "Um, I thought I should talk to you before I discussed this with anyone else." Joe knew that as soon as they got off the phone Leon would go to whomever he had talked to and ask them to keep it quiet. Which meant that by the time he got into the office rumors would be spreading like wildfire.

"All right. I'll see you in about twenty-five minutes." Joe switched off the phone and reflectively carried it into the house.

* * *

The second sign that morning was one that Joe forgot about in the chaos of that day and the terrible days that followed. It wasn't until later, when he first met the prospector, that he recalled the voice of warning that he'd received shortly before entering the office that day.

He had parked his car in the underground garage and was on his way to the elevator when he noticed the man with the grocery cart.

Joe barely gave him a thought other than to note that he would have to tell security to come down and roust the man out. He didn't know how the rough-looking man in the torn overcoat and ratty boots had gotten down there in the first place. It was supposed to be secure, entrance by permit only. And this street person obviously did not have a pass. Infinity couldn't have him harassing the employees for enough money to buy a bottle of cheap wine.

Joe was just walking past him, avoiding eye contact, yet still knowing somehow that he would hear the man's raspy voice call out, "Hey mister, can you spare some change?" Or maybe he even had a story worked out about the train fare that he'd mysteriously lost. Whatever it was, Joe had no time for it this morning. Under other circumstances he might have stopped. Probably even would have given him a buck or two and warned him to clear out before the guards came down. Just because a man had problems didn't mean that he wasn't still a human being. But today he had much bigger problems to deal with than this guy's sob story.

"Nice shirt, Joe."

He didn't know whether it was the line or just the voice that stopped him. They were both unique and unexpected. After college he had worked in New York for three years and he thought he'd heard them all. Everything from children that just needed a quarter to call home, to whole families that were down on their luck. But the voice that hailed him from behind the scraggly gray beard had a husky quality that was both deep and comforting. It could have come from the narrator in a feature film, or the host of a radio talk show. James Earl Jones had nothing on him.

Whatever it was, Joe paused and turned, made eye contact, and they both knew that he would stop. It wasn't just that the man had called him by name. "Joe" was a common enough way to call out to a stranger. "Hey Joe, can you spare a quarter?" had been the regular refrain of lots of the panhandlers he had seen. It was simply a coincidence. It wasn't until later that he came to question that assumption.

But he had appealed to one of Joe's vanities. It *was* a nice shirt. He had ordered it, handmade by an Italian tailor, just a few days earlier. It was a hand-woven blue silk with just enough black threads sewn in to give it an almost multilayered texture. Not that he thought the man leaning on the shopping cart could have recognized any of that, but he reflexively turned to say "Thank you," before he even realized what he was doing.

He started to turn away, and the man smiled at him as if to say "Gotcha," his deep brown eyes unremarkable and yet somehow familiar. Joe shook his head. The likelihood that the two of them had ever run in the same circles was slim to none; nevertheless, he dropped his hand into his pocket to grab a few bills. He would never have gotten this far in the business world if he couldn't recognize a good salesman, and this guy had put together a winning pitch. Dropping a five and a one onto the top of the bags piled in the man's cart, he winked and said "Good luck, buddy," before turning back to the elevator.

"Keep ya umbrella out. Gonna be a stormy one today I think." Again Joe was impressed by how well the man's voice resonated, even off the cement walls of the garage. But while he might well have trained at Julliard, it was obvious why he was living out of a grocery cart. It had been nothing but clear blue skies for the last week, and it looked to stay that way for at least another week. Obviously this guy was missing a few cards from his deck.

He spared one last glance for the man leaning against the cart. He was sure that the six bucks would have disappeared into the man's overcoat as soon as they left his hand. By now he should have been halfway to the nearest liquor store. But the only move he'd made was to rest his chin in one grimy palm, a worried, far-off look on his weathered face, as though he were looking past the confines of the garage at some distant thundercloud. He seemed so intent that Joe found himself following the man's gaze, but all he saw was row after row of expensive cars.

"I'll keep that in mind," Joe lied, before stepping into the elevator and punching the button for the top floor.

"Nah. Not yet ya won't." The man smiled grimly as the elevator doors closed.

CHAPTER 2

"Mr. Stewart, Mr. Kensington is waiting to meet with you," Abbey Vincens stated with a covert roll of her eyes, as though he couldn't see the red-faced man hovering over her desk. She only called him "Mr. Stewart" when he was meeting with someone important or when she was very annoyed. He thought that after having spent the last twenty minutes baby-sitting Leon, this was most definitely a case of the latter.

"Thanks Abbey. I'll meet with him now." Joe winked his understanding to her, and she returned an exasperated look that said, "Take him away from me now, before I skin and fillet him alive."

"Leon?" As he turned to his CTO, the man grabbed Joe's sleeve in one sweaty palm and pulled him toward the door to Joe's office.

"We gotta talk right now, Joe. I don't know how long I'm gonna be able to keep this hush-hush."

"Alright, alright, come on in." Joe swung the door open and ushered Leon inside. Unlike his den at home, which was decorated in dark wood and filled with so many books and pictures that it sometimes gave the appearance of chaos, his office here looked almost utilitarian. Centered on his chrome-and-glass desk was a trim gray notebook computer. The only other items on the desk were a black metal in/out box, a ceramic pen and pencil holder, his phone, and several pictures of his family.

Behind the desk a swivel chair stood in front of a black lacquer horizontal filing cabinet, its glossy top bare except for a neat stack of legal pads and a folded copy of that morning's *Wall Street Journal*. Above the filing cabinet was the single piece of artwork in the room, a framed copy of Arnold Friberg's painting, *The Prayer at Valley Forge*. The only other furnishings were a leather sofa placed directly across from his desk, and a circular table surrounded by chairs that stood in front of an enormous whiteboard on the far wall.

Joe was not a person that liked to spend the day cooped up in his office. He preferred ranging the manufacturing floors, stopping to meet the workers that ran the assembly line, or sitting in on departmental strategy meetings, enjoying being a part of the give-and-take that was what really shaped the company. He only came back to the isolation of this room when Abbey convinced him that it was absolutely essential. Now, guiding his obviously agitated officer over to the couch, he sat next to him and assumed his most calming voice.

"Now Leon, tell me what's wrong. Whatever it is, I'm sure we can fix it together."

Like a bobber popping to the surface of a lake, Leon jumped back up off the couch and began pacing around the room. "This isn't my fault. I had no idea that the designs weren't our own. I can't be every place at the same time. Of course I had to assume that if Research gave it to me we had created it, right?" He stared at Joe with the plaintive look of a child who has just been caught stealing cookies.

"Just calm down and tell me what this is all about." The knot in Joe's stomach was growing larger. Even for his excitable CTO this behavior was strange, bordering on bizarre. But before Leon could answer, the phone on Joe's desk buzzed and Abbey's voice interrupted.

"Joe, Stan Holtz is on the line." Stan was the chair of the board of Infinity Networks. His East Coast venture capital firm was the largest single holder of the company's stock. It was unusual for him to phone, as he preferred using e-mail to stay up to date on the latest numbers. As Joe got up to answer the phone, he glanced over at Leon, who had suddenly found something very interesting to look at out the window, and the knot in his stomach began to burn.

"Stan what's up?" Joe cradled the receiver between his ear and shoulder as he reached for one of the legal pads and grabbed a pen.

"What is going on down there?" Stan's voice was so loud that even Leon turned briefly around before quickly staring back out the window.

"What do you mean?" Joe tried to stay calm, but he could feel his fingers tightening on the barrel of the pen.

"What do I mean?" Stan was practically howling. The Brooklyn accent that only became obvious when he was excited or angry made him sound like a street thug now. "First I get some cockamamie phone call from some guy in your office feeding me a bunch of bull about nothing being his fault." Joe stared at Leon's broad back. *So much for not talking to anyone else.* "Then I get a call from the *Times* wanting to know how we plan on responding to a suit for theft of intellectual property and patent infringement."

As Joe scribbled the words onto the pad in front of him, he felt as though he had swallowed a meteorite, but he managed to keep his voice calm. "Listen Stan, I'm not sure what's going on. But I've got someone in my office right now that I think might be able to clear things up. Can I call you right back?"

"Make it quick. I've gotten three more messages while we've been talking." Stan hung up the phone leaving Joe with only a faint hissing noise in his ear.

As he set the receiver back down, the phone buzzed again. "Joe, what is going on? You've got a dozen people on hold for you right now." Abbey sounded as close to frantic as he had ever heard her.

"Abbey, hold all my calls please. I'm going to need a few minutes." Joe released the intercom button and turned his attention back to Leon who was rubbing his palms up and down the sides of khaki pants, his slick hands making a chirping sound like the world's largest cicada against the stiff fabric, as he continued to stare out the window.

"Leon, please come and sit down." As Joe waited, Leon turned away from the window and glanced anxiously toward the door before making his way back to the couch and collapsing down onto it.

"Now would you please tell me what is going on here?"

Coughing nervously into his fist, Leon opened and closed his mouth like a fish gasping for oxygen before finally blurting, "I really didn't know, Joe. When I got the first letters from their attorneys I figured that they were just another one of those small European companies trying to make a quick buck off of someone else's success. Who would have even considered that it might be true?"

Joe, finally losing his last shred of patience, slammed his fists on the desk, bouncing the ceramic pencil holder to the floor and sending pens and pencils showering across the carpet. Storming around from behind his desk, he placed his hands on the shoulders of his CTO—who looked like he was about to start weeping—and in a voice that by its very calm demanded attention asked, "That *what* might be true?"

Leon stared down at the floor, his cheeks bright red and dripping with sweat. "We stole their designs. We stole 'em. No other way to say it. For at least the last three years, maybe longer, we've been selling products based on someone else's designs." He shook his head. "No, not even just *based* on. We copied them circuit for circuit."

Joe stared at him, too stunned to speak. It didn't make any sense. Infinity Networks was a powerhouse, right up there with Cisco. They spent millions on research and development every month. They had scores of attorneys filing patents on everything they made and suing the pants off of anyone who even came close to infringing on what they had designed. It was not only illogical that they would steal someone else's designs, it was impossible. Or at least he would have said it was five minutes earlier.

"So what are you saying? One of our routers or something was designed by another company?" Joe asked, still trying to make sense of the situation.

Leon moaned as if he had just been punched in the stomach. "Not one of our routers. *All* of our routers, all of our switches, all of our hubs. This guy in Hungary is some kind of freakin' genius. And somehow one of our engineers got a hold of his designs. No one knew exactly where they had come from, but they were so much better than anything else on the market that we had to use them. I don't know who decided to copy them, but they did. And since then we've just been modifying the original specs."

"That's crazy. It would have turned up when we filed our patents." Joe fished a roll of Tums out of his pocket, started to take two, then thumbed four out of the wrapper and crushed them between his teeth.

"That's what I thought at first. But this guy is so small that he only filed locally. Our people are mostly on the lookout for products infringing on *our* patents, I guess these other designs didn't even show up on their radar."

Before Joe could completely comprehend what he was hearing, the intercom buzzed again. "Joe?"

"Abbey, I said I didn't want to be interrupted," Joe growled in the general direction of the phone. It wasn't like Abbey to ignore his instructions, and he had a sickening feeling that things were starting to slip out of his control.

"I'm sorry, but it's Jin Kwan. He says that it's urgent that he speaks to you now."

"Alright, put him through." Jin was the most levelheaded guy that Joe knew. As the company's Chief Financial Officer, he had ridden the same roller coaster that everyone else at Infinity had been on for the last eighteen months, but he had been sitting on the front of the first car with his mouth wide open. It had been up to him and Joe to take the brunt of the investors' criticisms when their stock had plummeted, calling in every favor they had with the analysts to get them to paint a fair picture of the company's stability and future growth potential so the market wouldn't pound them any worse than it had. If he said that this was urgent, then it was.

Joe pressed the speaker button, but before he could say anything, Jin was already talking. His voice sounded horse and tired as though he had spent the last few hours shouting. "Joe, they've halted trading on our stock."

Although he had spoken softly, the words crashed inside Joe's head like thunder. The NASDAQ only halted trading on a stock when there was an imminent announcement expected that could have a dramatic impact on the stock's value, or when there had been a drop so sharp that a freeze automatically went into effect. Since he knew that there was no announcement scheduled, that could only mean that the market had gotten wind of Infinity's problems even before he had.

"How bad is it?"

"Four and a quarter. But it would have dropped even lower if they hadn't stopped the carnage." Joe heard the door close behind him, and realized that Leon had heard everything. He shouldn't have put Jin on speaker. Leon would be rushing through the building seeding panic everywhere he went. He considered going after him, and then realized that it wouldn't make any difference. If there was one thing you could count on with employees of any publicly traded company, it was that they were stock watchers. If the stock was up, everyone was in a good mood. But when the stock dropped, productivity went down, sick days increased, and people generally griped about pretty much everything.

"Joe? You still there?" Jin's voice called out from the speaker-phone.

"Yeah." Joe dropped down into his chair. At least it was a Friday. That would give them the weekend to do some damage control before the market opened again on Monday. "How did word of this get out so fast anyway? I just heard about it myself."

There was a long pause on the other end of the line before Jin spoke. "You haven't seen the article yet?"

"No. What article?" Apparently Leon hadn't gotten around to telling him everything.

"Aw Joe." Jin's voice had changed, softened somehow. "I thought for sure that you would know more than I did. I was actually kind of ticked off that you hadn't given me any kind of heads-up on this. The paper says that we'd received several letters, but chose not to respond."

"What paper?" This was getting worse by the minute, and it wasn't even eight in the morning. It was going to be a very long day.

"Well apparently it ran about a week ago in some Hungarian local, the *Daily Goulash* or something. But the *London Times* picked it up this morning, and now it's all over the wires. The thing is . . ." Jin hesitated as if he were afraid to utter what he needed say to next.

"What?" Joe tried to force out a chuckle. "It can't get any worse, can it?" But on the other end of the line Jin's voice was dead serious.

"They're quoting an unnamed source as saying that you knew about it all along. They're saying that you knew Infinity's products were sub par, so you arranged the theft of the designs. That you figured it was such a small company you would never get caught." He sounded as though the words were being forced unwillingly from his mouth. "I know it can't be true . . . but this looks really bad."

It was like a long nightmare that he couldn't awaken from, and for a moment, he considered pinching his leg to see if he might possibly wake up. "Is there anything else?"

Jin seemed to be considering his words carefully before speaking. "Joe, I'm talking to you as your friend here, not your CFO. You need to protect any assets you have as quickly as you can. You might even want to consider bankruptcy."

"What?" It was as if Jin had suddenly started speaking another language, one that sounded like complete gibberish. This was definitely bad, but what did it have to do with his personal finances?

"When you bought the Infinity stock last fall, you borrowed money from the company to do it."

"Of course I did, but that loan was backed by—" the enormity of what Jin was saying suddenly hit him and it was like running full speed into a wall. The collateral he had used for the loan was the rest of his Infinity stock. If it had dropped to nearly four dollars? He quickly ran the numbers in his head and the figure was astounding. "I'm more than five million dollars in the hole?"

"And that's if the stock doesn't drop any more on Monday, which I wouldn't bet on." Jin's voice was an emotionless monotone.

"But I put up the house too."

Jin paused again before asking cautiously, "Joe have you talked with Stan this morning?"

"Yeah, he called just a couple of minutes ago. But what does that have to do with anything?"

"Maybe nothing. But I've been getting some strange feelers out of New York this morning. And a lot of the questions have been specifically about our liability on your loan."

"You don't think that they would try to . . ." Joe's words hung limply in the silence between them. They both knew that, as Chairman of the Board, Stan could be a powerful ally, but once his hackles were raised he wouldn't hesitate to bite.

"I'll do everything I can to help you Joe. But you know as well as I do that my hands may be tied on this one."

"Yeah, I know. Thanks for the warning, Jin." Joe leaned woodenly back into his chair, feeling like every muscle in his body had suddenly seized up on him, before he reached out to press the intercom button. "Abbey can you please get Stan on the line?"

* * *

It was nearly eight that night before the phone finally stopped ringing. Abbey had gone home a half hour earlier. Reluctant to leave Joe alone, she had only acquiesced when he promised that he would be right behind her. Staring out the window at the setting sun reflecting off of the other buildings around him, Joe tried to understand how things could have fallen apart so quickly. It seemed as if it had been a thousand years since he'd come into the office, and at least a million since he'd rolled out of bed that morning.

He felt like the cat in one of those *Tom and Jerry* cartoons after the mouse has just hit him in the head with a ten-pound sledgehammer, staggering woozily as floating shapes circled around his head. Except that, instead of stars and moons or cute little chirping birds, the shapes he saw were skulls and crossbones, red dollar signs, and big black question marks that buzzed in and out of his sight like giant mosquitoes.

Ten years ago, against the well-intentioned advice of most of his friends, Joe had left a high-paying job as the vice president of a major chip manufacturer. Using his own money and anything he could scrape together from friends and family, he had introduced Infinity Networks' first product. His small business networking solution, at half the cost of the competitor's and twice as easy to set up and maintain, had been an instant hit.

Over the years he had tramped through hundreds of miles of tradeshow aisles, met with scores of reporters, and done more demonstrations than he could ever hope to count. He had raised money when times were good and preserved it when things slowed down. He had been accused of everything from brilliance to incompetence, and at certain points had agreed with both. But not once during those years had anyone from reporter to board member even hinted that Joe Stewart was dishonest. Not until today.

Infinity had issued a press release that morning. If he had his way it would have been short and sweet, "Lies, lies, lies!" But by the time they had drawn up something that the board members and lawyers could all agree to, it was so watered down it sounded like an admission of guilt. *We are currently investigating . . . to the best of our knowledge . . . no intentional wrongdoing.* It was garbage. All he needed to do was get on a plane and go meet with these guys. The company's name ended up being Cognitive Computing Solutions. Run by a Hungarian college professor with Ph.D.'s in engineering and mathematics, their company didn't make in a year what Infinity made in a week.

Joe was certain that this was all just a big misunderstanding. If they really had infringed on any CCS designs, they would pay them damages. It probably wouldn't even make a dent in Infinity's quarterly earnings. And if it did, so what? It wasn't like most companies were showing huge profits this year anyway. They'd take their medicine, fire anyone who had knowingly broken the law, and get back to business. Which is what he had told the board on their hastily scheduled conference call. He was sure things had hit rock bottom, which meant that it was time to start bouncing back up, when Stan had dropped the biggest bombshell on a day that had been packed with enough TNT to last a lifetime.

"Listen Joe," Stan's voice came over the speakerphone, "we've been talking things over and we think that maybe it would be good for the company if you were to step down."

"What?" He was sure that he must have misunderstood. This was *his* company. He had poured his own blood, sweat, and tears into it. And what had Stan put in? Money that for the most part wasn't even his.

"It's probably only temporary. Until things have a chance to get sorted out. We'll say that you're taking some time off to be with your family, kind of a leave of absence."

"Are you crazy?" Joe could hear Stan's sharp intake of breath on the line, but it didn't matter. What he was suggesting was so ludicrous as to be laughable, if it hadn't also been incredibly dangerous. "Do you have any idea how the market would react to that?"

"Joe, the market has reacted, and now is the time for us to act quickly before it can get any worse." Stan's voice had gone from the velvety purr that he used to sell investors on his latest round, to the cold steel that he used when he was shoving a deal down some helpless company's throat. "You've lost the confidence of the public, Joe. Frankly it doesn't matter a whit whether you're guilty or not. The investors need to know that the board is taking action—moving quickly to find the problem and squash it. And as far as the rest of the world is concerned, you're the problem."

"I won't do it." Stan might be doing the talking, but he was only one member of the board. These were guys Joe had worked with for years. Some of them since even before he had started the company. Jin was on the board, and Joe had been the one who'd hired him.

He'd made a lot of money for all of them, and if nothing else they would at least remember that.

"I'm sorry to hear that, Joe. Because if that's your final decision then you leave me no choice but to fire you."

"You can't do that, Stan. That requires a majority board vote." He was taking a risk, but the other board members weren't stupid. They had seen him pull the company out of some tight spots. Maybe not anything this bad, but they had to know that he was much better equipped to handle it than anyone else.

"I propose a motion that Joe Stewart be removed as CEO effective end of day today. I further propose that the outstanding balance on his company loan be called immediately, as a result of his termination."

"I second the motion." That was Karl Sterlington, the senior partner of Sterlington Capital. Sterlington made most of their money piggybacking on Stan's deals, so it was not surprising that he'd join Stan on this. But there were seven voting board members including himself. He would be required to abstain, but that meant that Stan still needed a minimum of two more members to go his way.

"Lee?" Stan asked the founder of more than a dozen successful technology companies. Joe was confident that Lee would vote against this lunacy. He was one of the first people Joe had asked to join the board.

"I agree."

"Jin?" Stan continued. Why was he starting with Joe's stalwarts? Surely he had to realize that Jin would vote with his own CEO on this . . . unless the decision was a foregone conclusion. Had Stan taken a straw poll in advance and then, confident that he had the necessary votes, put the screws to the other board members?

"Sorry, Joe." Jin sounded drained, and Joe couldn't help but feel sorry for what this must be costing him.

One by one, he listened to the people he had worked with and trusted for years vote to remove him from the company he had come to love almost like a child. Each assent was like another spear, piercing his flesh and twisting, until numbly he listened to the last board member vote against him.

"Then with one abstaining member, voting is unanimous. We'll make the announcement tomorrow. Are there any other issues?" Stan asked, as though they had just agreed on what they would have for dinner. When there was no answer, he continued. "Then Jin, I assume that you will take care of this. Joe, I wish you the best of luck. I'm sure that you'll do just fine, as will Infinity." And with that, the call ended with Joe sitting frozen behind his desk, unable to believe what had just happened.

His thoughts were interrupted by a knock at the door to his office. "Come in," he called, wondering who would be there so late.

The door swung slowly inward and Jin stuck his head through the opening, looking embarrassed and uncomfortable. "If this is a bad time," he started, and then, realizing what he had just said, flushed even further.

"It's okay. I'm just packing," Joe said, nodding toward a single cardboard box, only half filled with belongings. It was hard to believe that this was all he had accumulated after more than a decade of leading Infinity Networks.

"I just have some papers for you to sign." Jin stepped through the doorway, still looking as though he expected Joe to begin shouting at him at any moment.

"Sure, just leave them on my desk. I'll stick them under your door on the way out." Jin looked down at the floor, but didn't come any further into the room, and Joe had a sudden flash of understanding.

"Oh, I see. You're also supposed to make sure that I leave the building without planting any bombs or hurling myself out the window. Is that it?"

"Something like that," Jin mumbled.

Joe quickly flipped through the papers. It was the standard termination paperwork he had approved many times over the years for other employees who had been let go, but he had never imagined that he would ever need to sign them himself.

"If you want you can have an attorney look them over," Jin suggested.

"No, they're fine." Joe filled in his signature at each of the appropriate places and handed them back to his CFO. *Actually,* he corrected himself, *my previous CFO, now that the termination was official.* He should probably have pushed the board for more favorable terms. He still held the leverage of being able to give the company a black eye. But even if he no longer worked there, Infinity was his baby and he couldn't fathom bad-mouthing it. Besides, whatever fight he might have started the morning with had been completely drained out of him by the day's events. All he wanted to do was go home and get this behind him.

Removing the electronic building key that had been on his ring longer than his car or house keys, he handed them to Jin along with his ID card and cell phone. Jin took the key and badge but handed back the phone. "Keep it. You've got all your numbers programmed into it, I'll just have the bill transferred into your name."

"Thanks." Joe took the phone, his eyes beginning to mist at the small act of kindness in a day filled with so much pain.

"You'll be back Joe. They'll change their minds once they've had a chance to think about it." Jin looked slowly around the office, as if realizing for the first time how wrong it would seem to have anyone else in it.

"I don't think so. Too many people would end up looking bad if that happened, and everybody's going to be looking to cover their flanks." Joe picked up the pitifully small box of his personal effects. He briefly considered taking the painting as well, and then decided that he'd leave it for whoever took his place. They would probably just have it removed, but maybe the image of the country's first president kneeling in prayer beside his horse would inspire the new CEO to run the company with the same respect that he'd run it with.

As he stepped into the elevator for what might be the last time, Joe knew that over the next few weeks he would do a lot of soul searching about what he should have done differently, but for now he was content to watch the lighted numbers count down to the garage level and let his mind shut down. He could take comfort in the fact, that for tonight at least, he wouldn't receive any further blows.

The bell chimed, signaling that he had reached his destination, and Joe stepped out of the elevator, shifting his belongings to his hip as he pulled his car keys out of his pocket. Unlocking his car, he dropped the cardboard box onto the passenger seat, got in, and then, as he pulled the door closed, noticed something tucked under his windshield wiper. Suddenly irate, he reached through the open window to pluck the offending piece of paper off his windshield. He'd told the guards to keep people from coming in here and littering the automobiles with flyers. But it wasn't a flyer that he found tucked between his fingers as he pulled his hand back into the car. It was a five-dollar bill and a one. Scribbled in spidery hand-writing across the top of the five were the words. "I thought you might need this more than me."

He knew that the sentence should mean something to him. For some reason his mind wanted to associate the money in his hand with a thunderstorm. He tried to think of why that might be, his overtaxed mind struggling to make a connection that he was sure would have been simple under other circumstances, but what little concentration he could muster was broken by the electronic ringing of his cell phone. Dropping the bills into the box, he picked up his phone and checked the caller ID on the small glowing screen.

The number flashing on the phone was his home, and with a sickening start he realized that through the chaos of the day he had never called Heather. The story must have been on the TV and radio all day. How had he been so thoughtless? She had probably tried to call all afternoon, but with the phones ringing off the hook couldn't get through until now. He had been so caught up in moving from one crisis to another that he hadn't given his family a thought all day. She must be panic-stricken.

"Heather."

"Oh Joe, I'm so glad I got through to you. This is so humiliating." Heather sounded drained.

"I'm so sorry sweetheart, it's just been a madhouse down here. But I should have called you earlier." He had promised her when he started the company that he would never put work ahead of his family, but today he'd done just that.

"How could you have known?" At first her words confused him. Of course he had known, he had been right in the middle of all this. But then he guessed that she was asking how he had known that *she* would be aware of the day's events.

"I'm sure it was all over the news. It was selfish not to call you as soon as everything started."

"The news? Tia and I were at Angela's school all day helping out with the bake sale. I haven't been home long enough to watch TV. But do you think this is actually big enough to make the news?"

Heather sounded completely bewildered, and for the first time Joe realized with a sinking feeling that they might be talking about two different things.

"What are you talking about?" He felt sure that he didn't want to know the answer. He couldn't take much more today without cracking completely.

"About our son getting arrested. What are *you* talking about?"

CHAPTER 3

It was nearly eleven before a slab-faced police sergeant finally approached Joe and Heather. In one hand he held a clipboard stained with coffee-cup shaped circles on the bottom, while with the other hand he regularly stuffed bites of a thick ham-and-cheese sandwich into his mouth. Watching him methodically churn his way through each mouthful as he studied the sheets of paper on the clipboard, Joe was reminded of a cow mindlessly chewing its cud, and mentally labeled him as Officer Holstein.

"Mr. and Mrs. Stewart?" he called out around a lump of partially masticated meat. Joe stood, happy to get out of the curved plastic chairs that were a painful reminder of his grade-school days, and beside him Heather rose slowly from her seat. Joe knew how uncomfortable she was here. He wasn't exactly enjoying it himself, and he took her hand protectively in his.

"Right here, Officer."

The police officer turned toward the two of them, starting to feed another bite into his wide mouth, and then stopped with his sandwich in midair as recognition flashed in his eyes. Double-checking the clipboard, he shook his head and barked a harsh laugh. "Man this sure hasn't been your day, has it?"

"No it hasn't," Joe agreed wearily.

Removing a stray crumb of cheese from the corner of his mouth with a surprisingly delicate pinch of his thumb and forefinger, the sergeant studied Joe as if wanting to ask him more about what he had heard on the news, but then seemed to think better of it. Tilting his head toward the hallway behind him, he popped the last of his sandwich into his mouth, swallowed it, and said, "Well, why don't you two come with me and we'll get this taken care of."

Joe and Heather followed the back of his blue uniform down the precinct hallway and into a large open room filled with desks. The room was crowded with police officers and a variety of men and women, both young and old. Some of them seemed at home here, as if they were regulars—prostitutes in cheap, garish outfits, and rough-looking men whose bloodshot eyes bore witness to years of hard drinking. A few of the people, though, looked as out of place as Joe felt, glancing around nervously as if afraid they might run into someone they knew. But none of them looked happy. *There aren't many happy reasons,* he thought, *to be sitting in a police office late on a Friday night.*

Sitting down behind a dark gray desk, its laminate surface marked with years of cigarette burns and ancient scars, Officer Holstein swept aside a brown paper sack and a plastic baggie that held a few last potato-chip fragments, and waved them to another pair of plastic chairs. Leafing through the papers again, he nodded and then slapped the clipboard down onto the desk with a sharp crack.

"You are the parents of Richard Spencer Stewart?" he asked them, as though they hadn't had to show their driver's licenses when they had first come into the station.

"Yes." They both nodded.

"I see." He seemed to ponder this bit of information for a moment, hooking one finger into the collar of his stiffly pressed uniform shirt and pulling it away from his thick neck before continuing. "Your son has been involved in some very serious criminal activity today." Sitting next to Joe, Heather gave a small sharp gasp and covered her mouth with one hand. This seemed to be the response that Officer Holstein was looking for, because he nodded knowingly at her and then turned to Joe with an expectant look on his face.

"We understand," Joe said between gritted teeth. It had been an incredibly bad day that didn't show any promise of getting better, and all he wanted to do right now was get his son and go home. There would be plenty of time later to discuss the details of Richie's crimes, since he was going to be grounded for the rest of his natural life.

The police sergeant must have registered the impatience in Joe's voice, because his face tightened and he read through the rest of the report quickly. "According to the arresting officer, your son was part of a group of boys and girls that broke into a house a few blocks away from their high school. While illegally in the residence, they consumed more than a dozen bottles of spirits from the owner's wet bar, swam in the pool, and from all appearances, at least a few of them made use of the home's bedrooms for a little extracurricular activity." As though he had just told an amusing, if slightly off-color joke, he looked up from the paperwork with the beginning of a "kids-will-be-kids" grin on his face. But seeing the identical pale, almost sick looks on Joe's and Heather's faces, the grin disappeared.

"We also recovered several grams of coke, marijuana, and a baggie full of pills." The ball that had been burning in Joe's stomach all day, apparently deciding that enough was enough, was trying to force its way up out of his throat, and despite the fact that he'd eaten nothing all day, it was all he could do to keep from throwing up. Drugs, sex, alcohol, these were things that other kids got involved with, kids whose parents didn't care about what they were doing and who they were hanging out with. Not Richie.

It seemed like just last Sunday Joe had watched him preparing the sacrament and thought how responsible he looked in his white shirt and tie. Richie was a *good* kid. He pulled good grades, helped out around the house. He was the kind of kid that every parent wished they had. But the man in front of him had just shattered that image. Beside him, Heather fumbled through her purse for a handkerchief that she used to mop up the mascara that was dripping down her cheeks.

Whether because of the tears, or because of his earlier indiscretion, the police officer's face seemed to soften a little and his voice took on a note of compassion that Joe wouldn't have thought him capable of. "Listen ma'am, it's probably not as bad as it sounds. Your kid doesn't have a prior record, and he claims that he wasn't aware that they were in the house illegally." Sliding open a desk drawer, he pulled out a box of tissues and handed them across to Heather. Nodding gratefully, she pulled several of them from the box and dabbed at her eyes between quiet sobs before blowing her nose and crumpling the tissues into a ball.

"I see a lot of parents come through here," he continued, dropping his eyes from Heather's distraught gaze, "but most of them couldn't give a rat's behind about what their kids have been doing. All they care about is getting in and out of here as quickly as possible." Joe suddenly found the backs of his hands extremely interesting, his earlier pride in what a good parent he was significantly diminished.

"You seem like a nice lady. I can see that you're really worked up about what your kid's done." He glanced briefly at Joe, with a look that seemed to be less than generous, and then turning back to Heather said, "He's lucky to have a mom like you. It's important for a kid to have at least one good example to look up to."

"What are you implying?" Joe asked, for the first time realizing that the police officer's praise had all been directed toward his wife.

"I'm not implying anything." The cop gave Joe a hard stare before looking away. "I'm just saying that sometimes when the pup looks up to see what the big dog's doing, maybe he gets the idea that it's okay to stretch the law a little here and there."

Joe couldn't believe what he was hearing. Where could this guy possibly have gotten the idea that he had set a bad example for Richie? Then, like an icicle sliding up the back of his spine, came the terrible realization of what the reporters must be saying about him on the news. "Look, whatever you might have heard, it's all lies. I haven't broken the law."

"Hey I'm not making any kind of judgments here." The police officer raised both hands in a peace gesture, and Heather, who had still not heard any of the news reports, watched the conversation with total bewilderment. "It's just that the apple doesn't always fall so far away from the tree."

He flipped around the clipboard so that it faced Joe and Heather and slid a pen across the desk. "We haven't been able to contact the owners of the house. They're on vacation somewhere in Mexico. So we don't know whether they'll want to press charges or not. But at the very least there's going to be the matter of the drugs. If you'll sign this release, we'll remand your son into your custody until the judge schedules a court date."

Joe watched Heather fill out the forms while noticing from the corner of his eye the suspicious way that Officer Holstein was studying him. It was unbelievable that a few insinuations from a talking head could convince a total stranger that he was some kind of criminal. Infinity had donated thousands of dollars to the Policeman's Benevolent Association every year. He had sat at the same table with this man's chief, and yet from the way the officer was watching him, he might as well be a convicted murderer.

Thank goodness everyone wasn't that impressionable. This guy was probably the kind of person who grilled all of his neighbors when he found a pile of dog manure on his lawn, sure that they were intentionally targeting his property. And yet as Joe let his gaze travel around the room, it seemed that Officer Holstein wasn't the only one giving him that look policemen seemed to save for accused criminals. The look that said, "You can deny it all you want, but we know what you really are."

Two desks over, another blue-uniformed officer with a long thin face, and a nose that looked like it had been squeezed by a giant pair of pliers, was staring at him as he talked on the phone. When Joe looked across at him, he quickly turned away, but the look of distaste stayed on his face. And on the other side of the room, a couple of plain-clothes detectives in shirts and ties talked animatedly with one another as they looked in his direction. Were they really *all* staring at him, or was he just being paranoid? It didn't matter. Either way, he could still feel eyes watching him—judging him.

Feeling his face flush with anger and humiliation, Joe quickly dropped his eyes to the desktop. It might be bad for a day or two, but things like this always blew over. Once people heard the truth, they would realize that he was the same person he had always been. He was a respected leader in the community, and that wouldn't change just because he had lost his job. Leaning toward Heather, he took her hand, now as much to receive her support as to offer his. Squeezing his hand she flashed him a fragile smile, her eyes still watery but strong.

"All right then. This should do it." Officer Holstein took the clipboard from Heather, gave it a quick once-over and added his signature. "Now if you two will just go back up to the front desk and take care of the bail, I'll go into the back and get your boy."

* * *

"How do you explain yourself?" Shoving a stack of rock magazines from the only chair in Richie's bedroom that looked even halfway accessible, Joe perched on its edge and stared across the room at his son.

"Dunno." Richie lounged on his bed staring up at the ceiling. Other than a halfhearted, "Sorry Mom," when he had been escorted out of the holding cells, this had been the limit of his response. Joe had endured it on the drive home, not wanting to upset Heather any more than she already was, but now that they were alone he was determined to get some answers.

"Do you have any idea how it made your mother and me feel having to come bail you out of jail?" He didn't know what he was hoping for, an explanation, an apology. Something. Anything but the infuriating little grunt that Richie accompanied with a quick shake of his head, his spiked hair casting a porcupine-like shadow on the wall behind him. Taking in the pictures tacked to the walls, Joe tried to remember when he had last taken a close look at Richie's room. Posters of cars and sports stars had been replaced by violent-looking men surrounded by barely dressed women. At some point in the last year he had taken down the model airplanes that used to hang from strings on the ceiling and replaced them with a series of images that at the very least looked dark, and maybe even a little satanic.

"Don't you have anything to say?" Joe had to stop himself from reaching out and shaking his son just to get some kind of response.

"So what, if I say I'm sorry and I'll never do it again you'll just forget about it?" Richie sat up on the edge of his bed, his hands planted on the knees of a pair of jeans that looked at least two sizes too big, and for the first time Joe noticed his black-painted fingernails.

"Absolutely not. Other than the last few days of school, you won't be leaving this house alone until the end of the summer."

"Then what does it matter what I say?" Richie flopped back onto the bed rolling his eyes. "You want to ground me? Fine, go ahead and do it. Take away my allowance, whatever, but don't go acting like you care one way or the other what I have to say. Why don't you just get out of here and leave me alone?"

Joe couldn't believe what he was hearing. He and Richie had always been friends. He had gone with him on his fifty-mile hike last summer, and at the end of it when he had bought the whole troop ice-cold root beer floats, they had joked around like best buddies. When had things suddenly turned so adversarial? Had it really been that long since he'd taken the time to sit down and talk to his son?

"Richie, have you been using drugs?" He couldn't believe he was asking this question. It just seemed so inconceivable, and yet obviously something was wrong.

"Yeah, that's it. Blame it all on me." Richie's cackle sounded almost like a sob, but his mouth never lost its grin and his eyes seemed to be glowing with some kind of internal fire. "I'm a coke-head, Dad. Maybe you should get me into rehab so I won't be around to sully the Stewart name. Oh, no wait, I guess it's too late for that."

"What did you say?" Joe got slowly up off of the chair and started toward the bed, his pulse throbbing like drums in his ears.

"Yeah, I heard all about it. One of the girls was looking for MTV when we saw your name on the news. All the other kids thought it was real cool to have a crook for a dad." There was no question now that Richie was crying. Tears dripped down from his eyes to the corners of his mouth, but still he continued to grin. "So how's it feel, Dad? All I did was break into a house, but you screwed people out of millions of dollars."

Joe felt his hand rising of its own will, but he could only stand there watching it, his entire body quivering uncontrollably with pent-up rage and frustration. That a member of his own family, his child, would believe that he was capable of something like that! And yet wasn't he somehow at fault if he hadn't taught Richie any better?

"Yeah go ahead, hit me." Richie was screaming now, his own hands closed into fists that he shook in his father's face. "You pretend to be so good. Teaching Sunday School, going to all those charity dinners. But you're a fake. You're a liar, and I wish you had never had me!"

It was the earring that finally made Joe snap. As Richie shook his head back and forth, spittle flying from his mouth with each of his accusations, Joe caught sight of something sparkling from his left ear. Leaning closer, he saw that it was a silver skull, tiny diamonds glittering from its eye sockets, centered on a silver crucifix. As his hand flew forward he shouted, "What did you do to your ear?"

He hadn't meant to swing that hard. He was actually trying to pull back even as his arm began to move forward. But his foot slipped on the pile of magazines and his body shifted forward in the direction he was swinging. As his open palm connected with the side of his son's face, he could feel the shock of the impact travel up his arm like a rocket, and the force of the blow took Richie by surprise, spinning him across the bed and knocking him against the wall.

For a moment there was total silence, and then from behind him Joe heard a small panicky voice crying out, "Addy, no! Addy, no!" And he turned just in time to see Angela, eyes wide with terror, turn and run from the doorway where she had been standing. "I—" he started, but she was already gone. Something silver slipped from where it had caught on the cuff of Joe's shirt, and dropped against the side of his shoe. He reached down and picked up the crucifix earring. On the back, instead of a pin, was a magnet. Turning back to face Richie he could see that his son's cheek and eye were already beginning to swell on the spot where a bright red handprint stood out against his white skin.

"It's a fake," Richie whispered, and then buried his face in his pillow.

* * *

Tired beyond exhaustion, Joe collapsed onto the foot of his bed, back crumpled forward, elbows buttressed against his knees, his face buried in his hands. Across the room, Heather rocked Angela in the oak glider and crooned a lullaby that Joe hadn't heard her sing since their daughter was a tiny baby.

"Cackle, cackle, cackle, says the old gray hen. Gobble, gobble, gobble, says the turkey then. Baa, baa, baa, says the old black sheep. Bow, wow, wow, says the doggy in his sleep." After a few minutes Angela's sobs turned to sniffles, and eventually into the steady inhales and exhales that signaled she was finally asleep. Sometime later the bedroom door swung open as Heather carried Angela out to her bed, and her footsteps disappeared down the hallway.

On some level these sounds registered dimly in Joe's subconscious. But if asked where Heather was or how Angela had gotten into her bed, he would have shaken his head in complete bewilderment. His mind seemed unable to concentrate, drifting across a sea of worries.

If it had just been one thing, he could have focused perhaps and found a way to manage it. But his mind jumped from one image to another, staying only long enough for him to recognize the futility of the situation before racing on to the next problem. Richie's swollen face, his job, Angela's cries, the possibility that they could lose the house, the police officers staring accusingly at him in the squad room. Like an obscene carousel, each of his worries whirled through his brain, leaving him almost breathless.

"Let it go," he muttered to himself. "Just let it go for tonight." Rising from the bed, he rubbed his hands briskly across the stubble that had coated his cheeks over the last eighteen hours, and tried to shake loose some of the cobwebs that filled his mind. It was good advice, advice he had given to literally hundreds of his employees over the years. *When you begin to feel overwhelmed by a situation, let it go. Turn your mind to something else. Sometimes the valves and pistons in your brain can get so hot that they start to seize up. When that happens you need to let the little guys inside your head come rushing in with the oil and water. They'll cool everything down, lubricate all the machinery, and when you least expect it a solution will come to you.*

He'd been through worse before. Finding out about Heather's cancer had been a hundred times worse than this. He just needed to turn his thoughts to something else for a while. *Easier said than done,* he mused. *How do you just turn off the fact that for the first time in your life, other than a swat on the rear when they were little, you have struck one of your children, or that you have just lost everything you had spent the last ten years of your life building, or the mortgage coming due on a house you thought you would own forever, or . . .* "No." He snatched the television remote control off of the nightstand and clicked the power button—looking for some kind of distraction. "You will not let this beat you."

On the far side of the room a section of the oak cabinetry rotated revealing a 35-inch TV. He vaguely noted that on the screen Steve Young was explaining to an attractive young woman in the car with him that he was a lawyer. It was a commercial that Heather normally laughed at every time she saw it. They were both die-hard 49ers fans. But now it was just a meaningless jumble of sounds and colors that he stared at dumbly, hoping for some relief from his own thoughts.

Hearing Heather's footsteps in the hallway, Joe returned to the bed and began to unlace his shoes. Trying to conceal the anguish he felt inside, he pretended to concentrate on the screen, but as Heather sat down on the blue-and-white checked spread next to him, he turned to face her.

"How is Angela?" He spoke carefully, like an uncertain child stepping from stone to stone across a fast-moving stream.

"She's sleeping now." On the bed beside him, Heather's face was the mask of serenity that he had been striving to achieve, but her hands trembled slightly as she struggled to undo the dark blue buttons of her blouse, and he thought that perhaps she too was trying to keep her deeper feelings hidden. Joe nodded silently as he dropped his shoes to the floor at the foot of the bed.

"She was pretty upset." Heather's hands, which seemed to have given up on unbuttoning her blouse, began to rise tremulously toward her face, but she forced them back down to her tightly pressed-together legs with a faint sigh that sounded almost musical. "Mmmmm," as if she were preparing to sing. A single tear trickled down the curve of her pale white cheek, and although Joe wanted desperately to reach out and wipe it away, he felt incapable of doing so. It was as if he were clinging precariously to the side of a cliff, and if he let go they would both fall.

"Richie was pretty upset too." She stared at him with such obvious pain on her face, her eyes silently begging him to make everything all right, that he forced his mouth into what he hoped looked like a smile and placed his large hand across the tops of her two smaller ones. Swallowing felt like forcing a tennis ball down his throat, but he did it anyway, painfully, repeatedly, until he thought he could trust himself to speak.

"I know. I'm sorry. I didn't mean to—" But whatever words he had meant to say were swept from his mouth as he suddenly heard his name coming from the television. He and Heather turned in unison toward the screen and Joe saw that the commercials had given way to a rerun of the ten o'clock news. The picture zoomed in on a stylishly dressed black woman. Her perfectly coiffed hair and dark jacket emphasized her deep-set eyes. Looking up from a stack of papers, she faced the camera and flashed a quick smile.

"Topping the news tonight, a local businessman faces some serious allegations." A picture of Joe appeared in the upper right-hand corner of the screen. But rather than using the standard publicity photo that the company provided to journalists for just such purposes, the television station had dragged up a shot that he thought might have been taken when he was addressing the city council a few years earlier about the dangers of increasing corporate taxes. In it he was frowning, his eyes narrowed and his brow furrowed with anger. It made his face look more like a serial killer than a business man.

"Joe Stewart, former CEO of networking giant Infinity Networks, has been forced to resign today by the company's board of directors, under mounting charges that he was behind the theft of designs from a small Hungarian engineering firm."

"Joe?" Heather whispered beside him, but he found himself unable to turn away from the screen. Driving to and from work every day, he had passed his share of terrible accidents, and he had always been dismayed by the way people slowed down to stare at the grisly scenes. He had never been able to understand why people would want to look at a blanket-covered body or a bloody windshield. But now he thought that he was getting a taste of what they must feel. He knew what was coming, felt the fear of it gnawing at his heart, and yet he still had to see it for himself.

The picture switched from the anchorwoman to a girl whose reddish-blonde hair framed a face that looked young enough to still be in high school, although a text bar identified her as Jessica Tremont, a member of Infinity's public relations department. *Throwing her to the wolves*, Joe thought. *That way if she said something that the company might want to retract later, they could get rid of her easily. She probably thought it was a big opportunity. Might even be gathered with her friends in front of another television set somewhere in the valley eating popcorn and marveling at her moment of fame.*

"We at Infinity Networks are deeply concerned by what we are learning, and we fully intend to cooperate with the authorities to see that justice is served. We are currently conducting a thorough internal investigation of the matter and . . ." She continued to drone on with the usual company line until one of the reporters called out, "Ms. Tremont, is it true that Infinity believes that Joe Stewart, your former CEO, is responsible for stealing another company's designs?"

"No," Heather shouted at the screen, her hand suddenly clutching Joe's shoulder.

It was obvious that Jessica had been waiting for this question since the interview began, but she seemed to mull it over carefully before stating, "I'm afraid that I really can't comment on that matter at this time."

"But doesn't it stand to reason that the board would not have moved so quickly if they didn't feel he was guilty?" the reporter pushed forward.

On the screen, the blue-eyed PR flack smiled, the gleam in her eye conveying to the world exactly what *she* thought and then repeated, "No comment."

The picture switched back to the anchorwoman, but Joe's photo above her right shoulder had been replaced by a jaggedly downward spiking graph. "Infinity's stock plummeted on word of the day's events, down almost twenty dollars, from twenty-four dollars to four and a quarter." Heather's fingers tightened on Joe's arm, and he knew that she was doing the same math in her head that he had done earlier.

"And now here's Vick from the finance desk in New York to tell us what this all means." As the screen split to show a clean-cut man with large round spectacles, Joe finally managed to break his eyes away from the TV long enough to find the remote and stab at the power button.

"They didn't really fire you?" Heather shook her head slowly back and forth, her eyes filled with a look of pain and bewilderment. What Joe wanted more than anything was to turn off the lights and bury his face in the pillows, hoping that somehow morning's light would bring some sort of sense to the day's events. But Heather needed an answer—deserved an answer.

Rising from the bed, he walked to the nightstand on his side of the bed and laid the television remote next to the alarm clock. He wished that he could tell Heather that it had all been a terrible misunderstanding, that by this time tomorrow everything would have worked itself out. But it was like he had told Jin earlier; there were too many people that were going to have their hands clamped firmly to their backsides for the next few weeks protecting their rears. He didn't think this was just going to blow over.

Turning to meet his wife's eyes, he nodded. "Yeah, they really did."

"But why?" She pounded one of her fists against the mattress in frustration. "You didn't. I mean you wouldn't—" her tears dissolved into an anguished sob, but for one brief moment Joe was afraid that he had seen the slightest hint of doubt in her eyes before she dropped her face to hide the grief that he could hear in her voice.

In an instant he was back across the room, his arms wrapped around her, her head buried against his chest. "Oh no, sweetheart, never. It's lies, all of it. Filthy lies by people who are more afraid of what others think about them than what they think about themselves." Feeling her hot tears against the front of his neck, he pulled her closer still. He could stand anyone's doubts but hers. He didn't know what he would do if he ever lost her trust.

"What are we going to do?" Heather's words were muffled by the front of Joe's shirt, but he could hear the fear in her voice clearly, and it brought back memories that were still too painfully fresh.

"We'll work it out, honey. We'll work it out." As Joe held her close, he prayed to God that he was telling her the truth.

CHAPTER 4

"Daddy!" Joe was pulled from a haze of confused dreams by the scream of his oldest daughter. For a moment he thought he remembered standing in a grove of tall trees having a conversation with a man whose leathery brown face and deep-set eyes seemed to have weathered everything the world could throw at him. The man had said something about the trails of man. But that didn't seem to make any sense. Maybe the man said *trials* and he had just misunderstood. Joe thought that it might have been important advice, at least it had seemed that way in the dream, but before he could remember anything more, the peace of the Stewart household was once again shattered by a shriek that seemed to emanate from somewhere downstairs.

"Daddy. There's a man!" If Debbie's words hadn't had the impact of a cattle prod on Joe, the panic in her voice would have, jerking him out of bed and halfway down the stairs before he was even completely awake. As he reached the base of the stairs and spun left past the banister, Debbie's voice was joined by Tia's. Their housekeeper was shouting out a stream of Spanish so fast and thick that Joe could only catch a few words. But the words that he did catch, "hombre malo," or *bad man*, made his heart leap into his throat.

Now he could hear that their voices were coming from the kitchen, and as Joe raced through the downstairs hallway, he grabbed the closest thing at hand to wield as some sort of weapon. It was a crystal vase, still filled with water and tulips. Under other circumstances he might have appreciated the irony of racing toward an intruder with a vase full of freshly cut flowers, but as he listened to a new round of screams, his mind was filled with images of his daughter and Tia under attack, and all he could think of was coming to their rescue as quickly as possible.

Crashing through the double swinging doors that separated the hallway from the kitchen, Joe was prepared to see anything from a knife-wielding psycho to a hardened criminal dressed in an orange prison jumper and brandishing a pistol. But the sight of a young man with long dark hair, and dressed in a neat pair of jeans and a yellow polo shirt backing away from Tia, who was waving a batter-covered spatula menacingly in his direction, was so unexpected that for a moment all Joe could do was stand there frozen, a look of puzzled confusion on his face.

"What's going on here?" Still holding the vase high above his head in his left hand, as though he were auditioning to be the Statue of Liberty, Joe stared around the room, trying to make sense of the scene before him. With the exception of the man standing a few steps inside the partially open French doors, the kitchen looked pretty much like it always did. Doughy balls popped and sputtered in a large iron skillet on the stove next to an oil-soaked paper towel, on which cooled dozens of powdered sugar–covered doughnut holes. On the granite-topped island in the center of the room a silver whisk lay against the rim of a mixing bowl, streamers of egg yolk dripping slowly down its side.

But the airy kitchen that was normally a strictly enforced no-commotion zone, was now anything *but* calm. Tia, a white smear of what looked like flour spread across the side of her nose, was advancing steadily toward the would-be assailant, her spatula held out in front of her like a dueling sword. Behind her, her eyes wide with anger, fear, or possibly some combination of both, Debbie stood barefoot, dripping water onto the dark blue tile floor. Her blonde hair was plastered to the sides of her head and down her back, where it disappeared beneath a beach towel.

"I was out by the pool when this guy suddenly stepped out of the bushes and attacked . . ." Debbie began, pulling the towel more tightly around her as she glared at the man from behind Tia's shoulder.

"I didn't attack anyone." The young man said, brushing a stray lock of curly brown hair out of his eyes and starting toward Joe, one arm extended as though he wanted to shake hands.

"Get back or I will cut off your head." Tia started forward, and from the look in her eyes, Joe had no doubt, dull spatula or not, that she would try to make good on her threat. Apparently the intruder felt the same way because he backpedaled quickly toward the door.

"Tia, please put down the spatula. I don't think that it will be necessary to behead anyone today." Then noting the flash in her deep brown eyes, Joe continued, "But if he makes a single wrong move I give you complete freedom to cut away." Tia nodded gravely, but lowered the utensil only a little.

"Now then, what are you doing in my back—" Joe began, but his words were cut off by two bright flashes, accompanied by the low whir of an electric motor. The combination of the light and sound was a familiar one to Joe, having spent a great deal of time in the public spotlight, and his mind instantly recalled what he would have noted immediately if it hadn't been for all the confusion. Around his neck the young man was wearing a dark black strap. It was attached to an expensive-looking 35-millimeter camera, which the man now held up to his eye as he snapped a quick series of photographs.

A reporter. Joe's emotions suddenly went from slightly befuddled good humor to bubbling rage. It wasn't enough that these jackals had made yesterday a living hell for him, painting him to the whole world as some kind of criminal. Now they were invading his home, trespassing on his private property, and—

"Hey sweetheart, do you think you could drop that towel for a picture or two?" The photographer turned his camera toward Debbie and quickly squeezed off a couple more shots. "You might even make the cover of the Sunday insert."

"Get out!" Joe roared. In two quick strides he was across the room, ripping the camera from the man's hands. Completely ignoring the strangled squawks of the photographer, who had to duck out from under the camera's strap to avoid being yanked from his feet, Joe snapped open the back of the camera and unspooled the film in a long trail of ruined images.

"Hey you can't—" the man sputtered. But apparently Joe could, as he grabbed the back collar of the man's shirt and dragged him out of the kitchen and toward the entryway, the man's loafers rattling across the tile floor like a poorly made marionette. Throwing the front door open, Joe was amazed to see that the entire street in front of his house was filled with news vans. Dozens of reporters jostled each other on his front lawn, and as he swung the door open, they all converged toward him like a cloud of gleaming-eyed ravens.

"Mr. Stewart, is it true that you've hired the same team of attorneys that defended O. J.? Can you comment on the allegations that you have been having an affair with your assistant? Did your wife file for divorce? Is this another Enron?" Ignoring the questions and the inquisitive lenses of the cameras, Joe shoved the photographer out the door, and the man barely avoided falling down the front steps.

"What about my camera?" the man demanded, sounding more confidant now that he had an audience of reporters behind him.

"Here." Joe tossed the camera to him, and he bobbled it for a minute before clutching it to his chest.

"You owe me for a roll of film too." He glanced back over his shoulder, swinging his long dark hair in a graceful arc, as he made sure that the cameras were getting all of this.

For a moment, Joe considered slapping the man's outstretched fingers away or just slamming the door. But then he noticed the vase still clutched in his left hand, and miraculously still full of flowers and water. "Take this." He shoved the vase forward and into the surprised photographer's hands, splashing water across the man's shirt and down the front of his pants. "That should cover it." Turning away, he closed the door, ignoring the shouts of the men and women in his front yard.

"Do you want me to call the police?" Tia asked, startling Joe, who hadn't realized that she had followed him to the front door.

Joe shook his head, remembering the looks the officers in the precinct had given him the night before. "No, I think we are just going to have to live with the paparazzi hounding us until this thing blows over."

"Paparazzi?" Tia asked with a quizzical frown.

"It's what they call these kind of people in Europe."

"Well I call them vultures," Tia said, miming a surprisingly good imitation of the long-necked carrion eaters.

Smiling, Joe put one arm around the small woman's shoulders and gave her a quick hug. "Then they better not mess with us, because we're far from dead." Joe started up the stairs, and then stopped and turned back toward Tia, lowering his voice.

"Maybe you'd better take the phone off the hook too. I don't think they've discovered our unlisted number yet, but it probably won't take them long to get it." He thought of how brittle Heather had looked the night before. "I'll probably need to talk to them sooner or later, but for right now I think it would be better if we all had a little peace and quiet."

"Sí," Tia nodded and hurried back into the kitchen.

It probably had not been the brightest move, Joe thought, tossing that kid out the front door in front of the hungry eyes of every major news affiliate in the area. He could just imagine what tonight's news-cast would look like. But just the thought of anyone hurting his family made his pulse start pounding all over again. He'd taken this risk knowingly when he'd made a public figure of himself. The company spent millions of dollars every year making sure that the press knew Infinity Networks very well, and by association Joe Stewart. It stood to reason that when things turned upside down for him, the press would be there to follow the story just as closely.

"But they better leave my family out of this," he muttered to himself, slamming one fist against his thigh and then wincing at the rash that was growing more painful by the day. He would need to get that looked at soon, but there was someone else he needed to meet with first. Slipping into a comfortably loose pair of jeans and a sweatshirt, he quickly ran the electric razor over his face and threw a couple of hand-fuls of water on his hair before pulling it into some semblance of neat-ness with a black plastic comb that he tucked into his back pocket.

Stepping back out of the bathroom, he frowned slightly at the sight of Heather still lying curled up beneath the blankets on her side of the bed. Normally she and Tia were the first ones up in the morning. Of course after last night, who could blame her for wanting to sleep in a little. It was just that seeing her there, dead to the world with the sun up for hours, was an uncomfortable reminder of the darkness that she'd gone through after her surgery. Leaning gently over her face, Joe brushed his lips against one bed-warm cheek. Still she lay unmoving, her chest rising and falling gently with each hushed breath. *Well, let her rest*, he thought. *She deserves it.*

Beginning to descend the stairs, he reached into his pocket to fish out his car keys, and then paused. He needed to apologize to Richie.

He'd never hit him before, and even now the thought of it made his stomach clench and his face flush with embarrassment. He should have done it right after their argument, before he had gone to bed, but he'd been so tired. And neither one of them had been in any frame of mind to talk.

"Richie?" Joe called softly. As he swung open Richie's door, he wasn't surprised to see the blinds drawn tightly shut, letting precious few of the sun's early morning rays into the dim room. Richie wasn't exactly known around the Stewart household as a morning person, and after last night he probably just wanted to sleep in. But it was important that the two of them work things out now, before any more time had gone by and feelings got any harder than they already were.

"Come on Richie, up and at 'em." Joe reached out to shake his son's shoulder. "You can go back to sleep after we—" Joe stopped suddenly as he pushed the blankets away revealing a line of neatly arranged pillows beneath them. Pulling the blankets all the way off the bed, he saw where the pillows had been pulled into a slight curve to more closely resemble a sleeping body. Blood suffused his cheeks as he realized that Richie must have sneaked out of the house that morning before anyone else was up.

"Oh no." Joe threw the blankets back down onto the bed and walked out the door.

"Addy?" Sometime between when Joe had come out of his room and his discovering Richie's absence, Angela had crept out of her bedroom, and now she stood at the head of the staircase waiting for him. Though still wearing the footed pajamas that she loved, she had for some reason decided to add the Mickey Mouse hat they had picked up at Disneyland the year before. It was dark blue with a yellow bill, and from each side sprouted a pair of big black Mickey ears.

"Hey Princess." Joe took a deep breath, trying to recover from his anger at Richie.

"Mama seepin," she said seriously, glancing toward the partially open door of the master bedroom.

"Yeah, Mama's sleeping," Joe nodded, kneeling down to look into her eyes. "She's pretty tired. She had a long night."

Angela nodded, her blonde curls bouncing up and down beneath her cap, and seemed to think this over. "Mama sad?" she asked.

"Oh no, sweetheart. Mama's not sad, she's just needs to get some rest." It wasn't really a lie. At least he hoped it wasn't.

"Hey," he said, trying to change the subject, "you didn't by any chance run into a mystical blue unicorn in search of a fairy princess to turn it white again last night, did you?"

But this morning she only shook her head, refusing to take part in their normal morning ritual. "Itty breda?" she asked pointing one finger toward Richie's closed door.

Thinking that she wanted to know if Richie was asleep too, Joe nodded, now crossing the line into out-and-out fabrication. "Yeah, Richie Brother is sleeping too. Maybe you should just go down and have some breakfast and leave him alone for a while."

"Wutchy breda no seepin." Angela shook her small head vehemently. "Wutchy bye bye." She had caught her father in a lie, and the look she gave him, both accusatory and knowing, was one that he would not have thought a six-year-old capable of, even one without Down syndrome. Not for the first time, Joe wondered how much might be going on behind those wide blue eyes that she was just incapable of expressing.

"Did you see him leave?" he asked.

"Um-hm-hm," she nodded adding the extra syllable as she always did when she wanted to give extra emphasis to her agreement. "Wutchy breda sad. Say, 'berra quite, don tell.'"

"Well don't worry," Joe said pulling her pajama-clad body close to him. "As far as I'm concerned you've been quiet as a mouse. Your secret's safe with me."

Pulling back from him for a moment, Angela stared up into his eyes and asked earnestly, "Addy sad?"

"No—" he started to say, and then seeing that look in her eyes again added, "Well maybe a little."

"Ohn be sad," Angela said, her eyes big and round. And then breaking into a smile, she removed her cap, pulled him close to her and whispered, "Anjwa give patafwy kiz," as she brushed her tiny eyelashes open and closed against his cheek.

* * *

"Mitch," Joe spoke into the hands-free microphone built into the visor of his Lincoln Navigator. "Sorry to be calling you on a Saturday morning."

"Joe?" Mitch sounded surprised, and something else that Joe couldn't quite read.

"I didn't wake you up, did I?" Joe asked, belatedly realizing that it was barely 9:00 A.M. on a Saturday morning.

"No. Not at all. In fact I just got back from doing a 10k with some guys in my running club," Mitch paused for a moment, seeming to choose his words carefully. "I heard that you had some problems yesterday."

"That's putting it mildly." Joe cornered the big vehicle smoothly into the alleyway between the Rite Aid pharmacy and the Albertson's parking lot, slowing for a couple of elderly ladies pushing a half-filled shopping cart out of the store before joining a line of six or so other cars in the McDonald's drive-thru lane. If Tia had known that he'd passed up one of her delicious feasts for a mass-produced breakfast sandwich, she would have told him off first and had his head examined second, but he'd wanted to get out of the house and meet with Mitch as soon as possible.

"So what can I do for you?" Again Joe sensed a note in Mitch's voice that sounded almost like apprehension, and it caught him off guard. Mitch Stevens had been his personal accountant since before he started up Infinity. They went way back together. Both had served together in the Palo Alto stake's high council. They played softball on the same city league team, and each year they celebrated the birthdays of their youngest children with a joint party.

"Did I catch you at a bad time?" Joe asked, trying to understand what was wrong with his friend.

"No, it's not that." Mitch coughed nervously. "Listen, um, you're not in jail or anything are you? Because, you know I'm an accountant not a lawyer, and I don't really know much about those kinds of things."

"Jail. You think I'm calling you from jail?" Joe let his friend's words sink in. Is that what even the people who knew him thought? Did they believe that he was capable of doing the kinds of things that the press was accusing him of? Had his decision not to bad-mouth Infinity been taken by everyone as an admission of guilt?

"Well, no. I mean, it's just that with everything they've been saying on the news I just . . ." Mitch let the words fade away into an uncomfortable silence.

"Mitch, you've known me for what, fifteen, sixteen years now?" Joe eased his car forward as the woman in front of him completed her order and pulled around the corner of the red-and-gold building. "I'd hope you know me better than that." He ordered a sausage McMuffin, juice, and hash browns as Mitch mumbled an excuse-filled apology.

"Listen, don't worry about it," Joe cut him off. "I know you didn't actually believe any of that. But the reason I called was, I wondered if I could swing by your house for a few minutes and have you take a look at my books. One of the guys at work thinks that Infinity may call in the loans I bought my stock with and you know that I put up the house as collateral."

"Well, Bev wanted to drive over and visit her folks this afternoon," Mitch started.

"Not a problem," Joe said around a bite of English muffin. "I can be there in five minutes and we can get everything wrapped up in under half an hour."

"I guess that would be okay," Mitch hesitantly agreed. Joe still wasn't sure what was wrong with him. But he thought they would both feel better once they'd had a chance to talk things over.

"Great then. I'll see you in five minutes." Joe stuffed the rest of the sandwich into his mouth, grimacing at the greasy-tasting meat, and pulled out across the intersection toward his friend's house.

When he knocked on the front door of the beige Tudor, Mitch answered quickly. He had pulled on a pair of red sweatpants, but he was still wearing his sweaty T-shirt. In the living room Mitch's wife glanced up curiously from a black-covered book with a picture of some kind of circuit board on it that Joe remembered seeing in a Church bookstore.

"Hey Bev," Joe called out as he followed Mitch back down the hallway. "That book any good?"

"So-so." Bev shrugged and looked quickly back down at her book as though embarrassed to be caught watching him.

Following Mitch past the dining room and into his office at the back of the house, Joe settled into one of the dark leather chairs lined up side-by-side behind the large cherry desk and watched as the accountant pulled a thick file from a cabinet made from the same dark red wood. Spreading out the pages, Mitch turned on a calculator and began tapping in figures.

"So what did the stock close at? Four and a quarter?" Mitch asked absently as he totaled a column of numbers scribbled onto a yellow legal pad.

"Yep." Joe grimaced, as he thought about the huge one-day drop and the additional drop that would probably occur on Monday.

"And what did the house appraise at last year?" Mitch continued.

"Three point five." Joe said.

"Probably have a hard time getting that for it now. But still it's as good a number as any." After a few more minutes of shuffling papers and entering numbers, Mitch sighed and sat back in his chair.

"It doesn't look good." Mitch ran one hand across his balding head and slid his glasses up on his forehead, making him look like an aging World War I pilot.

"How bad?" Joe leaned forward across the desk steeling himself for the worst.

"Even if you could liquidate everything at today's prices, which may not even be possible with word of your troubles getting around," Max spun the legal pad to face Joe and tapped at a number near the bottom of the page, "you're still more than three million in the hole."

"Three million?" Joe dropped back into his chair, the strength suddenly sapped from his body like water disappearing through a straw. "And that includes everything? Bonds, 401k?"

"That includes everything. Right down to your wife's Christmas account and your kid's college and mission funds." Mitch kept his eyes glued to the papers in front of him as he delivered the verdict.

"Well there must be something we can do," Joe nearly pleaded. "Isn't there some way we can protect the house and some of the money until—"

"Joe," Mitch interrupted him, "I think it might be better if you got a new accountant. I can recommend some very good people."

"What?" Joe asked, sure that he had misunderstood. "There's no way I'd ever go with someone else, Mitch. I trust you completely. If you need to bring in some outside help, that's fine. But you're the man. Always have been, always will be."

"I don't think you understand," Mitch said, still not looking up from the papers.

"What is it, the money?" Joe asked. "Because I'll make sure you get every dime. I can even pay you in advance. I'm not looking for pro bono."

"No, it's not the money." Mitch finally looked up from the desk.

"Then what is it?" Joe asked bewildered. Whatever had been bothering his friend and accountant was finally coming to a boil.

"Look," Mitch laughed uncomfortably, "you know that I handle the accounts of a lot of pretty wealthy people. And most of them are LDS."

"Sure." Joe nodded. "I probably sent half of them your way."

"Don't make this any more uncomfortable than it has to be." Mitch slid back in his chair.

"Look Mitch, whatever you have to say, just spit it out."

"Okay, the thing is, you know that with the market the way it is I'm struggling just like everybody else in the valley. So I can't afford to lose any more accounts without really taking it in the shorts."

"But that's just it," Joe said, still lost as to the point his friend was trying to make. "I'm giving you business. How would that make you *lose* accounts?"

"You really don't understand, do you?" Mitch lifted an expensive-looking pen from his desk and spun it open and closed. "If people start associating me with you, they're going to take their business somewhere else. You know, birds of a feather and all that. I'm still your friend and all, but I just can't afford to take that kind of risk."

As Joe stood up from his chair, his legs seemed to sway and waver beneath him. "Mitch, I told you I didn't do what they said. In a few days this whole thing is going to blow over. If you dump me now, I'm going to have a devil of a time trying to get someone else up to speed quick enough to help me out of this. What kind of a friend is that?"

"The kind of a friend who makes you face the truth." Although Mitch remained in his chair, his voice took on a high wavering timbre that Joe remembered from the times he would argue with an umpire over what he felt was a blown call. "You may not be willing to admit it, but this kind of thing doesn't just happen overnight. I don't know what you've gotten yourself into, and frankly I don't want to know. But I think money is the least of your worries. I've got to tell you my friend, I've seen people lose their temple recommends over less than this."

"I can't believe you." Joe spun away and wobbled down the hallway, his fists clenched into tight balls. Hurrying past Bev, who was now not even pretending to read the book in front of her, he pulled open the door and stumbled down the front steps.

"I have to avoid even the appearance of evil," were the last words he heard Mitch call out as Joe slammed his car door closed and started the engine.

CHAPTER 5

Beeeeep. A blaring horn reminded Joe that the traffic light in front of him had turned green, and he pulled quickly out into the intersection, waving weakly in apology to the driver behind him. As he approached Riviera Boulevard, the street that led back to his house, he abruptly turned left instead of right. Even on a Saturday morning the streets of Palo Alto were crowded with rushed drivers, trying to reach their destinations just a little faster than the person in the next car. But Joe thought that he would rather face a horde of rude motorists than fight his way back through the crowd of reporters surrounding his house to face his family just now. He needed to get his head on right, before he said or did something he might regret.

Passing one of the many parks spread throughout the city, he watched idly as a group of young boys and girls raced up and down a chalk-marked field, kicking and chasing a black-and-white soccer ball. On the sidelines parents called out encouragement and suggestions. It hadn't been that long ago that he had been one of those parents, cheering Debbie and Richie in their games. He thought that in another year or two Angela might even be up to giving it a try. But now he watched the men and women with longing, envying their seemingly carefree moments.

Mitch's words still echoed in his head. *This kind of thing doesn't just happen overnight.* Was there any truth to that? *Was* he responsible for this in some way? Could he have done something that might have prevented it?

"No," he spoke aloud in the quiet interior of the car, slamming one hand down onto the leather-covered steering wheel. Turning randomly through a series of streets that led away from the residential areas and out toward the shopping district of the city, he spoke half in prayer and half just to help himself clear his head. "This isn't my fault. There was no way I could have been prepared for this kind of thing. So why did You let this happen to me God?" Joe pulled to the side of the street, the car idling next to the curb as he wiped a stray tear from his eye with the back of his hand and bit back a sob of frustration.

"You let me build up this successful company, I know You did. There were so many times when I could have failed, probably should have failed. But You were always there for me, helping me find a way to make everything come together. So why now? Why even let me get to this point if You just planned on pulling the rug out from under me when everything was going smoothly?" The silence in the car was palpable, not that Joe expected a voice to miraculously answer him, but it would have been nice to feel some kind of comfort or at least direction.

This was the thing he had feared most since the day Debbie had been born. Prior to that, he had always felt like he and Heather could pretty much play things day to day, taking chances in his career. Taking time off from work to go back to school or even just because they felt like it if they'd wanted to. But the day he had looked at that tiny infant, he had felt a new weight on his shoulders. As her father, it was his responsibility to make sure that she would always have at least the basics; food, shelter, and clothing. But more than that, he wanted to see that she would never want for anything. And with each additional child, the feeling had only grown stronger.

"Is that why all this is happening?" Tears now flowed freely down Joe's cheeks. "Is it because deep down inside I was afraid that something like this really would happen? Is my family being punished for my fear? Is my fear a lack of faith?" But whether the answers were not forthcoming, or he was just unable to hear them through his anger and frustration, Joe felt no closer to the truths he was seeking, and at last he pulled back out into the street, angrily sweeping the wet streaks from his face.

Unconsciously, Joe realized, he had driven to one of the areas where Richie and his friends liked to hang out. Trendy upscale shops had been replaced by record stores, although Joe guessed that they really weren't *record* stores any more, no vinyl in any but the collectable shops. Boutique theaters crowded shoulders with coffee shops and clubs, now dark, recovering from late Friday nights and preparing for late Saturday nights. Most of the sidewalks were empty at this time of the morning, but a few groups of stragglers hung out here and there sipping coffee and, as often as not, taking long drags on cigarettes. Joe wondered whether they were early risers or still going from the night before.

Black overcoats and T-shirts seemed to be the dress of choice. Girls and boys alike wore dark eye makeup, black nail polish, and short, spiked hair. One of the guys at work had told him the style was called "Goth." As in Gothic, Joe assumed. But to him it just looked dark and depressing, as though death wasn't coming soon enough for these kids, and they felt like they had to hurry it up.

Turning right, he noticed a twenty-four-hour video arcade and slowed down to look inside. Across from the arcade, beside the open door of a shop called Hairzilla, a boy and girl were locked in a tight embrace against a brick wall. At least he thought it was a boy and a girl. One of them was wearing a black leather mini-skirt that hugged tightly at her narrow hips. Her blonde hair was streaked with black tiger stripes and sprouted up in every direction from dozens of hair clips. The other figure was harder to make out; he wore a pair of dark wraparound sunglasses, although they were both still standing in the shadows. His hair was dyed bright green and spiked out all over his head like a frozen fireworks display. Joe figured that maybe the kid had just blown a decent chunk of change on his new doo.

Finding the arcade empty except for a couple of boys that looked to be no older than seven or eight, Joe glanced into his rearview mirror and caught sight of Green Hair breaking out of his embrace with Tiger Stripes. *Probably needed to come up for air,* he thought. As the two of them turned to walk up the sidewalk in the other direction, he noticed that the guy was wearing the same type of leather jacket that Richie had been wearing the night before. Thick chains hung down from each pocket as though the wearer might need to lock it to a phone pole while he wasn't using it. *Did they all shop in the same stores to get just the right look?*

As Joe began to pull away from the arcade, Green Hair turned for a quick backward glance over his shoulder, and something about the boy made Joe slam on his brakes. That couldn't have been Richie, and yet something about that face looked so familiar. Dropping the big four-wheel drive into reverse, he checked to be sure that the street was clear behind him and then pressed the accelerator, quickly catching up to the couple. At the whining sound of the car reversing toward them, the kids picked up their pace and then stepped through the door of one of the shops.

Pulling over so quickly that his right rear tire ended up halfway over the curb, Joe killed the ignition and swung open his door. Leaping down to the street, he circled the front of the car and stopped before the shop that the couple had disappeared into. He assumed that it was a music store, although from the strange designs painted on the outside of the window, it could have been a voodoo shop for all he could tell. His only clue was the Cyrillic-looking lettering at the bottom of the pane that said new and used CDs were cheap.

Opening the door and stepping into the dim interior, he was pleasantly surprised by the music playing softly over the store's loudspeakers. Not that he recognized it. He wasn't even sure what the style was called. But he had been expecting something that sounded like trash cans being cut open with chain saws, and instead this was more like bongo drums being accompanied by woodwinds with the sound of some kind of bird or animal in the background. It was actually very pretty, and for a moment he almost forgot why he had come into the store.

But then remembering Green Hair and Tiger Stripes, he quickly scanned the interior of the small store. The entire store couldn't have been more than a few hundred square feet, four aisles of new CDs were arranged alphabetically by artist, while the used CDs were stacked in shelves that lined the walls. Cameras were mounted in all four corners of the single room with signs warning that shoplifters would be summarily hanged and then prosecuted to the full extent of the law. Although the painted-over windows and limited lighting left the store in an almost cavelike gloom, it was obvious that the man behind the counter and Joe were the only two in the store.

"Did you just see two kids come in here?" Joe asked. The pale man, who looked to Joe—now that his eyes had adjusted to the dark—to be no older than Richie, only shrugged. But for just a second after Joe asked the question, his eyes had darted to the opposite side of the room. Crossing slowly to the other side of the store, and carefully checking each aisle to make sure that no one was ducked down beneath the displays, Joe stopped before the far wall. Unlike the other three walls that were lined with shelves from top to bottom, this wall was draped with black fabric from floor to ceiling. Now that he was closer he could see the fabric swaying gently back and forth.

Reaching one hand tentatively forward, Joe pulled at the fabric and it slid to the side, revealing a small cubical with two chairs and two sets of headphones. A sign on the wall read *Listening Room* with a small handwritten subtitle that read, "We are still watching you!" This cubical was empty, but it was obvious that the entire wall was lined with similar "listening rooms."

Working his way down the wall, Joe slid open each of the curtains until at last he stood before the final space. Slowly moving aside the black fabric, he was not surprised to see the boy and girl cowering in the back corner of the room. Although Green Hair was still wearing his wraparound sunglasses, Joe now had no doubt of who it was.

"Richie," he said softly, and the boy looked toward the ground, his arm still wrapped protectively around the girl, who looked scared to death. "Richie, I would like you to come home now." For a moment, Richie looked as though he was thinking about trying to push past his father to make a run for it, but then his shoulders slumped as he nodded sullenly.

"Yeah whatever."

Joe sighed with relief. He didn't want to have to make a scene, especially with the way he knew that both of them were feeling this morning. "Would you like me to give your friend a lift somewhere?" he asked.

The girl shook her head, eyes wide, and squeaked out a quick, "No."

* * *

"Heather?" Joe ran one hand lightly over his wife's shoulder, but she only moaned a little and buried her face deeper into the pillows.

"Honey, it's almost noon." Joe continued to sit on the edge of the bed lightly rubbing Heather's shoulders and back, his eyes filled with concern. "You really need to get up and have something to eat."

"Just a few more minutes." Heather rolled across the bed away from his touch, the blankets twisting around her body like a cocoon.

"Why don't I just have Tia bring you up a tray?" Joe asked.

"Mmmm," Heather moaned something indecipherable that Joe decided to take as a yes.

"Tia, could you bring up a plate of toast and fruit? And maybe some juice too," Joe spoke into the intercom, pressing the button for the kitchen.

"Yes Mr. Stewart," Tia's voice answered quickly. "I have some very nice grapefruit."

"Thanks Tia, that would be perfect." Joe turned for another worried look at his wife before going into the bathroom and closing the door behind him. Could Heather be experiencing a setback? It was probably nothing, and yet sleeping all day had been one of the first signs before.

Two years ago, if someone had suggested to him that Heather might be using sleep to hide from her problems, Joe would have told them they were crazy. Heather was a warrior. No matter how big a challenge might be, she took it head on, grabbing it by the horns and wrestling it to the ground until it cried "Uncle."

He remembered the time when she had been stake Relief Society president, and two of the wards had ended up booking the gym for the same night for their annual Enrichment night programs. Both of the ward Relief Society presidents were adamant that they had booked the building first and that it would be absolutely impossible for either of them to change their dates now. The stake presidency had been in a near panic, sure that all-out war was about to break loose.

But Heather had calmly sat down with both sisters, listening to their carefully laid-out plans with the patience of a saint. Then, as if it should have been obvious to everyone, she outlined an elaborate evening that would combine the best of both of their programs into a multi-ward gala extravaganza. It had been a huge success, and several surrounding stakes had asked the sisters to help them with their plans.

That was just the way she was. What other people viewed as an insurmountable problem, she viewed as an exciting opportunity. She would no more have run from a problem than she would have abandoned her children. But after the last year, he wasn't sure what to think.

It was as if the cancer had slowly eroded the strength that she had always relied on to carry her through difficult times, and when her body had finally given out, her mind and spirit hadn't known how to cope with it.

Still, that was months ago, and she was doing so much better now. It had just taken her some time to build her reserves back up. She had probably had a tough time getting to sleep last night. After a good rest and something to eat she would be fine.

As Joe stepped into the shower, his thoughts turned from Heather to Richie. The ride home had been about as quiet as expected. He had tried to get Richie to open up to him, but the conversation had been mostly one sided.

"Are you hungry? Do you want to stop and get a burger or something?" Joe had asked his son, who sat slumped against the passenger door, as far away from his father as he could get.

"Huh-uh."

"Who was the girl?"

"Just somebody."

"Richie, you know how we feel about you dating girls outside the Church. It's not that a girl inside the Church is necessarily any better than one outside the Church. But if you could just find some friends with your same standards to—"

"She is," Ricky cut him off.

"Is what?"

"Mormon. Kayla is a Mormon."

"Oh." Joe turned to stare at Richie, trying to decide if he was telling the truth or just trying to yank his dad's chain, but it was impossible to read his expression behind the dark sunglasses. "Would you mind taking those things off?" Joe reached across the seat and pulled the sunglasses from his son's face, exposing a badly swollen left eye, black and blue around the lid, and fading to a sickly yellow toward the bridge of his nose. Joe's heart plummeted.

"Richie, I'm so sorry." Joe's hand trembled as he tried to set the glasses down on the dashboard. "I didn't mean to . . . I mean . . . you have to know I would never intentionally hurt you. I'm just so sorry."

"'S okay" Richie picked the glasses up off the dashboard and put them back on, tucking his hands into his jacket pockets and turning to look out the window.

They had driven the rest of the way home in silence. Joe had a million things that he wanted to say, but his mind kept replaying the scene from the night before, his hand connecting with a jarring thud against his son's eye, and his tongue remained glued to the roof of his mouth.

I'll talk to Richie, he thought as he stepped out of the shower and toweled off, enjoying the steamy solitude of the bathroom, *just as soon as things calm down a little.* Slipping into his robe, he eased the bathroom door open and peered out at his wife. Although the tray of food lay untouched at her side, at least she was awake. A puzzle magazine lay open across her lap and she was busily filling in the blanks of an anagram or crossword, or some such thing, with a black ballpoint pen. That was just like Heather too. He had never seen her use a pencil, even on the *New York Times* crosswords.

Maybe she was going to be okay after all.

* * *

As Joe drifted into a fitful sleep his mind was still troubled by the seemingly infinite number of problems he had to face. How was he going to right their financial situation? He needed to find a replacement for Mitch, but going to a complete stranger with such a personal matter just felt wrong; like hanging his dirty laundry from a flagpole.

And sooner or later he was going to have to come clean with Heather, telling her about the possibility, however remote, that they might lose their house. He would have talked to her about it already, but being around her right now was like being with a zombie. She had eventually roused herself from the bed. He and Tia had even talked her into eating some dinner. But she seemed to be lost in her own world most of the time, and she had gone back to bed before the nine o'clock early news even started.

At least Richie had been okay. He had spent most of the day in his room; coming out briefly to eat, and then returning just as quickly. After dinner Heather had gone into his room to talk to him for a while. She had been in there almost an hour before returning to her own room and delving back into her puzzle magazine again. So maybe he could talk to her tomorrow and find out what she'd been able to learn.

He had finally gone out to make a brief statement to the reporters still gathered in front of his house. It had been short and to the point. He had not known anything about the possible design theft until he had been informed of it Friday morning like everyone else. To the best of his knowledge no charges had been filed against him, and unless they were, he had no intentions of hiring a lawyer, publicist, or anyone else to represent him in the matter. He was sure that the reporters had come away from their brief discussion frustrated. He had refused to lay blame or name names. He wouldn't even comment on the ridiculous rumors that had been floating around, and he had no plans for pursuing any legal action against the company at this time.

It wasn't what they wanted to hear, and it had been his experience that when reporters didn't get what they wanted, they found ways to invent things. But that was their problem. He had said everything he was going to say, and that was that. He didn't know whether it was his statement or the appearance of the Palo Alto police, encouraging the reporters to move their vehicles, but for the first time since that morning, the street in front of his house was finally quiet again.

So many worries, he thought drowsily, *and so little concrete direction*. It was like being lost in a trackless wilderness. Where no one knew how to find you, might not even have known you were lost in the first place, and you had no idea which direction led toward safety and which led deeper into the forest, into the blackness where anything might be waiting for an unwary traveler to step within striking distance.

It was with these thoughts swirling dreamily through his head that he finally drifted off to sleep. Leaving behind a world in which he only felt lost, to emerge into a world in which he truly was. He had thought that nothing could match the last forty-eight hours for stress, and at times outright fear, but he was wrong.

"Heather?" Joe called out into the woods, but the rising gusts of frigid air whipped the words away as soon as they left his mouth. He shielded the sides of his face with his hands, trying to block the pine needles, bits of dust, and debris that stung his eyes before disappearing out into the darkness, and searched for any sign of his wife. She and the children had been right behind him just a few minutes ago, but now all he could make out were the tree branches swaying back and forth wildly, as though intentionally trying to point him in the wrong direction.

Heavy black clouds raced across the night sky, erasing what little light the stars and moon had provided, and suddenly his vision was limited to only a few feet in front of his face. A fat drop of icy water splattered against the back of his neck, another struck his bare forearm, then another.

"Heather? Debbie? Richie? Angela?" His words now carried a new sense of urgency as he cupped his hands to his mouth, shouting into the night. He didn't know how they had become separated, but he knew that he needed to find his family and get them to safety fast. This felt like it was going to be one of those mountain storms that his father had called widow-makers.

In the mountains, squalls could come on with a speed unbelievable to those who had never experienced them. Unwary travelers caught out in such a storm, especially at night, could find themselves not only disoriented, but experiencing temperatures that plummeted from cool to freezing in minutes. Slapping at his arms to keep them warm, Joe turned in a slow circle, straining his eyes against the darkness, searching for a flash of movement that might signal his family was somewhere nearby.

As though some unseen power had suddenly flipped a switch, the clouds overhead released their fury in a downpour that instantly soaked through Joe's pants and shirt, while the wind gusted to near-gale force, turning the frigid drops of water into stinging bullets. Were Heather and the kids out in this? The thought made his heart race, and he felt the first stirrings of all-out panic.

Maybe they had turned around and headed back down to the car, he thought. *When the wind had picked up. Sure. They had probably called out to him, and thinking that he'd heard, doubled back on the trail. They were safe for the time being, but if he didn't get back soon, they might decide to start looking for him.*

"I'm coming!" Joe tried vainly to shout above the roar of the rain and wind as he turned and began to jog back down the hill. But before he had taken a half dozen steps, something hard slammed across the bridge of his nose, dropping him to the ground and sending bright sparks of color shooting across the backs of his eyes.

Rising slowly, he rubbed one hand across his nose and then pulled it sharply away, gasping at the hot pain it caused. He must have been cut pretty badly. Reaching cautiously forward, now almost completely blinded by the sheets of falling water, his hand touched the thick pine branch that he had run into.

He had gotten turned around a little—there had definitely not been any branches across the trail when he'd hiked up it. But the path had to be somewhere nearby. Holding his hands out before him like a blind man, he tried first one direction and then another. But no matter which way he turned, after only a few steps, scrub brush and tree branches met his touch, and he fought to keep from giving in completely to the panic that was rising like hot bile in his chest.

He couldn't be lost. How could he save his family if he couldn't even save himself? The trees, which had begun moaning softly when the wind had first picked up, now wailed and screamed as though the gale was causing them physical pain. For a moment he thought he heard Angela's voice calling his name. But the wind was blowing so wildly now that he couldn't tell which direction it had come from, or even if he had actually heard it at all.

"Angela!" he screamed, as a huge gust of wind nearly lifted him from his feet.

"Addy!" Again Joe thought he could hear Angela's shrill voice breaking and echoing out of the swirling rain, and his heart leapt into his throat. His baby was out there somewhere caught in a storm that would suck the life from her if he didn't reach her soon. Bulling his way through the thicket of trees and brush in the direction that he thought her voice had come from, he slipped and fell to his knees. A wave of shivers racked his arms and legs as he tried to push himself up out of the dirt that was quickly turning to a slippery muck.

"Annngggggeeelllllaaa!" he bawled out her name. "Where are you?" Straining to hear her voice again, he held perfectly still, muddy hands resting on the knees of his water-logged jeans. The only answer was the wind, now screaming through the branches above his head. Something in the sound of the rain changed, but he couldn't place it until a hard object struck the side of his face and dropped down into his collar. Reaching inside the front of his shirt, he pulled out a ball of ice the size of a marble.

"Nooo," he moaned. Angela wouldn't last an hour in this.

Suddenly the darkness was rent by a flash of light, followed by a huge boom that Joe could actually feel pulse through his body. Behind him, what sounded like a rifle shot preceded a thunderous crash as a tree collapsed beneath the storm's onslaught. Joe rose to his feet, trying to regain his bearings. But as quickly as the light had appeared, it was swallowed back up again by the black.

"Oh please, Heavenly Father, help me find my baby," he cried. "I'll suffer whatever I have to, only please, please, don't let me lose my angel."

Again the night sky was lit up by a flash of lightning, and in that brief instant of light, he saw what looked like an old man beckoning to him. Jumping to his feet, he ran toward the figure, calling out for help. "You there, do you have a light? My daughter is out in the woods alone and I—" He reached where he thought the man had been and waited, but there was no answer.

Either the clouds had thinned a little or his eyes had begun adjusting to the darkness, because he could now faintly see the trees blowing to and fro around him. But the man was nowhere to be seen. "Hello?" he screamed above the sound of wind and the pounding of the hail. But there was no answer. Had he imagined the man? Had he been so desperate for help that he had hallucinated him? Straining to peer through the darkness, he suddenly noticed a patch of white standing out against the dark trunk of a tall pine just to his right.

Walking closer, he raised up to his toes and ran his fingers across the rough bark and then across two smooth white scars. A blaze. Someone had used a hatchet to mark this tree trunk. Slowly rotating in place, he searched the other trees around him until, about ten feet away, he noticed another blaze. Searching the ground between the two trees he could just make out the indentation of a well-used path. Hopefully it would lead him to someone who could help him organize a search party.

Keeping his eye on the second patch of white, he walked quickly along the trail. The next mark was a little further away, but it was just as recognizable, standing out in the dark almost as if it glowed with a light of its own. The trees were thicker here and the rain and wind had less impact. He moved from a quick walk to a jog, and then finally to a brisk run, trusting his feet and eyes to keep him on the trail. Although the marks seemed to be leading away from where he had last heard Angela, he had a strong feeling that he should keep following them. Whoever had marked this trail would help him rescue his family.

He wasn't sure how long he ran along the barely seen trail, occasionally losing his footing but always jumping back to his feet and continuing on. Abruptly the trail came to an end, and just as abruptly, Joe realized that the storm had ended as well. Although it was still dark, a few stray stars broke through the clouds now and then, giving just enough light to let him see that he was standing on the banks of a lake. It was small, no more than five or ten acres in size he thought. But it looked deep. And something about it was very familiar. Had he been here before?

"Addy?" Angela's voice drifted faintly on the night air from some distance away.

"Angela! Princess come this way!" Joe called out at the top of his lungs. "It's safe here."

"I cumbin." Angela's voice cried out, sounding just a little closer.

"Oh thank you." Joe's heart was filled with gratitude and he dropped to his knees and bowed his head. "I—" he began to pray. But something felt very wrong. Opening his eyes he looked slowly around the clearing. He wasn't alone. There was something out there, hiding in the trees, just out of sight.

He listened intently, straining to hear a movement or a breath. But although Joe knew that it was still there, it was utterly silent. *That's how I know it's there,* he thought. *By the silence. It's so deadly that silence accompanies it like a shroud. All living things burrow into the ground or huddle in their nests, or lay shivering in the brush, too scared to even run when it approaches.*

And suddenly Joe knew why it was there. It wanted Angela. It had been stalking her, following her through the darkness waiting to pounce. It sensed her goodness and was attracted to it like a shark to the scent of blood.

But then Joe had called her and now it could wait for her to come to it—crouching silently, powerful muscles flexing, glowing eyes tracking her progress as she drew ever nearer. He had to warn her now before she got any closer. "Run!" he tried to scream, but his throat was locked with fear. He tried to get to his feet to go to her but his body was a block of ice.

"I cumbin Addy." Her voice was just around the corner now, and Joe could feel the thing's hunger radiating through the trees like waves of heat.

"Oh Father, please protect her," he begged silently, eyes screwed tightly shut, chin clamped against his chest. Suddenly a hand dropped onto his shoulder and he cried out in terror, eyes snapping open, sure that he was about to face death.

"Don't be afraid." It was the old man who had shown him the trail.

"Who are you?" Joe gasped, even as his mind, for some inexplicable reason, kept repeating, *The homeless man, the homeless man.*

"Know your enemy," the man whispered, his breath hot against the cold of the night air. "And protect that which you deem most valuable."

"Addy!" Angela screamed. And for the second time in the last twenty-four hours, Joe leapt from his bed to the sounds of one of his daughters screaming.

Throwing his bedroom door open, he raced down the hallway and burst into Angela's room. Lying on her bed, her eyes wide with terror, Angela screamed out, "Addy help me!" And Joe skidded to a stop. Spread across his youngest daughter's bed, tangled in her hair, and scattered across the floor were hundreds of shards of broken glass. And down the front of her face and hands dripped dark trails of what was unmistakably blood.

CHAPTER 6

"Okay, I think that should wrap it up." Officer Holstein closed his notebook and turned from Joe to look down at Angela who was lying in her parent's bed cradled in Heather's arms. Bandages with various Disney characters prancing across them covered several scratches on her hands and face. She had been a trooper through it all, not even crying when Heather squirted the antiseptic on her cuts.

"You feeling okay soldier?" the officer asked, and with a quick movement of his hand, that even Heather and Joe were unable to follow, magically produced a cherry-red lollipop that he presented to the little girl.

With a smile that could have defrosted icebergs, Angela nodded and took the candy. "Ein okay," she stated confidently. "Ein tut guy."

The policeman looked bewildered by her slurred speech, but Heather squeezed her tightly, being careful not to touch any of her cuts, and agreed, "You are a tough guy."

"The toughest." Officer Holstein patted her hair gently, and then looking back at Joe tilted his head toward the stairway. "Can I have a few more minutes with you?"

"Sure." With a last worried backward glance at his daughter, Joe turned and followed the policeman down the stairs.

"You wouldn't by any chance have a cup of coffee anywhere around here would you?" the policeman asked as they entered the kitchen.

"Sorry. We don't drink coffee," Joe said. "But I could get you a glass of juice or a soda."

"Probably for the best anyway. The caffeine does a number on my stomach. But it helps me stay awake through the night shift." The officer shifted his gun belt slightly as he lowered himself into a chair. "Actually water would be fine."

As Joe lifted a glass from the cupboard and carried it to the refrigerator, he mused about the odds of drawing the same policeman that had taken the report on Richie. *If he thought that I was a bad father then, what must he think now?* Joe wondered. Returning to sit on the other side of the table from the thick-faced officer, he slid the glass and a plastic bottle of water across to him.

"It's a miracle that none of those cuts were more serious. I've seen a piece of broken window like that take an eye out before." Unscrewing the white plastic lid with a cracking sound as the safety seal broke, Officer Holstein ignored the glass and swigged the water straight from the bottle.

"Not to mention the brick," Joe nodded with a shudder, imagining what kind of damage *that* could have done if it had hit his daughter instead of landing harmlessly on the carpet beside her bed.

"True enough." A second swig nearly drained the bottle, and Officer Holstein wiped his mouth with the back of his hand. "We'll check it for prints of course. But it's nearly impossible to get anything off that kind of surface. You're sure you don't have any idea who might have tossed it through your window?"

"I would imagine any of the thousands of people who lost money on Infinity stock on Friday. But no, no one specific."

"Well you can narrow that number down by one. I've got a solid alibi." The police officer fixed Joe with a stare. *Oh just my luck,* Joe thought, *he was an investor too.* "But whoever it was," the officer continued, "he had a pretty good arm. It takes a fair amount of strength to heave a brick through a second-story window."

Joe nodded silently. Angela would sleep in someone else's room until things calmed down. He was still more than a little rattled by the terrifying dream, although he hadn't told anyone else about it. After the brick incident, it would be hard to even let his daughter out of his sight.

Crumpling the plastic bottle, Officer Holstein screwed the lid back on and arched it toward the trash can. It bounced off the wall and ricocheted into the plastic bag that lined the dark blue container. "Two points," he said, getting slowly up out of his chair. Joe followed him as he walked back through the hallway, stopping to pick up the brick, now sheathed in a clear plastic bag, off of the table, and the two men stopped in front of the door.

"You know," Officer Holstein said softly, glancing toward the stairway, "this may be none of my business, but I would keep on eye on your wife as well. She didn't look any too good herself. In fact, if I didn't know better I'd say . . ." He paused for a minute, before shaking his head. "Well she just looks pretty tired."

"I will," Joe said opening the door. First this guy tries to tell him how to raise his son, and then he thinks that Joe needs help seeing how hard his wife was taking everything. Of course she looked tired. After the last couple of days, who wouldn't? Outside, the morning sun was just peeking above the eastern foothills. In another couple of hours they would need to be getting ready for church, and what they all needed most was a little peace and quiet.

The police officer looked as though he was considering saying something more, but finally he shook his head and stepped out onto the walkway. He began to walk straight to his car, but just as Joe was beginning to shut the door, he stopped and turned back.

"Hey, I meant to tell you. I saw your little press conference thing on the news."

"What did you think?" Joe asked, sure that he already knew the answer.

"Pretty weak."

Joe nodded. It was more or less what he had expected.

"I liked it," the police officer said as Joe's eyes widened in surprise. "Guy blusters and shoots his mouth off about how he was wronged and how he's gonna sue everybody, you can count on one hand the times they're ever telling the truth. But, the devil take my soul if I'm lying, I almost believe you *are* innocent." Before Joe could respond, the big man turned around and continued out toward his car.

* * *

By the time the police officer left, everyone in the house was wide awake. And although Joe and Heather urged the kids to go back to bed, Joe thought that Angela was the only one to actually fall asleep. Little kids were funny that way. Maybe it was because so many of the things they experienced were new to them, but they seemed to be almost elastic in nature, recovering in a matter of minutes from what could take an adult weeks to get over. It might have been nature's way of helping them avoid total sensory overload.

And yet those memories were stored away somewhere, where they could be replayed over and over in later years when the impact might be much more traumatic. The possibility kept Joe lying awake in his bed, watching the minutes slowly change on the digital clock. As he listened to Angela's quiet snoring, he wondered if the night's events would come back to haunt his daughter some day, the way that they were haunting him now. He didn't know what he would have done if she had been more seriously injured or, Heaven forbid, killed. Could he live with the guilt of knowing that, at least to some extent, it was his fault? He was glad that he didn't have to find out.

Again his thoughts returned to his dream. It had seemed so real, with none of the usual vagueness or incongruities that seemed perfectly acceptable during a dream, but that made even the most frightening nightmare laughable in the daylight. He could still feel the icy water soaking his skin and the unspeakable terror that had turned his body as cold as the rain when he realized that he was incapable of protecting one of his children. Wrapping his arm around the soft fuzziness of his daughter's pajama-clad body, he pulled her tightly toward him.

"Top kwishin me," she complained, eyes still tightly shut, and squirmed out of his grasp.

"Sorry," he whispered. Realizing that any possibility of further sleep was gone, he rolled quietly out of bed, trying not to disturb either the girl or the woman he was sharing it with.

"Where are you going?" Heather asked. Apparently she hadn't been able to get back to sleep either.

"I thought I'd make some breakfast," he answered quietly. Sunday and Monday were Tia's days off, although she never left with less than five meals stored in the freezer.

"I can do that," Heather started to get out of bed, but Joe motioned for her to lie back down.

"Stay with her, in case she wakes up," he said. And then flipping an imaginary spatula, he added, "Besides, I learned to make a pretty mean waffle on my mission."

"You don't use a spatula to make waffles." Heather smiled with an expression that looked almost like her old self. "Just don't burn the house down, okay?"

"No fires." Joe assured her. Seeing her smile that way was like having a thick rusty chain unwrapped from his heart. He hadn't realized how much of the weight of raising the family Heather carried until he had been without her for six months, and he knew that the children felt the same way. He hoped that spending a quiet Sabbath at church with their friends would do them all some good.

Downstairs, Joe searched the kitchen cabinets fruitlessly for a box of pancake mix, before realizing that Tia probably made everything from scratch. Oh well, time to switch to plan B: toast, scrambled eggs, and bacon. None of those required him to read a recipe.

Cracking eggs into a silver bowl, careful not to get any shells into the runny yellow mixture, his mind returned to the dream, especially the last few minutes of it. What was the source of evil hiding in the trees? And why had it only been interested in Angela instead of him? Hadn't the troll in the story of "The Three Billy Goats Gruff" waited to eat the biggest of the three brothers? But as Joe recalled, the biggest brother had knocked the stuffing out of the troll when he finally showed up. Was the creature afraid of him then? He didn't think so.

Then there was the man. Joe hadn't been able to see much of him, just a quick glimpse of his dark eyes, and then he had moved away to whisper into Joe's ear. But something about looking into those eyes, or maybe listening to the husky voice had been an incredibly familiar, almost deja vu-like, experience.

He had told Joe not to be afraid. Then he had whispered two things to him, just before the dream ended. Something like, "Know who your enemy is and protect your valuables." It actually sounded kind of like the advice Richie's PeeWee football coach had given the boys on their first day of practice, Joe thought with a half-smile.

That hadn't been the exact wording though. Joe thought harder. "Protect that which you deem most valuable." That was it. Well that was easy enough. Hands down, his family was what he deemed most valuable. But what was he supposed to be protecting them from? It went back to the question of knowing his enemy. But had the man been talking about a specific enemy, like the person who had thrown the brick, or something huge like, say, a famine? Pouring the eggs into a skillet and sprinkling in a handful of grated cheddar cheese, he mused that it sounded like something out of Genesis. He could really use a good interpreter of dreams.

He pictured Joseph wandering through the kitchen door. "You see the pine trees represent seven months of declining consumer confidence," Joseph, who looked an awful lot like Donnie Osmond in Joe's imagination, pontificated, "and the rain represents a rebounding stock market. I'd recommend that you short Yahoo, and put half your money into utilities." Oh well, with his luck the interpreter would only speak Egyptian, and he still wouldn't be any better off.

As he laid the plates of steaming eggs and bacon on the table, Joe realized that he hadn't heard the sound of the any of the upstairs showers running. On the clock above the sink, the hour and minute hand were both in the vicinity of the eight. He understood Heather letting Angela sleep in a little this morning, but Debbie and Richie should have both been up by now.

Brushing off his hands on the dark gray cotton of his sweat pants, he climbed the stairs two at a time and called out, "Hey everybody, out of bed. Breakfast is on the table, and we need to get moving if we don't want to be late for church." Halfway up the staircase, he paused to see if his shout elicited some sound of action from above him. When the house remained silent, he continued the rest of the way up.

"Rise and shine everyone. We need to be out the door in an hour." Joe knocked first on Richie's door and then Debbie's, making sure that he heard signs of movement before he continued down the hall. Slowly easing the doors to the master bedroom open, he was surprised to see that Heather was still in bed, doing one of her puzzles. He assumed that the lump under the blankets next to her was Angela.

"Hey hon," he whispered, "breakfast is ready. Do you want to eat or shower first?" Heather glanced up from her magazine with a look that was almost bewilderment.

"Church starts in a little over an hour," Joe reminded her. She checked the clock and then looked over at Angela before shaking her head.

"I don't think that she should go out after what happened last night. Maybe I'll just stay home with her," she whispered back.

"Oh, all right," Joe nodded slowly. He hadn't thought about it, but Heather was probably right. It *had* been a pretty traumatic night, and maybe it would be better for Angela to just stay home and get some rest.

"I'm not going either." Joe hadn't realized that Richie had walked up behind him.

Wheeling around, he took in the fact that his son had apparently slept in the same clothes that he had been wearing the day before. "Oh yes you are," Joe countered. "And while you're in the shower, try to wash that dye out of your hair too."

"It's permanent," Richie sneered. "So unless you want me to embarrass you in front of all of your friends, you're just gonna have to let me stay home."

"I don't embarrass easily. Now get in there and get cleaned up." Joe pointed toward the bathroom.

"Come on man. You know that everyone'll be staring at us. They're all gonna think that you, ya know . . ." Richie stuck his hands in his pockets and stared uncomfortably at the floor.

"You think that everyone at church will believe what they heard on the news?" Joe asked. He could feel his pulse starting to pound. "You think that people who have known us since before you were born are suddenly going to take some reporter's words over mine?"

"Yeah, maybe." Richie refused to back down. From her bed, Heather silently watched the two of them argue.

"Well I don't believe that. But if a few of them do, that's their problem. I know that I'm innocent here, and that's all that matters." Joe's voice was low now, but if anything it was more powerful than before as he waited for Richie to look up and meet his eyes before continuing. "I guess we'll both just have to take a chance that we might be embarrassed in front of our friends."

"No, Dad. Richie's right. Everyone's just going to stare at us like some kind of sideshow freaks. It's not like we're all going to go to hell for missing one day of church." Sometime during Joe's conversation with Richie, Debbie had come out of her room, and now she walked down the hallway toward them in her long white robe, her arms folded firmly across her chest.

Joe turned to look at her, shocked that he was hearing this from his oldest daughter, who he felt sure would have been backing him up. "It's not about getting punished for not going. It's about taking the sacrament, and feeling the Spirit. It's about showing gratitude for everything Heavenly Father has given us."

"Oh yes. I'm feeling grateful today." Debbie's words were hot and biting, almost spiteful. "Let's see, I'm grateful for having my dad lose his job, and I'm grateful for having a gazillion reporters turning our front yard into a circus. I'm grateful for losing all of our money, which believe me, Dad, I am aware of, even though you haven't felt the need to inform us of it. Oh yes, I almost forgot, I'm especially grateful for having some lunatic nearly shred my little sister. I guess that about covers it."

Joe felt as though someone had slammed him against a wall, knocking all the air out of his body. He had no idea that this much anger had been percolating inside his children. Shaking his head, almost at a loss for how to respond, he said softly, "It is where Heavenly Father wants us to be, and we *are* going."

"How do *you* know what Heavenly Father wants? It isn't exactly like He's been taking us into His confidence lately, is it? Or did you just forget to tell us that He whispered to you last week that He was about to hit us over the head with a sledgehammer? If there is a God at all Dad, *I* think He hates us." Debbie's words hurt far worse than Richie's had because they were coming from someone who he had been sure had a testimony. His son was still going through the ups and downs of adolescence, but was it possible that he had let his first-born child reach the point where she was about to leave home without a sure knowledge of God's love for His children?

"I . . ." he faltered, turning to Heather for some help. But she was staring down at Angela, her hands clutching at one another as though she were searching for a lost coin. "I don't understand . . ." he started again, but he was saved from having to say anything further by an explosion of covers next to his wife.

Somehow Angela had gotten turned around in her sleep, and the first thing to pop out of the blankets was her feet. A second later they disappeared as she spun around and began tunneling out of the blankets, pushing the pillows out ahead of her like an excited mole. Even before her head cleared the last of the covers though, they could all hear her exuberant voice calling out, "Choochy-chooch. Ina go choochy-chooch."

* * *

"Just a reminder that the young men and young women will be meeting together today in the cultural—" Brother Halpertson, the second counselor in the bishopric, seemed to lose his place as Joe led his family up the aisle to one of the two only available benches, both of which were located at the front of the chapel. Joe was sure that they made quite a sight as they trooped up to their seats.

Richie, with his dark glasses and green hair, hated wearing ties, and had only finished pulling his into a sloppy knot in the car, leaving it hanging a good two inches below his buttoned collar.

Angela wore a huge grin, her pink flowered dress brushing against the tops of her white shoes as she clung to Richie's shirtsleeve, nearly skipping down the aisle behind him. She loved church, and waved to all the people they passed, calling out, "Hedo," to everyone she knew and some that she didn't. She seemed completely oblivious of the myriad of bandages crisscrossing her hands and face.

Joe thought that he and Heather both looked as if they had struggled to remember which shoe went on which foot, a point not far from the truth. As it was, Heather had finally settled for a pair of pantyhose that had a small run on the back of her left leg, and Debbie had pointed out to Joe as they entered the building that he was wearing the wrong jacket for his suit pants.

Of the five of them, Debbie was the only one that looked normal, and she of all people had been the hardest one to talk into coming to church.

As they slid into their bench, Bishop Jacobs stood up and whispered into Brother Halpertson's ear. The second counselor's narrow face suddenly flushed as he looked away from the Stewarts and back down at the list of announcements in front of him. "We will now prepare for the sacrament by singing from page . . ."

Joe watched Angela place a hymnbook in Richie's hands as she waited expectantly for him to open it to the correct page. Richie tried to ignore her, but her persistent smile eventually won out. Angela sang every hymn enthusiastically, whether she knew the song or not. Joe had never really determined whether that was because she loved music in general or due to the fact that she almost always substituted the words "Oh, do you know the muffin man?" at the top of her lungs when she didn't know the correct lyrics.

As he sang the hymn's words from memory, Joe tried to relax and feel the Spirit, but feeling anything other than frustration seemed almost impossible. It had taken everything he had to get them all out the door that morning, and the family's harsh words and arguments lay heavy on his heart.

Listening to the words of the dark-haired sixteen-year-old priest who was blessing the sacrament, ". . . and keep His commandments which He has given them, that they may always have His Spirit to be with them . . ." Joe wondered if his family did have His Spirit with them. And if not whose fault was it that they didn't?

A few minutes later, a young man in a white shirt and tie carried his silver tray of bread to their bench. Heather took the tray from him, but quickly passed it across to Richie without taking a piece of bread. Richie seemed to hesitate, but he too passed the tray across to Angela without taking any. Angela popped a small white square into her mouth, and then, noticing that Richie hadn't eaten any, took a piece for him and tried to press it into his mouth. Refusing to take it, he pushed her hand gently but firmly back down. Before she could try again, Debbie took the bread from her hand, and placed it into her own mouth with a roll of her eyes.

Taking the tray from his daughter, Joe tried to catch Heather's eyes. Why had she chosen not to take of the sacrament? Did she feel that they were unworthy to partake because of this morning's argument? But she had her eyes tightly shut as if in prayer. Finally he took one of the smaller pieces from the tray and swallowed it woodenly. It seemed to catch in his throat for a moment before going down.

* * *

"Hey if it isn't the famous Joe Stewart." Mike Tanner sat down in the folding metal chair next to Joe and held out one freckled hand toward him. Returning his grip, Joe smiled, as always, at the way his gregarious fellow high priest vigorously pumped his hand, up and down, up and down, as though trying to draw water.

"More like infamous these days," Joe grimaced.

"Aah, I wouldn't worry about it." Brother Tanner waved his hand through the air as though shooing away a fly. "I hear that ex-crime bosses are in big demand on the talk-show circuit."

Overhearing Mike's words, a few of the other men in the room glanced curiously toward the two of them, and for just a second Joe thought that he might have been serious. It had been that kind of week. But then seeing the mischievous smile that, along with his fiery red hair, made his friend look like a seriously oversized elf, Joe relaxed. He guessed it was nice to see that *someone* found humor in his misfortunes. "You keep that up Tanner, and I'll see that you get saddled with filling the next three cannery assignments."

"A fate undoubtedly worse than death." Brother Tanner shook his head knowingly.

"Brethren." Tim Brown, the high priest group leader, stood up in front of the twenty or so men crowded into the small classroom. "If I can have your attention, today is the fourth Sunday of the month and so Brother Parkins will be our instructor."

Several of the men around the room moaned quietly. And one of them whispered, "Guess I won't be getting back in time to watch the Giant's game today." Brother Parkins was somewhere in his late eighties. He was hard of hearing and very opinionated. These attributes by themselves wouldn't have mattered much to the men in this room, many of whom shared at least one of those qualities. But he was also extremely long-winded, often letting his lessons run twenty minutes or more overtime, which nearly every man in the room considered a cardinal sin, and his lessons tended to ramble just about anywhere his thoughts carried him.

"With that in mind," Brother Brown continued, trying not to show that he had heard the whispers, "we will dispense with any announcements, and let Brother Parkins begin his lesson."

Brother Parkins stepped gingerly up to the table and laid a large stack of books on its top. He wore a dark flannel three-piece suit year round, regardless of the weather, and carried a gold-handled cane that he often rapped on the table for emphasis. His white hair was combed up into a pompadour that he liked to tell people made him the spitting image of David O. McKay. Although Joe rather agreed with

Brother Tanner, who said that he thought that Brother Parkins looked more like the Mr. Cold Meister character from one of the old animated Christmas specials.

Joe thought that they had chosen the fourth Sunday of the month to let Brother Parkins teach, because that was the one lesson that was not taught from the manual, and he had never seemed to have much use for that book anyway. Instead, the fourth Sunday's lesson was to be taught on a subject chosen by the First Presidency, based on selected conference addresses, scriptures, and occasionally other materials.

"Ahem, well then," Brother Parkins began, snapping at a loose fold of skin on the front of his neck like a rubber band, "I had planned on using the topic selected by the Brethren, but events of this past week convinced me otherwise."

"Probably picked up one of those tabloids and discovered that Elvis was really Joseph Smith's great, great, nephew," Brother Tanner whispered under his breath, and several men around him laughed quietly. But something about the way Brother Parkins had looked toward him as he was mentioning the past week's events gave Joe an uncomfortable jolt in the pit of his stomach.

Brother Parkins *was* old, and he did tend to ramble, but he was not senile. He was quick to decide whether something was good or evil. In his opinion, everything fell squarely on one side of the fence or the other, and once his mind was made up, he defended his decisions forcefully. And he did know his doctrine. The men around the back of the room, especially the younger ones, liked to joke about him behind his back. But Joe had noticed that few of them were actually willing to disagree with the elder statesman of the group to his face. His tongue was quick and sharp, and they had learned through sad experience that Brother Parkins could leave almost any of them looking foolish in front of their peers.

Turning toward the blackboard, the instructor took a piece of chalk between his bony fingers and printed the words "Wickedness NEVER Was Happiness." Facing the class again, he set the chalk deliberately back onto the tray at the base of the board and wiped the white dust from his dry hands with a sound like two pieces of sandpaper rubbing against each other.

"The Lord will not be mocked." Brother Parkins nearly shouted the words, his reedy voice silencing everyone in the room. Picking up his Bible, he tabbed quickly to the page he was looking for. "Proverbs 11:27–28," he sternly announced. "'He that diligently seeketh good procureth favor: but he that seeketh mischief, it shall come unto him. He that trusteth in his riches shall fall: but the righteous shall flourish as a branch.'"

Looking slowly around the room, as if daring anyone to disagree with him, he narrowed his eyes and pointed a finger at Brother Marcum, the ward clerk. "Do you know what that means, young man?"

Brother Marcum, who couldn't have been younger than fifty, and like many of the men in the room made a living that often reached seven figures annually, seemed too surprised to speak for a moment, before recovering his nerve enough to stammer, "Well I would say that the Lord is telling us that we should not focus on our riches. That is, we should seek for spiritual wealth before seeking for material possessions." He risked a quick look up at the instructor, and then quickly began fumbling with his scriptures as though searching for a misplaced bit of wisdom.

Brother Parkins glared around the room, a disappointed look on his face, before asking, "Would anyone else care to hazard a guess as to why that nugget of wisdom was included in the book of Proverbs?" Judging from the silence around the room, no one did.

"Well then, let me share another story that you might be familiar with," Brother Parkins said, his voice deceptively quiet. "As you may remember, there was a certain young man who came unto the Savior upon the coasts of Judaea. And this young man sought what we all seek brothers: life eternal.

"Now this man claimed to have kept the commandments. He told the Savior that he had kept them from his youth up. And yet when Jesus Himself commanded the young man to go and give all that he had to the poor so that he too might become a disciple, he went away sorrowing."

Clucking his tongue against the roof of his mouth, Brother Parkins again let his eyes travel the room before stopping on Mike Tanner. "Brother Tanner, you seem to be full of wisdom today. Why don't you enlighten us with understanding on why this young man went away from the Savior sorrowing so."

Mike's face blushed even more red than usual but his voice sounded under control, maybe even a little amused as he answered. "As I recall, the scripture states that his possessions were great. So I would have to assume that this young man valued his earthly riches above the treasures of Heaven. It would therefore stand to reason that he sorrowed because he felt unable to make the sacrifice necessary to earn exaltation." Leaning back in his seat, he folded his beefy arms across his chest and grinned. "So what do you think Brother Parkins, do I pass?"

Brother Parkins wrinkled his nose as though he smelled something foul. "Barely Brother Tanner, C minus at best. You see, you have only stated what anyone can find by reading a verse or two. You have regurgitated the words that you found on the page. But in order to truly understand the scriptures, you must delve deeper. You must scour the pages, drilling down between each and every word to find the *real* truths hidden within."

The instructor's voice took on a new sense of urgency. "My brothers in the gospel, I tell you that despite what this young man may have claimed, he was a liar and a thief. A liar because no man who truly kept the commandments of God would ever pass up the chance to become a disciple of the Savior for any amount of riches, and a thief because he stole precious minutes of the Savior's time. Wasting his breath with lies which the Lord quickly revealed.

"And Brother Stewart do you know what happened to that young man after he left the Savior that day?" Brother Parkins suddenly turned to face Joe, the taut skin of his broad forehead now furrowed down so tightly that his bushy gray eyebrows actually seemed to overlap each other. Somehow Joe had known all along that this discussion was going to turn back to him, and he felt a greasy sheen of cold sweat coat his arms and back as he tried to recall any further mention of that particular story in anything he had read.

"I don't think so," he answered, feeling somewhat confidant that he was on safe ground.

"No I don't imagine you would. Although I expect that his shoes might fit quite snugly on your feet right about now." Brother Parkins smiled, his big, white, false teeth gleaming from between his gray lips like a hungry crocodile's. Joe could feel the tension in the room rising as several men began clearing their throats nervously and shifting in their chairs. But they held their tongues, perhaps hoping that this was just another of Brother Parkins' ramblings and that he would move on—soon.

"After that man went away, he felt the wrath of God pour down upon him like a hurricane at his door. All that wealth that he had so carefully hidden up, through evil dealings with other dishonest men like himself no doubt, was snatched away from him. His fine linen was turned to sackcloth, his beautiful jewels to glass, and tinkling cymbals to rust. And do you know how *I* know that Brother Stewart?" Joe shook his head silently forcing himself to keep his temper under control. But around him, he could see several of the brothers glancing at each other as if deciding who should say something.

"I know it," Brother Parkins nearly crowed, "because I believe the Lord when He says 'he that seeketh mischief, it shall come unto him.' and 'He that trusteth in his riches shall fall.'"

Raising his arms up and outward as though preparing to conduct an orchestra, his voice filled with an almost manic energy, Brother Parkins called out to the rest of the men. "Brothers, a terrible, terrible thing has happened to every one of us this week. Just terrible." Out of his lips the word sounded as though it rhymed with *gerbil.*

"A wolf came into our little flock wearing the guise of the sheep. He might have fooled some of us, although I must say that I've had my doubts all along, but he didn't fool the Shepherd. No he did not. His deeds were seen and marked in the book of He who watches us all. And now his acts have been made known, and he has felt the lash of God come down upon his back."

"Don't let him bait you," Mike whispered to Joe under his breath. "He's just looking for a fight, and you don't have to give it to him." And yet even as he listened to Mike's advice, Joe could feel himself getting ready to tell the old man what he thought of him and his "lesson".

"Brother Parkins, maybe we could just go back to the lesson that the brethren had outlined for this week." Tim Brown, the group leader interrupted before Joe could speak.

Shaking his head slowly back and forth as though it pained him greatly, Brother Parkins said, "I'd like to, Brother Brown, I truly would. In fact, I for one have completely forgiven my brother for his sins against me already. But true forgiveness from God can only come with true repentance, and repentance cannot come without one freely admitting that he has sinned. I will not stand by and watch a man who I still love take that speedy path down to hell, without speaking to him clearly and yes, even painfully."

Overriding Brother Brown's attempts to stop him, Brother Parkins now turned to face Joe directly. "Brother Stewart, denying the truth will not do you any good. Will you now admit your guilt and free yourself from the weight of your sins?"

"Brother Parkins, that is really quite enough—" Brother Brown began, but Joe cut him off.

"No, it's all right, Tim. Maybe it's for the best that we get all this out in the open anyway." Taking a deep breath to try and calm himself, Joe turned to his accuser and looked him firmly in the eye.

"Brother Parkins, I believe that you have spoken from your heart. But you are misguided and misinformed. You have taken upon yourself a role that belongs to the Lord. You have judged me, and in your eyes I came up short. But let me tell you all," and now Joe's eyes took in every face in the room, both those who seemed embarrassed by Brother Parkins's accusations and those who looked as if they might, to some extent at least, agree with him, "when I am judged of the Lord I *will* be found clean.

"Despite what any of you may have heard on the news or just picked up from the local rumor mill, I have been honest in my business dealings. I have never stolen or encouraged anyone to steal any designs. And I have never committed any type of fraud on my employees or my investors."

"Proverbs 12:15," Brother Parkins spat out. "The way of a fool is right in his own eyes."

"Yes," said Joe, picking up his scriptures and walking to the door, "but I think that in chapter twelve it also says 'Deceit is in the heart of them that imagine evil.'" As he walked out of the classroom, he thought he heard more than a smattering of applause.

CHAPTER 7

Except for Angela's constant chattering, the ride home from church was a quiet one. In the passenger seat, Heather watched the cars passing by them in the other direction with an almost robotic concentration. Something was festering inside her. Joe could feel it lying just beneath the surface of her seemingly calm exterior like the malignant tumors that had grown silently but deadly within her body. But until she was willing to talk about it, there was nothing he could do to help her.

After sacrament meeting he had taken her aside to talk, but she had only given him a blank smile.

"Wrong? What could be wrong on a beautiful Sunday morning with my family in church?" Her eyes had avoided his, dancing up to the pulpit, across the back of the chapel, looking anywhere but toward his concerned gaze.

"Heather, we need to talk. You didn't take the sacrament and you've been so distant since this all started."

"I'm fine, really." She had kissed him on the cheek, her lips brushing coolly across his skin. "Now I have a class to teach and I need to go to the library and check out some . . ." For a second she had looked dazed, almost lost, then she was back again, ". . . pictures. I need to get some pictures." She had turned and walked out into the hallway without looking back.

Reaching across the Navigator's plush seats, Joe took her hand, hoping to get at least a smile. But she continued to stare intently out the window as though there would be a test later.

"So," he said, looking into the rearview mirror at Debbie, "what was your Sunday School lesson about?"

"Same old, same old." Debbie rolled her eyes. "Faith, prayer, repentance. It's pretty much the same thing every week. Just wrapped around a different story and somebody's idea of a new object lesson that we've all seen a hundred times before."

"Well, with that attitude I'm not surprised you didn't get much out of it."

"Come on Dad. Do you really think anyone in the class cared about the lesson? All they could talk about was you. 'So like, is your dad going to jail?' 'I heard he was working with the Russians,' 'Are you guys gonna be on *America's Most Wanted?* Hyuck, hyuck.' It was a blast."

"I'm sorry." Joe slowed for a stoplight and signaled to turn left.

"It's not your fault. Look, I know you didn't do anything wrong. But this is really hard. I'm graduating on Tuesday. Do you know how it's going to feel knowing that all of my friends and their families are going to be gawking at me? Do you have any idea how it feels to have people blaming you for something that you have no control over?"

"Yeah, I think I might." Joe glanced back at Richie who was leafing through a magazine. "Should I ask what you learned about in class?"

"Didn't go." Richie continued to flip through the magazine, although Joe had no idea how he could see anything through his dark glasses.

"I see."

"We sinkt," Angela piped up.

"You did?" Joe asked, glad that someone seemed to have had a good time at church. "What did you sing?"

"Jezaz ants to be a submrine," Angela answered brightly, and immediately launched into the chorus.

"Yes, well don't we all?" Joe commented. As they rounded the corner, their house came into view, and Joe found that he was not especially surprised to see a short Asian man wearing dark glasses standing in his front yard taking pictures of the house. There were bound to be a few reporters who straggled in over the next few days, sure that they had found the scoop that no one else had.

Pulling into the driveway, Joe swung the car door open and started across the lawn. Apparently the man had not heard them pull up, because he continued to snap pictures as Joe walked toward him. Behind him, Heather and the kids were getting cautiously out of the car.

"Excuse me, but you are trespassing on private property." The little photographer nearly fell over at the sound of Joe's voice. *Now,* Joe thought, *he'll start trying to snap pictures of me.* But instead, the man dropped the camera so that it hung from the strap around his neck and removed a card from his shirt pocket. Although he looked startled, he showed no signs of moving off the lawn as Joe walked toward him.

"Look, I'm not doing any interviews and you are not allowed on my lawn." Joe folded his arms across his chest, ignoring the card that the man offered him.

"Oh, very sorry." The man half bowed but continued to stand his ground.

"Besides, aren't you a little late? The rest of the reporters were all out here yesterday."

"Reporters?" the man asked with a confused look, the hand with the card still partially extended.

"Yeah. What, are you a photographer from some out-of-town paper?"

"I'm not from a paper," the man said, once again offering Joe his card. "I'm a real estate agent." For the first time, Joe noticed that the camera hanging from the man's neck was not one of those professional numbers with multiple lenses, but a simple cheap 35-millimeter, like something that you might pick up at Target.

"Real estate?" Joe took the card and read the name of a local broker.

"Yes, I knocked on the door, but no one answered." He looked as though he thought Joe should have been expecting him. "You will be selling the house?" A wave of nausea washed over Joe as he realized who the man was and what he was doing.

"Look, I think that you better leave." He took the man by the arm and began escorting him away from the house and back to the sporty black car that was parked in the street. But before they had taken more than three steps, Heather was standing in front of them. She was breathing hard as though she had just completed a sprint, which Joe realized she must have to have gotten there so quickly. She had lost one of her shoes on her way across the lawn, but seemed not to notice it.

"What do you mean, sell the house?"

"Yes, yes," the man bobbed his head and grinned, seemingly unaware of the streaks of color rising high across the cheeks of the woman in front of him. "Sell the house, that's right."

"Get out," Heather screamed, raising her hand. Joe barely had time to grab her arm to stop her from hitting the confused man. "This is *my* house. You leave it alone."

"I—" the man stuttered, staring at a seemingly crazed woman hissing at him like an alley cat. Reality finally seemed to dawn on him though, as she pulled her arm free from her husband and bore down on him again.

"If you ever come near my house again I will rip you limb from limb." The man turned hastily, nearly tripping as he watched Heather closing on him from over his shoulder, and ran for his car, the camera swinging crazily from his neck.

"You will *not* take my house," Heather screamed again as the car accelerated away from the curb.

"Go, Mom," Richie said, a note of amazement in his voice, as Heather watched the car completely out of sight before turning and storming into the house.

* * *

"How dare you not tell me about this? This is my house too. Did you think that you could just keep everything a secret somehow? That I wouldn't notice anything was wrong until a moving van pulled up and started taking everything away? You are the most arrogant, self centered . . ." The words tore through Joe's brain like twisted metal, and yet they were the most wonderful sounds he could imagine. True, they meant that Heather was angry, no, worse than that, fuming, enraged, incensed, but at least she was alive. Finally something had pulled her from the torpor that seemed to be sucking her in like a great black maw, and for that he was almost pathetically grateful.

If only the words had been real and not all in his mind.

Looking across the room at his wife, sitting in the hand-carved rocking chair that her great-grandfather had brought with him across the Atlantic, Joe thought that most people would have seen a perfectly contented woman. A woman obviously lost in one of the many delightfully obtuse puzzles in the magazine she held folded back on itself while she carefully printed her answers in a back slanting hand so neat it almost looked like calligraphy. If they listened closely enough they would realize that she was softly humming that most saccharinely sweet of all LDS hymns, *Love at Home*. The scene would have been practically bucolic if it hadn't been for the fact that she had been working on the same magazine, humming the same hymn for almost five hours straight. He knew because he had been there watching her the entire time.

For the first few hours he had continued to hold out some kind of hope. After all, it wasn't like she was catatonic or anything. If you spoke to her she would respond. But her answers, when she spoke at all, were never more than a word or two, spoken in the flat emotionless monotone of a ticket taker at a movie theater. "Three doors down on the right. Next." And she never looked up from the page she was working on, as though she were hiding. Almost as if she were afraid of what her eyes might give away.

It wasn't until he had taken Heather's hand, to lead her down to the kitchen and the slightly blackened grilled cheese sandwiches and the soup that were about the limit of Debbie's cooking ability, that he realized the extent of her trauma. As she unfolded herself grudgingly from her chair, she had dropped the magazine to the night table, and Joe's gaze had fallen to the upside down crossword puzzle, nearly three quarters completed. At first he thought his eyes were playing tricks on him. To the uninitiated, crossword answers can look like gibberish, three-letter words for Nigerian peninsulas that one would never find in an ordinary dictionary. But as he turned the magazine around and looked closer, he saw that although each square was filled in, it was the same group of letters over and over.

Flipping back through the pages, he saw with growing horror that it was the same for every puzzle. EVERYTHING IS FINE EVERYTHING IS FINE EVERYTHING IS FINE. Page after page of the same three words, as though her mind was stuck in an eternal loop. And unlike her normal printing, these letters looked almost like incisions. Three sharp slashes for an *N*, a single gash for an *I*. How long had she been doing this? Judging from the number of puzzles in this magazine alone it must have been days. The sheets fluttered loosely to the carpet as Joe's numb fingers dropped the publication and he stared at his wife's lifeless downturned eyes. It was happening all over again. The sleep, the mood swings, the long, nearly catatonic states. He stared into his wife's eyes looking for some sign of recognition.

"Maybe if we go back to the doctors they can help you this time."

"No doctors." If he hadn't been right next to her, he wouldn't have been able to make the words out, and the brief flash of life disappeared from her eyes as quickly as it had come. But the message was clear.

"Then what? What do you want me to do? I know this is my fault, but how can I help you if you're not even willing to help yourself?" The tears that had turned Joe's vision into a kaleidoscope of blurred images spilled over his lids and dripped down his face, but if Heather realized that his words were directed at her she gave no indication. He knew that he could make her go back to the psychiatrists and physicians they had seen before. But if they had been unable to help her then, what made him think things would be any different now? And the pressure of all the examinations and medications might just push her completely over the edge this time. It seemed as if every alternative promised only to make things worse than they already were.

"A little help here?" Joe stumbled backward onto the bed, his hands raised toward the ceiling. His words were no longer directed to his wife but to his God. Maybe they *were* irreverent, but he felt irreverent.

"What do You want from me? Why are You doing this? You want my blood? Fine, then take it!" He turned his arms wrist up, hands flattened down toward the floor as though preparing to have them slit. "Take my life. It's the only thing I seem to have left now. But please, don't hurt my family.

"However I've offended You, whatever I've done, it's on my head. But they're innocent, can't You at least see that? Please, God, I've tried to be a good man. I've tried to obey the commandments. I've gone to the temple, I've paid my tithing, I've kept my covenants. If any of that means anything to You at all, leave . . . them . . . alone."

Jamming his hands against his mouth, trying to muffle the strangled sobs that tore from his throat, Joe bent nearly double in his armchair, his forehead touching his knees. The anchors that held the web of his life together were beginning to snap, each broken strand singing through the air like a live wire. And with each break, he could feel the center becoming more unstable, more out of control. He would hold on as long as he could. He had to. But more and more it was starting to feel like some kind of collapse was inevitable.

Sliding his hands up from his mouth to his head, he entangled his hair between his fingers and pulled. The instant pain in his scalp acted like kerosene on an open wound, shocking his nerves so that his mind was forced to shift from the internal pain to the external for at least a few moments. Only when he felt like he was a little more under control did he finally raise his head.

Across the room, Heather had once again picked up the magazine, and held it pressed tightly between her white-knuckled fingers. Her lips, now silent, were pressed together so tightly they almost disappeared—her mouth a small horizontal slit. No longer looking down, the deep green irises of her unblinking eyes seemed to have shrunk somehow, adrift in a sea of white, as a single tear writhed slowly down the side of her jaw.

* * *

"Got to help . . . dangerous . . . killer . . . have to stop." Joe rolled onto his side, thrashing out of the sweat-damp sheets that clung to him like a sticky shroud, and instantly every joint in his body seemed to explode with pain.

"Whad I do las night?" The words came out in a horse rumble that he could barely recognize as his own voice. He was reminded of a phrase his grandfather used to mutter after waking from an especially poor night's sleep. *I feel as if a thousand Russian soldiers marched across my tongue last night in their stocking feet.* Only in Joe's case, they hadn't stopped with his tongue. They had continued right down across his chest, stomach, legs, and feet, paying especially close attention to his shoulders and hips. And it felt as though one of them had even tried to run his bayonet down Joe's throat for good measure.

Cracking his eyelids partway open allowed the morning sunlight to shine directly into his exposed eyes, and he instantly snapped them shut as the optic nerves screamed out in protest. The closest he had ever come to drinking anything alcoholic was when, at the age of ten or eleven, he and a group of his friends had each taken a sip from a lukewarm bottle of beer that one of them had lifted from his dad's stash. Thinking that it tasted like horse pee, Joe had instantly spit it out on the ground. But he thought that now he might be getting a taste of what a hangover felt like. If it was even half this bad, he was amazed prohibition had ever been lifted.

"Can't be sick," he croaked. "Too much to do today." But pressing his palm to his forehead produced a warmth that he felt pretty sure was higher than it ought to be. A long low growl rumbled from his stomach and a sudden loose feeling in his gut convinced him that, sore or not, he had better get into the bathroom quickly. As he rolled toward the side of the bed though, a fuzzy round bundle beside him voiced a high-pitched squeal.

"Angela?" Cupping the sun from his eyes with one hand, he squinted down at his daughter. "What are you doing here?" He was sure that she had gone to sleep on the pull-out in her sister's room. Maybe the brick incident had made her nervous to be too far from her parents.

"Oo sount fuddy," Angela giggled sleepily.

"Yeah well, you'd sound funny too if your throat was full of barbed wire." Joe coughed harshly, trying to clear up whatever gunk was coating his vocal cords, but it only seemed to make matters worse.

"Wire in yur froat?" Angela's small liquid voice turned the word *wire* into something exotic that sounded kind of like water, only better. The way she said it, you might even *want* to have it in your throat.

"Never mind. What are you doing in my bed anyway? I thought you liked to sleep with your stuffed animals?"

Angela's eyes widened as if this was the silliest question she had ever heard. "Oo calt me."

"I did?" Had he called her? He couldn't remember having done so. But maybe he had been dreaming about . . .

"Oo calt me and I cumbt." It was a little frightening to think that he had been talking in his sleep. In fact, if Angela had heard him from all the way down the hall in her bedroom, he must have been doing a lot more than talking. Maybe Heather wasn't the only one who was having trouble coping.

"Well thank you for *cumbing*," he smiled, running one hand across her soft bed-warm cheek. "But now the bathroom is calling me, so scoot on over."

* * *

"Hmm, interesting." Doctor Anjum, a stocky Arab with a studied, intelligent look on his face, gently prodded at the rash on Joe's thigh with a thick finger. "How long have you had this rash?"

"I'm not sure, maybe a week or two," Joe answered, trying to remember the first time he had noticed it. He thought that it might have been a few days after he and some of the other guys from work had gone mountain biking through the coastal redwoods. "But what does that have to do with the way I feel? Isn't it just the flu or something?"

"Maybe, maybe not." Raising the buds of his stethoscope to his ears, the doctor placed its cold metal against Joe's chest and back, listening intently to the instrument as he walked Joe through a series of inhales, exhales, and coughs.

"Does it hurt to chew or swallow?" he asked, pressing his fingertips lightly against the glands beneath Joe's jaw.

"A little," Joe admitted.

"Joints stiff?"

"Yes."

"Any pain urinating?"

"No."

"Ringing in your ears or sensitivity to noise?"

"Not that I've noticed." Joe was trying not to be paranoid, but the laundry list of ailments sounded much more serious than the common cold or flu.

"Sensitivity to light?" The doctor unclipped a small penlight from his pocket and flashed it across Joe's eyes.

"Ow, yes." Joe winced, pulling back from the light.

"Um hmm." Doctor Anjum clipped the light back into his pocket and returned to the rash. It had grown in size over the last couple of days, and now the largest of its concentric rings was nearly five inches across.

"Have you been out in the woods anytime in the last six weeks or so?"

Joe's mind instantly returned to the bike ride. "Yeah, a few of the guys from work and I did a twenty miler up near Santa Cruz. But I still don't understand what any of this has to do with—"

"Tick bite?" the small, intense man interrupted him.

"What?"

"Were you bitten by a tick?" The doctor turned and opened a cabinet drawer, sorting through a stack of papers before finding what he wanted.

"No. I'm sure I'd have noticed that." And yet something tickled at the back of Joe's memory. It was just as he was stepping into the shower the evening after the ride. As he stepped out of his shorts, hadn't he noticed a small black something a few inches below where the band of his shorts left a slightly pink ring around his waist? Brushing the protrusion off the outside of his thigh, he had noticed a slight stinging sensation and a small drop of blood. He had just assumed at the time that it was a thorn, or maybe a scab from one of the many cuts he always seemed to incur on those rides. But it *could* have been a tick.

Doctor Anjum laid the sheet of paper on the examining table next to Joe and traced his finger around a picture of a rash that looked identical to his. "Bulls-eye rash. It's one of the primary indicators of Lyme disease."

"Lyme disease." The words echoed ominously in Joe's ears. He remembered the flyers he had seen stapled to the bulletin boards at many of the local trailheads. This was serious stuff. As he recalled it could last for months. He couldn't take months of feeling as lousy as he did right now. Not with everything else that was going on.

"Are you sure?"

"No." The doctor folded his arms across his chest, leaving the sheet of paper on the table. "We'll take a blood test of course. But even those aren't completely accurate. Lots of false positives, and false negatives. But you have the rash. And your symptoms match those of the early stage of the disease. So we'll assume that you are positive and start you on antibiotics right away."

Joe nodded. That all seemed to make sense. But then a disturbing thought occurred to him. "What do you mean by *early stage* symptoms? What *are* the symptoms of Lyme disease? It doesn't get any worse than this does it?"

"Well, it can be as simple as a low-grade fever and fatigue."

"But?" Joe asked, fearing the answer.

"We really don't understand this disease completely. It's not like the common cold where we can predict pretty much what it will do to any given individual. Lyme disease can affect every organ of the body." He seemed to consider stopping there, but seeing Joe's persistent stare, sighed and continued.

"Symptoms can include everything from inflamed joints to respiratory infection. Vomiting, dizziness, hearing loss, double vision, headaches, facial paralysis, irregular heartbeat, liver infection, mental deterioration, loss of reflexes and coordination, even Multiple Sclerosis–like conditions in some cases."

Joe stared at the doctor, stunned by the magnitude of what he had just said. "But that's if it goes untreated? I mean the antibiotics should take care of it, right?"

"Mr. Stewart," the doctor said, placing his hand on Joe's shoulder, "you are probably getting worked up about nothing. You may experience few or none of these symptoms. But even if you do, four to six weeks of oral antibiotics will normally treat it. If it doesn't respond to one medication, we can switch to another or use a combination. We can even switch to an IV if that becomes necessary, which I highly doubt it will.

"What you need to do is go home. Begin taking the antibiotics and get some rest. If the symptoms get any worse or don't begin to abate in the next few days, call me and we'll try you on another type of antibiotic." Scribbling something onto his prescription pad, he tore off a small pink sheet and handed it to Joe along with a small cardboard and foil folder.

"Take this to the pharmacy and get it filled. Make sure you take two of these every day until they are gone—even if you start feeling better. The symptoms of Lyme disease are funny. A strong dose of antibiotics can seem to beat them into remission, but if you don't complete the treatment, they can return with a vengeance. In the meantime, swallow two of these with a glass of water. We might as well get your body on the offensive as soon as possible. Now go home, get into bed and stay there for a while."

Sure that's just what I'll do. If I can only convince the world to stop spinning for a few weeks until I get better, Joe thought. But he simply nodded and said, "Will do."

* * *

Joe was never sure how much his decisions of the next few days were affected by the events of that evening. How could he be, when he wasn't even sure if the events themselves had ever actually taken place? The hours after his doctor's appointment started out in a seemingly normal fashion. Don the sunglasses that kept the sunlight from frying his eyeballs, get in the car, drive to the pharmacy, trade the slip of paper for a surprisingly large, brown plastic bottle of surprisingly small yellow pills. It wasn't until he was pulling up to his house—had it suddenly grown much hotter?—that time began to stretch and distort, taking on the misshapen reality of a carnival house of mirrors.

How had he, for example, suddenly come to find himself lying in bed? He must have walked. How else could he have gotten there? And yet his hand was still reaching forward to take his keys from the ignition. Instead of keys, his aching fingers touched a glass of ice-cold water Tia was holding out to him. *Why are you here?* he tried to ask. Monday was her day off. Had he called and asked her to come in? He couldn't remember doing so. It was so nice of her to give up her day off. She was so great. He didn't know how they ever could have survived without her. He was going to give her a big raise, if he ended up with any money left. But the only sound that came from his mouth was a weak croak.

His parched throat cried out for the cool water. Even in the dim room he could see the condensation forming on the side of the glass filled with crystal-clear crescents of sweet ice as he tried to close his hot fist around it. Though he commanded his fingers to curve around the smooth surface, they refused to obey. Like the Tin Woodsman in *The Wizard of Oz*, his joints seemed to have rusted in place, and he realized with horror that the water he so desperately wanted was going to slip through his hand.

"I can't—" he whispered, but his words were cut off as he realized that Tia was no longer there. Instead, the glass of water was in the hands of a dark shape—perhaps a man—that he couldn't quite make out.

"Do you thirst?" The words sounded human, but the voice speaking them was nothing that human vocal cords had ever formed, and Joe found himself unable to answer.

"Drink from my cup and you need never thirst again." The voice was hungry, greedy, and now Joe could just make out two eyes glowing red from the depths of the dark shape before him. He shook his head numbly, or at least tried to. The fingers tightened around the glass and the water instantly vaporized, floating away in a cloud of steam. In its place was something black, murky, and foul. It smelled like swamp water as the figure forced it toward Joe's lips.

"I can give you back everything you have lost—your home, your health, your money." There was a low throaty chuckle, almost a growl, as the red eyes moved closer toward him. "I can give you your family. You can't protect them Joe. You'll lose them all. You already are. All you need do is ask. Ask me now of your own free will and I will protect you. It's so easy. All you need do is turn your back on the god that has mistreated you. Look into my eyes and say 'Yes.' It's such a little word really. You can even nod your head if the cat's got your tongue."

For just a moment, Joe considered the promise. It was tempting to turn it all over to someone else. The figure in front of him promised exactly what Joe had been praying for—a quick, clean solution to all of his problems. But then the words of the old man from his dream came back to him. *Protect that which you deem most valuable.*

"No," he gasped, his body shivering in violent spasms.

"Then drink." The foul solution was pressed to his lips, its dark stench—now more like something dead and decaying—invaded his nostrils. "It is of your own making."

Cold liquid filled his mouth, and he began to choke before realizing that Angela was now sitting on the edge of the bed, tilting a glass of ice water to his mouth. Somehow both the dark figure and his black concoction had disappeared. The ice in the glass had melted, but the water felt wonderful as it cascaded down the back of his throat. With her other hand, Angela brushed a sweaty mat of hair back off of his forehead. He started at her touch, her fingers were so cold, almost deathlike, before realizing that he was the one whose temperature was wrong. Closing his eyes, enjoying the brush of her tiny fingers across his brow, he must have drifted off, because he heard Angela talking to him, but her words were not the slurred syllables that only her immediate family could completely understand.

"Daddy?" It was one of those amazing transformations that could only take place in dreams or a Hollywood special-effects studio. It sounded like his daughter's voice, the same tones and inflections that he would have recognized anywhere, but her enunciation was clear and distinct. The voice he imagined she would have when her body was perfected and glorified in the afterlife.

"Daddy, you need to hurry."

"Can't even move. Too sick." In this dream, it didn't matter that his throat was cracked and rusty. His words seemed to be coming from somewhere else entirely, as though he were a ventriloquist dummy.

"They're getting lost." Again he was amazed by the voice of the dream-Angela talking to him, and he found that his mind was actually translating the words back into the way that Angela really would have said them, *Dear getn ost.*

"They're getting lost in the darkness and only you can find them."

"I don't—Who is getting lost?" Was it possible to dream about a dream? It must have been, because Joe suddenly found himself remembering the dream in which he had become separated from his family in a dark and possibly dangerous woods, and with the memory came the same sense of fear and urgency.

"You promised Daddy. You promised to find them all and bring us home." Angela's voice, which had been gently pleading, now acquired a desperation that he had never heard there before. "I can't get them. I'm trying, but I'm too little and I . . . I . . ." Into Joe's mind suddenly began flashing a series of images. *Richie, Debbie, and Heather are slipping beneath the dark surface of some impossibly deep water. Their eyes and mouths form wide O's of fear as their pale faces disappear into the murk. Angela paddles across the top of the water, her tiny hands stretching toward the receding figures. They reach up for her, but her arms are not long enough and Joe realizes with a sick dread that Angela is going to watch them drown.*

Now they are in a deep forest. Joe is somehow watching them from high overhead, perhaps from the vantage point of a circling eagle. He can see that they are lost in some kind of thick gray mist. They are trying to find their way out of the woods, but he can see that in the direction they are headed is a sheer cliff dropping thousands of feet to a bleak rocky wasteland that is littered with the bleached white remains of human bones. On a distant mountain peak, opposite the cliffs, Angela is shouting herself hoarse and waving her hands. It seems for a moment as if they might hear her, but her voice is not quite strong enough, and they turn back toward the cliff. Richie is the first to topple over the precipice, screaming as his body plummets through the air, but Heather and Debbie are hot on his heels.

But the last image is perhaps the worst. It is of a brightly lit house, welcoming light streaming out of its windows into a dark night. It is not a fancy house, his own is much bigger, and he can only see the outside. But he desperately wants to be inside of it nonetheless. He knows that there is a warm fire crackling on the hearth, and that in the dining room, a polished mahogany table has been set for five. The mouth-watering smells of fresh-baked bread and hot buttered corn issue forth from the kitchen. It is more than a house, it is a home where a family could live forever in blissful happiness. In fact it is his family's home. The doors are unlocked, just waiting to be swung open. But except for a small blonde girl staring out the window, her tear-filled eyes straining for any sight of the others who belong there, it is empty.

Joe woke with a start, his face feeling stretched tight, but slightly out of shape as though he had been weeping. It was a relief to have escaped those terrifying images, but looking around him, he realized that instead of waking, he had just slipped out of one dream and into another. He was no longer in his bed, but was now standing in the hallway just outside Debbie's room. He could smell the combined fragrances of perfume, hair gel, and nail polish that seemed to be the exclusive province of teenage girls. His oldest daughter lay on her bed, stomach down, chin resting on palms, knees bent so that her feet waved slightly back and forth in the air. The bright red nails of her cotton-ball–separated toes arced back and forth through the air like tiny skyrockets. Something about the way that the scene seemed to be taking place on the other side of a thick pane of glass reminded him of an old movie, but before he could place it, Debbie's voice interrupted his thoughts.

"I don't know. Mike doesn't get back from school until Friday, so I'll probably just go to some of the grad-night parties and hang out." From the angle he was watching her, Joe hadn't been able to see the phone plastered to the other side of her head, but now he could make out the curled white cord disappearing over the side of the bed.

Debbie laughed, apparently at something the person on the other end of the line had said, and bobbed her head. "Oh yeah, anything to get out of the house for a while. It's starting to feel like *One Flew Over the Cuckoo's Nest* around here. Mom's completely wigging out, Richie's on his way to Juvie if he's not careful, and Dad seems to think that if we all say a prayer it's somehow going to be all better. It really sucks when your retarded little sister is the most sane one in the house."

For the second time in as many days, Joe felt the air whoosh out of him as he listened to the words of someone who could not have been his oldest daughter. Who was this imposter that had taken the place of the little girl who had once begged to teach family home evening lessons?

"Puhleeese, I'm old enough to make my own decisions," Debbie answered into the phone almost as if she had heard Joe's silent question. "After seventeen years of brainwashing, it's about time I started thinking for myself. They think that just because you go to seminary at some obnoxiously early hour for four years that you're just going to fall in line with all the other good little Mormons. I'd just like to shake some of those kids who stand up there and talk about how they *know* that Heavenly Father lives. I mean how can they know anything about God?"

Whatever she heard seemed to stop her for a minute, and for the barest of instants Joe thought that he saw sorrow sweep across his daughter's face. But before he could even be sure of what he had seen, the look was replaced by a scowl. "Well maybe I did, but kids say all kinds of dumb things. I'll bet I was just trying to impress some guy at church. What I mistook for the Spirit was probably gas.

"Exactly," she smiled. "He's been gone since Christmas, and I'm not about to lose him to some Ivy League hussy. And what do you think Mom and Dad will have to say when they find out that their good little Mormon girl isn't so good anymore?"

Joe swung his fists forward to smash through the glass pane in front of him. But before his hands could reach the barrier, the scene in front of him began to dissolve into a swirl of color and he felt himself falling backward.

Arming a layer of oily sweat from his forehead, Joe leaned back against the pillows and tried to calm the frantic pounding of his heart. The Lyme disease or the antibiotic or maybe both had caused whatever strange dreams he was having. The doctor had even said that mental deterioration was one of the symptoms, and if this wasn't mental deterioration, Joe didn't know what was. Feeling like he finally had himself under some kind of control, he opened his eyes and gasped.

The face looking down at him from the darkness—eyes so bloodshot they might as well have been red; long pointed tongue lolling out from a lascivious grin; piercings covering ears, nose, tongue, cheeks, and even eyelids—exuded such pure evil, that for a moment Joe was sure he had been cast directly down to hell. It wasn't until he realized that he was looking at a poster that Joe sat up and saw that he had somehow ended up in Richie's bed. It was dark outside now, and the streetlights shining through the blinds on his son's window cast an eerie set of vertical light and dark bars across the bedroom.

Turning to see the shining red numerals of the alarm clock on Richie's nightstand, he was shocked to see that it was nearly eleven o'clock. Was it possible that he had actually been asleep for nearly twelve hours? And if so, why did he feel so completely exhausted? Sitting groggily up, he rubbed his eyes and then squinted in pain as a set of headlights lanced through the blinds.

In the street below, a dark sports car, its suspension lowered so that the front bumper nearly scraped the street, slowed in front of Joe's house before coming to a stop. From the shadow of a tree near the end of the driveway, a lone figure emerged and made its way cautiously to the driver's side window of the car. The figure in the street and the car's driver appeared to exchange something and then the car accelerated away from the curb with a squeal of tires.

From the window, Joe watched with a tired kind of knowing as the figure turned, stepped beneath the streetlight and glanced up at the house. Almost as if he could see his father watching him from the window of his bedroom, Richie paused before sticking something into his jacket pocket and walking slowly back to the house.

At the sound of the front door closing, Joe stood up from his son's bed and, for a moment as the floor began to spin under him, felt sure that he was about to fall. Reaching out to touch the bedroom wall, he traced his hand along it like a sailor holding to the ship's railing during a heavy storm and was able to keep his balance long enough to slip out into the darkness of the hallway. Below him, he could hear Richie coming up the stairs. He did not seem to be trying to hide the sounds of his footsteps, almost as though he wanted to get caught. At the top of the stairs, Richie turned toward his room and walked past Joe without so much as a glance in his direction.

Joe watched Richie slam two bundles onto his dresser. By the window's light he could just make out the tight roll of currency and the baggie filled with what looked like some kind of pills. Not even bothering to take off his jacket or shoes, Richie fell to the bed face first and, in the darkness, Joe thought he could hear his son crying.

"No." Joe staggered forward, his hands held stiffly out in front of his body as though he expected to encounter a brick wall at any moment, wanting to comfort his son and at the same time deathly afraid of actually reaching him. Touching Richie would mean that everything had been real, the dream-equivalent of pinching himself and feeling pain. As he drew nearer to the bed, he could hear that beneath his sobs, Richie was repeating something. His words were indistinct, muffled by his crying and the pillow his face was buried in, but Joe thought that he could just make them out.

It didn't make any sense. *None of it* had. But didn't the very nonsensical nature of it just reaffirm that this was some kind of horrible fever-induced nightmare? Stretching his hand toward his son's sweat-matted hair, he clamped his eyes shut at the last minute, and felt an almost intoxicating sense of relief when instead of hair his fingers closed on the rough softness of the blankets in his own bed.

It *had* been a dream. Angela had not suddenly lost her speech impediment, and Debbie didn't even know any college guys. He hadn't wandered through the house on some kind of wild journey of revelation. And he had not watched his son buying drugs from a shadowy character in front of his house or listened to him whimpering over and over the words, "I'm sorry Mom, I'm sorry, I'm sorry."

CHAPTER 8

Although the rest of the night held more confused dreams, none of them shared the same sickening sense of vertigo, of reality twisted and distorted into something black and dangerous, that the first ones had. Once he thought he heard Angela singing to him, only to realize that the voice was actually Heather's. Had he ever noticed how alike their voices sounded? She was leaning so close to him that he could actually feel the warm puffs of her breath against his cheek with each of her words. He might even have believed it had been real if she hadn't abruptly stopped singing and started to whisper words that he instantly recognized as coming from his own tortured conscience.

"I'm a failure, a terrible parent. All of this is my fault. Maybe if I hadn't been so selfish everything would have turned out differently. But it's too late now. I've messed up everything so badly, so very badly." At the sound of such complete misery in his wife's voice, Joe instinctively reached out to comfort her. But although he thought he caught the faintest scent of the body wash she used, his hand met only empty air, and before he could find the strength to open his eyes, he had drifted off again.

* * *

It was finally remembering the movie that woke him. *A Christmas Carol*, he whispered. That was what the dreams had reminded him of. It was that sense of being led from scene to wretched scene. Like Ebenezer Scrooge, he had been able to watch the unhappiness of those around him, but no one had been able to see *him*. "Surprised I didn't dream up Tiny Tim, asking God to bless us, every one."

Shading his eyes, he risked a quick peek around the room and was amazed to find that the morning light didn't bother him at all. His headache was gone too, and pressing the back of his hand to his forehead, he thought that his temperature had returned to normal overnight. Whatever was in those little yellow tablets seemed to have done the trick. Slipping noiselessly out of bed so as not to disturb Heather, he found the pill bottle and carried it into the bathroom. His joints complained at being asked to go back into action after nearly twenty hours in bed, but all in all he felt pretty good. After downing two of the tablets with a glass of tap water, he splashed a few handfuls of the cold water across his face and washed away the crust that had formed in the corners of his eyes. If only he could wash away the feeling of disquiet the dreams had left him with as easily.

A hot shower would go a long way toward making him feel human again, but he knew that he wouldn't be able to enjoy it until he proved to himself once and for all that what he had seen the night before had not been real. It should be easy enough to do. Unlike most dreams that faded quickly upon waking, the details he had seen were still vividly imprinted in his mind.

Leaving the bathroom, he crossed through the bedroom, stepped out into the hallway and paused in front of his oldest daughter's door. Swinging it slowly open, his first impression was the strong scent of nail polish that he remembered from his dream. But that was easily explainable. Like many teenage girls, Debbie obsessed about her nails, repainting them at least twice a week. His subconscious had merely added a detail that he had picked up from his years of being a father. It would be easy enough to check. All he had to do was walk across the room and look into the trash can. If she had actually painted her toenails last night it should have red-spattered cotton balls in it.

And yet he found himself loathe to move from the doorway. Even if he did find cotton balls there, what would that really prove anyway? It would only mean that she had painted her nails red since the last time the can was emptied. He would be getting himself all worked up over nothing. Just like the white telephone lying on the floor next to her bed, it simply showed that he had a good memory for details. So what if he couldn't actually remember knowing that Debbie's phone was white; there were probably hundreds, even thousands of details that were hidden away in the back storerooms of his mind just waiting to be recalled at the right moment.

Closing her door perhaps a little too quickly, he nearly chuckled at how close he had come to believing all that nonsense. Richie's room would clear up everything. There were no drugs on his son's dresser. He was willing to bet his life on that. And yet, his hand trembled and his breath caught as he reached toward the knob on Richie's door. He could stop now. Just turn and walk back into his bathroom, step into a hot shower and scrub his skin until it turned red. Every waking hour would make the memories fade just a little bit more, until finally . . .

"No." His voice was louder than he intended and he jumped a little at the sound of it, rattling the knob slightly. He had to look, had to know. He couldn't stand to go back to sleep that night facing the possibility of more of those disturbing images. He didn't know what he would do if he *did* find drugs there. But he knew that not knowing one way or the other would be worse. He reached for the knob, but before he touched it, it turned of its own accord and the door swung open.

Richie stood in the doorway, dressed in the same jeans and jacket that he always wore. His hair looked as though he had just crawled out of bed, but that was kind of the style that kids liked now, so it was hard to tell. At the sudden appearance of his father, he gasped a small squeaking noise like a bathtub toy, and stepped back into the room. His eyes darted to the dresser and Joe suddenly had a sure knowledge of what he would see there. His head seemed to turn with the agonizing slowness of a rusty piece of machinery to follow his son's gaze, but his mind had no need of visual confirmation. After all, it had registered what was there once before and it could upload the image much more quickly than any physical movement.

Before Joe's eyes actually found the dresser, he could see the two items laying there. The bills crushed together into a tube roughly the size of a stack of quarters, the baggie taped into a tight rectangle with what looked like white medical tape, pills bulging against its sides. The image was so vivid that his mind nearly rejected the report it received from his eyes. For a split second he was sure that he saw them there as clearly as he had the night before, and then with a nearly childlike surprise he registered that, except for the usual array of coins, scraps of paper, and various odds and ends, the top of the dresser was empty.

"What?" Again Richie's eyes shot away from his father and toward the dresser, but his hand moved to the pocket of his jacket.

"Richie what's in your jacket?"

"Nothin'."

"Empty your pockets."

"I said I don't have anything."

"Then you shouldn't have any problem showing me." Joe's voice sounded dead, even to Joe.

"Fine." Richie pulled a hand full of bills, mostly fives and tens, out of his right jacket pocket and handed them to Joe.

Joe fingered the bills. They were crumpled but for all he could tell that could have come from the normal wear and tear of being stuffed into a boy's pocket. He couldn't tell if they had been rolled up or not. He estimated there was about sixty dollars. "Where did you get this?"

"Allowance." Richie turned out his other pockets one by one until it was obvious that there was nothing else in his jacket.

"What about your pants?"

"Whatever." Richie turned out those as well. "What'd you expect, a rocket launcher or something?" Joe could see the anger blazing in his son's eyes, but there was something else there too. Something that looked almost like a mix between guilt and sorrow.

"Richie is there something you'd like to talk about? I want to help you if I can." For a moment, he thought that his son was going to confess to buying the drugs. He looked like he wanted to. But at the last minute, something seemed to change his mind, and he just shook his head.

"Okay. But remember that you can come to me any time."

"It's not that easy." Richie shrugged past him through the doorway and walked down the stairs.

* * *

Joe wasn't sure what had brought him back to Pleasant Hill, the Bay Area town he had grown up in. Perhaps it was his way of seeking some kind of emotional comfort. Heaven knew he needed some after his meeting with the accounting firm Mitch had recommended. At least they hadn't tried to tell him that he was being punished for breaking some unknown commandment. But that was the limit on good news. The only recommendation they made was to declare bankruptcy as soon as possible.

Driving slowly up Monument Boulevard he looked forlornly at the long rows of gleaming office buildings that stood where his boyhood home had once been. The walnut orchard that he and his friends built forts in had been gone for more than fifteen years and the bowling alley was now an apartment complex. Whatever comfort he might have been looking for had been bulldozed under and built over long ago.

He almost missed the plain brown sign in the confusion of street-lights and strip malls, but it might have been its simplicity itself that caught his eye. *Lafayette Reservoir—9 mi.* Lafayette Reservoir; the name called up memories of bike rides and fishing poles, digging red worms in the backyard with his father to lure the blue gills and occa-sional trout, and dickering with Mr. Genge, the Polish-speaking butcher, over frozen chicken livers for night fishing the big cats that prowled the lake bottom.

The memories brought back such feelings of youthfully innocent joy, that he was almost convinced to just keep right on driving. Nothing that good could remain unspoiled. It was probably polluted now, the pungent eucalyptus trees cut down to put in condominiums. And yet hadn't he come looking for just such a chance to recapture some of the faith and confidence of his youth?

Following the winding road that had expanded from two lanes to four since he last pedaled up it, Joe rolled down his window. The eucalyptus trees were still there after all, and he eagerly inhaled the scent of their aromatic leaves. He couldn't remember the last time he had wandered aimlessly, letting the road take him where it would. Building a successful company had taken an exceptional amount of control. He had made time for family vacations and as much one-on-one time with Heather and the kids as he could, but even those times had been carefully planned. He had somehow forgotten the simple pleasure of spontaneity.

Pausing at the gravel parking lot at the top of the dam, he was delighted to see that although some things had changed, the reservoir was much as he remembered it. Twenty or thirty feet away from the safety buoys that ringed the base of the dam, a pair of old timers slowly trolled from their aluminum boats, occasionally calling out friendly insults to each other about their angling skills. Another quarter mile down the road, a floating dock that might have been the very one he had spent hours jigging his bait up and down from, jutted forty or fifty feet out into the bluish green water. Either school must have let out a week early here or the warm June weather had been too attractive for kids to resist playing hooky, because dozens of bikes were parked helter-skelter along the grassy patch next to the dock's edge, and the voices of excited boys and girls knifed cleanly through the air.

Wheeling the big Navigator out of the gravel lot, he followed the paved road down past the dock and over a small rise where a group of older black men sat beneath the shade of a huge oak, their poles propped up on the kind of hand-carved wooden forks he remembered making himself. Finally he pulled off the road and into a dirt lot next to a grassy field where a group of teenagers were tossing around a football and a black-and-gold Frisbee next to a half-dozen peeling, green picnic tables. Stepping out of the car, he waved away the cloud of dust his tires had kicked up and inhaled the warm air.

Something about the tranquility of the spot, the combined smells of lily pads and oak leaves, dry grass and deep water, seemed to offer him a peace he had been unable to find lately. Although this looked nothing like upstate New York, he was suddenly reminded of the Sacred Grove in Palmyra, where the young Joseph Smith had gone in search of answers to his heartfelt questions. Was this why he had come here, to seek answers? He thought that it might be, although it seemed like an awfully long drive just to say a prayer. But maybe he needed this quiet to hear the answers he had been searching for.

Passing the tables, he left the grass and started up a small hill, shoving through the prickly bushes that seemed to grow closer together the further he climbed. After only a hundred yards or so he stopped to catch his breath, bending over, hands on knees, sweat beginning to drip from his forehead. Was this the spot? It certainly didn't look very promising. The trees that grew close together near the lake were spread farther apart up here, and looking down he saw that the primary groundcover seemed to be poison oak. It looked more like a sacred briar patch.

Maybe he would be better off closer to the water. Turning around, he again struggled through the brush, although at least gravity was working with him as he made his way back down the hill. Returning to the clutch of picnic tables, he stopped for a drink at the concrete fountain and surveyed the lakeside. A small ring of eucalyptus trees near the edge of the lake looked perfect. Serene, cool, and not a sign of poison oak—he could easily imagine receiving the answer to his prayers there.

Entering the shade of the small grove, Joe looked quickly around to make sure that his prayers would be uninterrupted before kneeling. The men with the propped-up fishing poles were not far away, but they seemed to be involved in a serious game of chess or checkers. To the other side of him, a tall stand of reeds blocked the view of the teenagers at the tables. Comfortable with the relative privacy of the spot, he dropped to his knees in the leafy dirt and bowed his head.

"Father," he began, "I have always tried to help those who were in trouble. Giving them food, money, or whatever help they might have needed. But now I'm in trouble and I can't seem to help myself. Everything's falling down around me. My wife is suffering, Father, and my children need guidance that I don't know how to give them. I've lost my job, my money, and it looks like maybe even my house now. I've got some kind of disease that sounds like one of the plagues from the Old Testament, and I don't know what to do.

"Heavenly Father, if I've done anything to bring this upon myself, I am truly sorry and I am willing to pay whatever the price might be. If I somehow got caught up in my work, or didn't spend enough time serving my fellowman, just let me know what I need to do. But please tell me where to go, what to do, give me some kind of sign and I'll—"

"Give you a hand?" Joe's eyes flew open at the unexpected sound of a voice next to him, and for a moment he thought that God had actually appeared to him in person. The man standing above him was framed by the afternoon sun in such a way that it was nearly impossible to make out anything other than his silhouette.

"I, uh . . ." Joe stuttered, unable to think of what to say to the heavenly apparition before him.

"Lose your lure did you?" The man stepped closer and Joe realized that it was just an old man with a thick white beard. His gnarled hands clasped his knees as he leaned over and searched the ground at Joe's feet.

"No. I mean, I didn't have a lure." Joe quickly rose to his feet, both embarrassed and irritated by the old man's interruption. Where had he come from anyway? Joe couldn't have been praying for much more than a minute or so. "Look, I was just trying to have a little privacy here."

"Oh I understand, say no more." The man straightened, his knees popping audibly as he stood up. "A man finds a good fishing spot, he wants to keep it to himself. I've got a few secret holes myself," he said with a wink. And yet he made no move to leave.

"Great day for fishing though, isn't it? Air's warm but the water's still cool enough that the fish'll come up to the top ta feed." He leaned against the peeling white bark of one of the trees and looked out over the water.

"Look, if you don't mind, I'd really like some time alone. I've got to get back to my daughter's graduation soon, and I've got to . . . well, I've just got to do some things."

"I had daughters myself. Six of them."

"Six? Six daughters?" Joe was fascinated despite himself. "What are you, Mormon or Catholic?"

"Oh, neither really I guess," the man chuckled, "although I am a Christian." Pulling out a piece of wood and a folding knife, he began to whittle on what looked like a rather intricate figurine of a woman on a donkey. Although it was less than a quarter done, Joe could already see that it was going to be beautiful.

"Listen," Joe tried one last time, although he had a sinking feeling that getting this man to move was going to be futile, "I don't mean to be rude but I really need a few minutes of privacy."

"Oh sure, you go right ahead and find yourself some privacy. I'm just going to hunker down here a spell and mind my own business," the man said, not bothering to look up from his work.

"Yeah all right, fine. I'll just find another spot, where I won't be in your way," Joe said stomping back up toward the road. Had he really thought that this lake was so tranquil? According to his watch, he had less than fifteen minutes before he needed to start back home. If he missed Debbie's graduation, she would never forgive him. And yet he still hadn't received his answer. Searching around, he saw that the only real privacy within walking distance was going to be down in the reeds near the edge of the water. The cattails would probably play havoc with his allergies, but at least he wouldn't be interrupted again.

Parting the head-high stalks, Joe pressed tentatively at the marshy ground with the tip of his loafer and winced at the dark brown water that welled up around his shoe. He had dressed to meet with an expensive accounting firm, not to go wading through a swamp. Was this really worth ruining an expensive pair of shoes? It was if he could get the answers he was looking for. Ignoring the slick sucking of the mud that oozed over the tops of his shoes and soaked his socks, he continued to slog forward until he was completely surrounded. Eyeing the water that was up to his ankles, he decided that it wouldn't really be necessary to kneel.

Bowing his head, hands clasped at his waist, he closed his eyes. "Heavenly Father, it's not like I need a sign in the sky or anything, if you could just give me some kind of clue then I—"

"Aah, now you've gone and discovered one of *my* secret fishing spots."

"What?" Joe spun around at the sound of the voice directly behind him and nearly lost one of his shoes in the thick goop. Struggling to keep from falling, he shot out one hand and grabbed the shoulder of the bearded man that must have followed him into the reeds. Although the man looked to be at least eighty, the shoulders under his short-sleeved khaki shirt were broad, and he held out one hand to steady Joe as easily as if he had been helping a child.

"Yep, these reeds are where those fat old big-mouth bass live. Just hop a green-and-yellow plug along the top of the water, and bam, he'll hit your line like an angry mule."

"What are you doing here? Why did you follow me?" Joe could feel himself loosing complete control of his temper at this bearded stalker. The man seemed as intent on hunting him as Ahab did the great white whale. But the man seemed to ignore his outburst entirely as he pointed back over Joe's shoulder.

"See there. There's a father teaching his son that very trick."

Turning to look despite himself, Joe saw nothing but long green stalks. "I don't see anything . . ." and yet just as he spoke, a breeze seemed to split the reeds in front of him, bending them gently back like blades of grass, and revealing a weathered wooden rowboat floating a short distance away. Seated on a bench at the center of the boat, a young father held the hand of a boy that looked to be seven or eight, and with a flick of his wrist helped him turn a smooth cast that sent a lure arcing through the air to drop only a few feet from the edge of the sand. Grinning, the boy began to retrieve the lure, giving the tip of the rod a quick twitch, and then reeling in the slack. Sure enough, on the third twitch, the water exploded a few inches from the spot where the line disappeared into the water and the end of the rod bowed with the pressure.

"Yep, nothing like fishing with your pap to shake the scales from your eyes."

"Scales?" As the breeze died, the reeds straightened, again hiding the boat from the two men's view.

"Yeah. Fish aren't the only ones with scales. The world can place scales on a child's eyes sometimes, blinding them from seeing what's important in life. And it's not just children that can be blinded either. Nope, no one's immune to scales."

"Yes, I guess." Joe nodded, and then, remembering why he was standing ankle-deep in this slimy black soup, he shook his head angrily. "Why did you follow me here anyway. Didn't I just tell you I was trying to get a little privacy? Why don't you go on up to the dock? I'm sure those kids would just *love* to get some of your angling tips. If I could just get five minutes of peace and quiet maybe I might be able to—"

"Hey you'd better get going," the man interrupted him. "Don't you have a graduation to get to?"

"Yes, and I. . ." Joe looked at his watch, realizing that he had used up his fifteen minutes. "Thanks a lot," he grumbled, shouldering past the man, his feet sending up geysers of green and black with each step.

"Oh, and you might want to think about changing those shoes before you go. Looks like you got 'em a mite wet."

Throwing open the car's door, Joe peeled off his muddy shoes and sopping socks and tossed them onto the floor behind his seat. This was great. He had just driven two hours and ruined a three-hundred dollar pair of shoes to listen to some crackpot give him fishing advice. Reversing out of the lot, his tires throwing up plumes of dust, Joe wheeled around and stopped to look down at the stand of reeds. Not surprisingly, the man was now nowhere in sight. *Now that he's managed to screw up* my *day, he's off to go bother some other innocent soul in search of a little quiet.*

But what was even more annoying was that, studying the stretch of dirt that separated the reeds from the road, he could only see one pair of wet footprints. "Not only is this guy some kind of expert fisherman, he also apparently walks on water."

* * *

" . . . and so, as we leave our childhood behind us to make our marks in the world, we free ourselves from the shackles of our parent's well meaning but often antiquated beliefs. We go boldly forward now to make our own decisions and, for better or worse, to set the course that our own lives will follow.

"So to the parents in this audience today, I say, 'Thank you for raising us, thank you for holding our hands through the days of our youth, but now it's time to let go.' And to my fellow classmates, in the graduating class of 2002, I say, 'Be free. Like the California condor, soar once again into the sky and don't let anything bring you down.'"

As Joe listened to the crescendo of applause that followed the remarks of the class valedictorian, he felt his stomach clenching and unclenching like a great cold fist. Is that really what these kids all believed? That everything their parents had taught them could be thrown out the window now because they had managed to pull passing marks through thirteen years of public education? Did they really think that because they got an A in history that they knew more than all the generations that had come along before them?

And yet it wasn't just the students standing and cheering. Parents in the stands were on their feet waving their arms in the air and whooping right along with their kids. Were they just so happy to have their children out of the nest that they didn't care what they did once they were on their own? If that was how they felt, it was no wonder so many of their kids ended up on drugs or in therapy.

Well at least Debbie was going to BYU. They had standards there. And yet, was that any kind of guarantee that she would be safe? If a kid wanted to get into trouble it was easy enough to find, even in Happy Valley. He remembered what she had said in his dream, or hallucination, or vision, or whatever it had been. *They think that just*

*because you go to seminary at some obnoxiously early hour for four years
that you're just going to fall in line with all the other good little Mormons.*

He knew he had to let her go. Like every other parent, he had to
trust that he and Heather had taught their children well enough to
make the right decisions once they were out of his sight. But that was
assuming that they had raised her right, had given her the tools to
cope with all the negativity that the world would throw at her. Up
until a week ago, he would have sworn that Debbie's testimony was
up to the challenge, but now he wasn't so sure, and the thought of his
daughter going out into the world without a sure knowledge that she
was a child of God scared him to death.

If only he had been able to get an answer to his prayers. He had
felt so close, so sure that he was about to learn something vital to the
welfare of his family, and then that crazy fisherman had shown up.
Looking back on it, the man's timing had been almost eerie. It would
have been funny if it wasn't so thoroughly frustrating. Still it had been
fun to watch that young boy catch what was probably his first fish.
He hoped that the father had remembered to bring a camera. He still
had a photograph of his first fish. A black-and-white of him standing
at the edge of the lake, a glistening fourteen-inch rainbow hanging
from the end of his line. In the background, his mother standing on
the front stoop of their cabin with a look of . . .

In his mind two images superimposed over one another and the
effect was like a slap in the face, actually snapping his head back on
his neck. Beside him, Heather turned as if he had said something and
stared at him before returning her dull gaze back to the stage where
students were walking up to take their diplomas.

The lake in front of his parent's cabin, his cabin now that they
had passed away, and the lake in his dream. They were the same. Why
hadn't he seen it before? Because he hadn't been there since before the
kids were born. It was too remote. No, that wasn't even the right
word, more like isolated. No electricity, no running water. No phone
service of any kind. He had gone with his father every summer as a
boy, and then a few times after his mission. But after he married and
began to have kids it had just seemed like too much trouble. Heather
worried that they were hours from any kind of medical help if something happened to the kids, and Joe's business concerns demanded

that he remain within contact of cell phones and e-mail. So he had just quit going. His father went up every summer, even after Mom had passed away, right up until the stroke that eventually took his life. That meant it had stood empty for nearly ten years.

And yet he knew with a certainty that he needed to take his family there. It was as if a skyrocket had been fired off in his head, illuminating the dark landscape he had been wandering aimlessly in. A barrage of images filled his head. Chopping wood for the stove. Diving into the crystal clear water from the dock. Paddling the canoe to the other side of the lake. Hiking through miles of virgin forest, the fresh smell of cedars and firs in his nose and the soft cushion of pine needles beneath his feet. It was perfect. The kids would love it, just like he had.

Could he even find it? It was a good twenty-five miles off of any roads you could find on a map. His grandfather had purchased it from the railroad in the late forties. Like many of the land grants the railroad had received from the federal government as an incentive for putting through lines, it was in the middle of nowhere. Surrounded by national forest on three sides, it could only be reached by navigating a puzzle of old logging roads and dirt trails that were barely wide enough to get a car through. He would need to install the winch on the front of the car, and they'd probably want the chainsaw too. They would need to bring food. He knew that his parents kept supplies up there, but who knew what kind of condition they would be in after ten years.

They would drive up Friday and stay through the weekend at least. No, why wait? There was nothing keeping them here. Why not tomorrow morning? It could be a surprise. He would tell the kids to pack a couple days worth of clothes, some books and games. This might be exactly what Heather needed to shake her out of the funk she'd been in. Wouldn't the old guy down at the lake be surprised if he found out that he had actually been the one to provide the answer to Joe's prayers?

CHAPTER 9

"Debbie, Richie, hurry up and get your bags down here. We want to get an early start," Joe shouted up the stairs.

"Eddy tart," Angela parroted from next to Joe, nearly dancing across the granite slab of the entryway floor. She had been this way since the night before, when he told the family that they were going away for a few days. Richie had been suspiciously optimistic, Heather noncommittal as she seemed to be about everything lately, and Debbie had openly rebelled, only agreeing to go on this "stupid trip," with the understanding that she was coming back on Friday night whether the rest of the family did or not. Only Angela seemed thrilled, almost as if she had somehow been able to peek into Joe's brain and glimpse the beauty of their true destination.

"Patafwy kiz. Patafwy kiz," Angela pulled at the tail of the long-sleeved denim shirt that Joe wore unbuttoned over a white tee.

"Oh, of course. How could I have forgotten?" He leaned down and took her face between his hands, warmed as always by the soft flutter of her eyelashes against his cheek.

"Duhkee go addy," she whispered in his ear as he brushed his own eyelashes against her pink cheek.

"You're welcome, baby," he said. And then, because he could barely control his own excitement, her picked her up and swung her around and around in the air. "This is going to be so great."

"Ate," she agreed.

Fwump. Richie's bag landed on the floor next to Joe. "Just tell me that we're not going to Disneyland again," Richie said from the top of the stairs. The year before, he had announced that Disneyland was not cool, a baby place, and he would not go there anymore. Privately Joe thought it was because a girl Richie had tried to pick up on in the Pirates of the Caribbean ride had told him to jump in the lake, but Richie's negativity was not going to get to him this morning.

"Not Disneyland," Joe said, hefting the single duffel bag. "Sure you've got everything? This feels pretty light."

"That's it," Richie shrugged.

"Underwear, toothbrush, swimsuit?"

"Swimsuit? You didn't say we were swimming,"

"Are you taking us to Huntington Beach?" Debbie called from upstairs, with almost a trace of enthusiasm in her voice.

"It's a surprise." If it would get them into the car more quickly, Joe would let them think whatever they wanted. Holding the bag up to Richie he asked, "So you want to pack it a little more full?"

"Whatever." Richie shrugged, but he took the bag and returned to his room.

When they were finally all loaded into the car, the morning sun was just beginning to peek over the eastern foothills. They would be slowed down by commuter traffic, but with the whole family in the car, they would at least be able to take advantage of the carpool lanes. Looking across at Heather, he thought about calling the whole thing off. He had hoped that getting out of the house might cheer her up. But she looked worse than ever this morning. Now not even bothering to spell anything, she was simply filling in the blanks of her puzzles with random numbers, letters, and in some cases meaningless squiggles. He had tried taking her to a doctor the day before, but she had locked herself in the bathroom for nearly three hours—only her monotonous humming indicating that she was even alive. No, he had to trust his feeling that he was doing the right thing.

"Debbie, would you start us off with a prayer this morning?"

"No, you go ahead, Dad."

"Richie?" he asked.

"Too tired," Richie muttered from the back seat.

"Okay, your loss." Joe bowed his head. "Father, as we leave our home this day, we thank Thee for the many blessings Thou hast given us. We ask that Thou would watch over and protect us. Help us to come closer together as a family. Please help us to overcome our trials and to remember why we have been placed on this earth. In the name of Jesus Christ, amen."

"Men," Angela nearly shouted. But Debbie only muttered, "That's a lot to ask from a couple of days at the beach."

"What's under the tarp?" Richie asked, peering over the backseat.

"Supplies." Joe ran through everything he had loaded that morning and the night before, hoping he hadn't forgotten anything. Gas for the chainsaw, kerosene for the lamps, extra blankets and towels. He had loaded all the nonperishables he could find, and an oversized ice chest, figuring they could stop at a grocery store on the way up and fill it with milk, lunch meat, sodas, and whatever else he might think of. But still he had the nagging feeling that he was missing something important. Soap, shampoo, toilet paper, well whatever it was, he could always pick it up on the way in.

* * *

UNKNOWN LOCATION, flashed in bright letters across the top of the car's global positioning system screen. A squiggly green line branching off from state highway 163, which itself was actually little more than a one-lane road, showed the series of lefts and rights they had taken over the last fifteen miles. The flashing red dot at the end of the line, surrounded by empty black space, was their current location. Not for the first time, Joe wondered if they had taken a wrong turn somewhere along the way. The roads they followed had gone from asphalt, to chip and seal, to gravel, and eventually to the red dirt they were traveling along now. He thought he remembered the boulder they had passed about a mile back—it looked kind of like a goose with a severely humped back—but he had thought the same about the huge burned-out pine, and that turn had led to a dead end that forced them to back the Navigator nearly a mile before they found a spot wide enough to turn around.

Beside him, Heather's head rocked softly back and forth on the pillow propped between her seat back and the window. In the back, Debbie and Richie were asleep too, having long since given up complaining about driving into the middle of nowhere. Angela, listening to a sing-along-songs tape on her Walkman, was staring out the window at the trees that, with elevation, had changed from predominantly oaks to lodgepole pines and cedars with an occasional aspen and cottonwood thrown in for good measure.

"Cracker?" he asked, holding a box back over the seat to her.

"No fanks." She shook her head, and returned to staring out the window, softly singing something that sounded like, "E I E I E I."

Ahead, the road split to the left and right. Stopping the car, Joe stepped out and examined the two alternatives. It looked like the main road, if he could call it that, continued to the right, disappearing behind a stand of aspens a few hundred yards ahead. The road to the left looked little wider than an equestrian trail, blades of dry grass and brush sprouting from the hump in the middle. The manzanita had overgrown both sides of the road, and he knew that the sharp red branches would scrape paint off the sides of the wide Navigator's body. Less than a hundred feet ahead, he could see where a tree had fallen across the road. Its trunk was too tall to use the winch, which meant he would have to cut through it. And yet something about that direction seemed so familiar. He almost thought he could remember his father stopping at this juncture and joking about the road less traveled.

"Well I've come this far," he said to a scrub jay watching him inquisitively from a large pinecone just off the side of the road. "Might as well keep going." The jay cocked its head, let out a hoarse caw and lit into the air.

Nearly four hours later the afternoon sun was beginning to turn red as it moved progressively lower in the western sky, and Joe was beginning to get seriously worried that they would have to spend the night in the car. Double-checking the cable that he had wrapped around yet another tree trunk, he waved to Richie, who engaged the winch. As he watched the log slowly being dragged out of the road, Joe placed his hands on his hips and leaned backwards, listening to his spine pop as rarely used muscles tried to pull back into shape. According to the GPS, they had driven nearly thirty miles since leaving the highway. Even with the backtracking they had done, that meant that they must have covered twenty to twenty-five miles. If they were heading in the right direction they should have been there by now, but except for the fallen trees and branches that limited them to only a few miles an hour, this narrow road looked just the same as it had for the last five miles.

He had turned left at the fork, scraping paint off the sides of the car just as he thought he would, and turned off onto two equally narrow tracks since then. Once they had joined an inexplicably wide road, its surface wonderfully covered with the almost asphalt-like chip and seal that logging companies used to make passage possible for the big trucks that hauled out the timber they cut. But less than a half-mile later the road had turned back into a dirt lane, so full of potholes and swales that it had rattled everyone in the car awake. If they turned around now they might be able to make it back to the main highway before nightfall.

"Hey Dad, what's that?" Richie was standing at the side of the road near where they had dragged the log, and pointing down the road. He still complained every time they stopped the car to move another log, but Joe thought his son looked like he might actually be enjoying himself a little. Turning, he looked back down the road in the direction Richie was pointing. Other than the wide slabs of glittering black-and-white granite that lined the roadside, there wasn't much to see.

"What's what?" he started to ask, thinking that his son had spotted a chipmunk or maybe a few deer, but then he noticed a metallic gleam in the center of the road, maybe a quarter mile away. The gate. He had forgotten all about that. He remembered his dad and granddad bringing it up on the back of a flatbed truck and welding it in place when he was about six. Concerned that one day the Russians would finally lose their cool and fire off a bunch of missiles, they had decided to secure the road in the event that they might all have to come up here and live one day. The gate was less than a mile from the cabin. He had been right after all, and they wouldn't have to sleep in the car.

"Wahoo!" he shouted, scaring a pair of quails into flight and earning disgusted looks from his two oldest children. "Come on, we're almost there!" He jumped into the car, nearly forgetting to wait for Richie before he accelerated down the rutted trail at an exhilarating eight miles an hour.

At the gate he hopped out, prepared to swing back the thick metal bars, then stopped cold at the sight of the small gold padlock hanging from the latch. He had completely forgotten about the lock. How could he have been such an idiot? To have come all this way only to be stopped less than a mile from the goal. Of course they could climb the gate and walk the rest of the way, but that would mean lugging all the supplies up as well. Examining the bottom of the lock he saw that it had six wheels embedded in its base, each numbered from zero to nine. How long would it take to try 999,999 combinations? A lot longer than he had.

Had his dad ever told him the combination? He must have, but with all the numbers Joe had to remember: driver's license, social security, phone numbers, birthdays . . . wait, birthdays. Hadn't Dad always used Mom's birthday when he had to make up a code? Joe thought that he had. All he needed to do was set the numbers to his mother's birthday and they would be in. Except that he couldn't remember his mother's birthday. He was lousy with dates, and Heather who *could* remember every important date, wasn't up to remembering much of anything at the moment. Through the windshield, he could see that she had picked up her puzzle magazine again, now that the car had stopped.

Come on, come on, he told himself. *You can do this.*

"No I can't." He yanked on the lock in frustration and it popped open in his hand. Removing it from the gate, he turned it upside down and saw that it was set to 961938. September 6, 1938. His dad had left it set to the right combination the last time he had come up as if he knew that he would not be coming back. In his head he could hear his father's gruff laughter. *Never could remember that one, could you?*

With a low sigh of relief he swung the gate open. The hinges squealed from a decade of disuse, but after a few feet the gate moved easily, and after forcing it against the thicket of blackberry bushes that had grown up to the edge of the road, he was able to clear enough space to pull the car through.

* * *

It was just as he had remembered it. The lake was crystal clear, created centuries earlier by the glaciers that slowly and methodically forced their way through the mountain's granite slabs, so deep toward the middle that he and his friends had never been able to touch bottom. The evening sun reflected off the granite, like millions of tiny diamonds. In the distance he could see mountaintops still capped with snow. He remembered hiking up to those caps and eating homemade snow cones. Walking slowly down to the dock he marveled at how fresh the air smelled. Find a way to pipe that directly to L.A. and people would pay millions for it. He stepped tentatively out onto the dock, wondering if the wood had rotted at all, and was delighted to find that it was still as solid as ever.

"Ebin." Angela's small voice reminded him that he wasn't alone, and he knelt down to look into her shining eyes.

"It is like heaven, isn't it?" She held out her arms and twirled around as though trying to take in everything at once.

"Ike ebin."

"We spent twelve hours in the car for this?" Debbie's voice split the evening like a rusty nail being pulled painfully from a piece of hardwood.

"Yeah, isn't it great?" Joe said, so lost in what he was feeling that he completely missed his oldest daughter's tone of voice.

"Dad, this place is a dump."

"What did you say?" he asked, not sure that he had heard her correctly.

"You expect us to sleep in that . . . shack? It's like some kind of relic from a scout camp gone horribly wrong."

Joe turned to look at the cabin, trying to see it from Debbie's perspective. He had been so caught up in his own memories of coming here as a boy, that he had completely overlooked how his family might react to it. Debbie had been imagining the Tahoe Hilton and he had surprised her with an abandoned fishing cabin— more shack than lodge—with no running water or electricity. It was no wonder she wasn't exactly thrilled to see it.

Originally built by his grandfather and then added onto over the years, the family cabin had been constructed with functionality, not beauty, in mind. Even *he* had to admit it was no architectural wonder. With the shutters latched closed and several of the shingles spiking up at odd angles, it looked a little like some of the abandoned homes you saw on urban street corners. And the fuchsia paint his father had picked up at a garage sale *was* a pretty silly color for the outhouse and the water pump.

But in spite of all of that, or maybe even a little because of it, the cabin looked pleasant—homey. It looked like the kind of place where you could put your feet up on the coffee table without being criticized. No one would ever tell you to take off your shoes before you walked through that doorway. And, dilapidated or not, it was the place to which the Spirit had whispered for him to bring his family.

". . . right now." Debbie's shrill voice again snapped at him.

"I'm sorry, I missed what you said."

"Dad, you can stay here as long as you want, cooking weenies over the campfire and reliving your boyhood days or whatever. You might even convince Richie to stay with you, although I doubt it. But in case you hadn't noticed, Mom is not well, and if anything happened to Angela, what would you do, holler for Smoky the Bear? And I am *not* going to start possibly my last free summer sitting in an eighty-year-old purple outhouse communing with nature. Now give me the car keys." Marching to the end of the pier, she held out her hand.

"This is a family vacation and we are all staying here together."

"I'm not staying here another minute. Now I mean it, give me those keys." She snatched at the key ring in his hand, but Joe lifted it up and away from her. He had never seen her like this. It was almost like Jekyll and Hyde, watching his polite, mild-mannered daughter turn into a screaming lunatic.

"Look, I don't know what this is all about. I hope it's not about some college guy that you want to meet." Her eyes widened, first with surprise and then with anger, and he knew that he had hit the mark. "But you are not going anywhere. We are going to stay here as a family for as long as we need to. And if you think that—"

"No!" Her scream seemed to fill the valley, shuttering through the trees and ricocheting off the top of the lake like a gunshot. In the distance a large bird, possibly an osprey, lifted off the water with a flurry of its powerful wings. Debbie lunged for the keys, slapping at Joe's hand as her weight knocked him backward. Struggling to keep his balance, his hand flew open and the keys sailed into the air and out over the water. For a split second they seemed to hang suspended between the setting red ball of fire in the air and its counterpart reflected in the lake, before splashing into the water with a dull plunk. Joe caught sight of a single shimmer of gold as they spun down into the darkness, and then they were gone.

* * *

Fear. Stranded with his wife and children in a cabin twenty miles or more from any hope of contact with the outside world, Joe *should* have been feeling an almost overwhelming fear. There was less than a week's food in the back of the car, and his keys were at the bottom of a lake so deep that they would probably be irrecoverable without scuba gear. Although Heather's key ring would still be in her purse, it only had keys to the house and her Mercedes. They drove each other's cars so seldomly that it made no sense to carry two sets of keys. He had no idea what kind of condition the cabin might be in, or how they would get back to the highway, and yet what he was feeling most was a deep sense of peace—a contentment so complete it was actually a physical sensation.

"But what are we going to do?" Richie tailed behind Joe with Angela close behind him, alternating his shocked gaze between his father and the spot about twenty feet from the end of the dock where the keys had disappeared.

"Well for starters we're going to get that cabin open and see what kind of condition it's in." Joe followed the still faintly visible path that led from the water up to the front of the house.

"But how are we going to get home?"

"Well at this point it looks like at least one of us is going to do some walking. It shouldn't be any worse than that fifty miler we went on with the Scouts a couple of years ago." Climbing the front steps he tried the front door, and finding it locked, stretched one hand up above the doorway.

"Should be right up around here somewhere." Joe walked his fingers along the top of the doorjamb, exploring the knotty surface of the pine log just above it. The mortar between the log and the jam was a solid seal except for one small chink where he thought he remembered . . . "Got it." His fingers closed on the brass key secreted in the hidden opening. It wasn't much of a hiding place really, the first place a potential intruder searched for a key would be under the welcome mat, had there been one, and above the door. But the lock wasn't really meant to keep people out anyway.

Anyone finds themselves clear out here deserves to rest their feet for a day or two in my place, Joe remembered his grandfather saying. Which was probably a pretty safe bet. Not even the hunters, with their cases of beer and ATVs, made it out this far. In all his years of coming to the cabin, Joe could count on one hand the number of times they had run across anyone. And when they did, it was either a hiker who was delighted to be invited in for a bite to eat, or someone so hopelessly lost they were ecstatic just to see another human face. No, the only reason for the lock was to keep out the raccoons, who could jimmy just about any kind of latch, and the rare bear looking for an easy meal.

Sliding the key into the lock, he released the dead bolt and then paused for a moment. There was so much riding on this little shack, as Debbie had called it. On it, and the few hundred acres surrounding it, swung possibly the future of his family. The notion seemed crazy, like something out of a Grimms' fairy tale. A magic forest with an axis so strong that it repelled Debbie like nothing he had ever seen before, while it pulled Angela to it like a magnet. But at the same time, it felt true that this seemingly insignificant "vacation" would forever alter the future, inexplicable perhaps, but true. The question was whether it would bring them all together or tear them apart.

"Are you gonna open the door or just stand there all day?" Richie leaned against one of the supporting poles of the broad front porch, hands in his jacket pockets, trying to look nonchalant, but Joe thought that his son felt something too.

"Okay, it might be a little dusty now. It's been a while since anyone was last here." Joe pushed the door open quickly and a cloud of tiny gray particles instantly danced out into the sunlight.

"Achoo, achoo!" Angela, who had been standing next to Joe, clutching his pant leg, waved at the haze, her face exploding into a series of surprised sneezes. "S'turty."

"Yeah, it is a little dirty," Joe agreed. Holding the sleeve of his shirt over his mouth and nose, he cautiously stepped across the small patch of light that the evening sun cast through the doorway and into the darkness of the cabin's interior. Fumbling his hand along the wall just to his right, he found one of the two windows that faced the lake. All of the cabin's windows were shuttered tight against both animals and the ferocious storms that often struck the area. Twisting the latch at the side of the window he swung open the pane, slid out the screen, and lifted the bar that held closed the heavy wooden shutters. As the warm, golden sunlight touched the interior of the cabin for the first time in more years than Angela had been alive, Joe was transported back to a time he had almost completely forgotten.

When his grandfather had originally built the cabin fifty years earlier, it had consisted of a single large room with a stone fireplace on one wall and a rectangular copper sink built into the other. His grandmother had cooked over the open fire and washed everything from potatoes to babies in the sink.

Over the years the cabin had grown. The fireplace still remained, its wide stone hearth taking up most of the north wall, but a wood stove had been added to the kitchen. Copper pipe had been plumbed in a zigzag pattern along the back of it, connecting to a storage tank beneath the sink so that the stove could be used not just for cooking and heating, but also as a kind of rudimentary hot water heater.

A second story had been added onto the cabin when Joe's father was old enough to help build it. The stairway, a steep narrow affair that ran along the back wall, had a flowered runner tacked down to it, providing a modicum of cushioning for the invariable times that people stumbled down it. But that was the only actual carpeting ever laid down. The rest of the floors were hand-rubbed pine with a smattering of throw rugs. The upstairs had been divided into two rooms; the master suite, as Joe's father had called it, really only differed from the other bedroom in the fact that it had a closet.

Everything necessary for survival was here, and yet so many of the things that the modern world considered necessary were conspicuously absent. There were no light switches or electrical outlets; instead kerosene lamps hung from the ceiling and walls. The kitchen counter, where one would expect to see a blender, microwave, and maybe an electric grill, instead held a hand grinder and a copper kettle. And at the back of the room against the stairway, where any self-respecting family would have placed a big color television, stood a hand-carved bookshelf, where titles like *A Tale of Two Cities* and *Little Women* sat side by side with *The Hardy Boys* and dozens of Louis L'Amour paperbacks.

How many evenings had he sat curled up on one of the big overstuffed chairs, exhausted from a day of hiking and swimming, and read himself to sleep next to the fire? There was such a sense of peace that came from going to bed not long after the sun had set and arising with the first rays of dawn—not because you had to beat the rush hour, but because you wanted to see what was over the next peak.

"How come there are sheets on everything?" Richie pulled back the cover from a brown-and-green sofa, raising a small dust storm.

"Take that outside," Joe said, coughing at the mouthful of grit that he'd just inhaled. "And don't touch anything else until we get some more windows opened."

"Soh-reee." Richie backed out the door and laid the sheet over the porch railing. "I was just asking."

"It's all right, just be a little more careful," Joe said, trying not to antagonize any of his children further. Debbie was still sitting in the car sulking, and he didn't need Richie mad as well. And the truth was that Richie had hit on something. Why had his father covered all the furniture with sheets? He couldn't remember him doing it any of the other times that they had come. There were plenty of other things to do, shuttering the windows, covering the pump, storing the tools, all the things that winter-proofed the cabin. But he had never covered the furniture before. Again, it was almost as if his father had known that he would not be returning, and that it would be years before his only child *did*.

"Wuz a ere?" Angela asked, pulling on a door in the back corner of the room, just below the point where the top of the stairs disappeared from view.

"Oh that just goes to the covered porch out back," Joe said. And yet when the door swung inward, it wasn't the back porch that came into view. Enough of the cabin's shutters were now open that it was possible to see that someone had added a room back there.

"What in the world?" Stepping through the doorway, Joe crossed to the back of the room and opened a window obviously built much more recently than the others in the cabin. Double panes would help keep this bedroom warm even though it was further from the stove than the upstairs rooms.

"Oh, wow." Richie, who had come back into the cabin with a scowl on his face, now stood openmouthed staring at a room that could only have been built with a boy in mind. On the wall across from the window, a huge stuffed trout was mounted beneath a pair of arched, bamboo fly-fishing rods. Next to the door, three black powder muskets hung from pegs, and on the opposite wall, a small bookshelf held titles like *Treasure Island*, *The Red Badge of Courage*, and *The Last of the Mohicans*.

The centerpiece of the room was a four-poster bed that stood nearly three feet off the floor. Each of the posts reached nearly to the ceiling, and as Joe pulled off the dust cover, he saw that instead of being lathed into the ornate spindles that were common on such beds, each of the thick pine shafts had been carved into a unique totem pole. The faces of eagles, bears, owls, and raccoons would look down upon whoever was sleeping in this bed.

"Peety." While Joe and Richie had been goggling, Angela had discovered yet another door, this one connecting the boy's room with what should have been the other half of the covered porch. Stepping into the doorway, Joe felt as if he had just entered a secret glen in an enchanted forest.

The walls had been painted with a mixture of ancient firs whose gnarled bark looked almost like faces, and a dazzling array of brightly colored flowers waving before a backdrop of snowcapped peaks. The bed in the center of this room required no dust cover, because yards of pink and white cloth hung down from the ceiling, forming a canopy that turned the bed into a magic castle of sorts. Lifting a cloth, Joe saw that four small wooden toadstools and one slightly larger one formed a table and chairs that were the perfect size for Angela.

"When did you do this, Dad?" Joe asked quietly. *And why?* Opening the window to get more light, he saw that each of the walls had been painted in the most intricate detail. Beneath one of the flowers gamboled a tiny wood elf whose eyes actually seeming to glimmer. But his dad wasn't a painter or a sculptor. He was a gifted mechanic, and a decent carpenter, good with a screwdriver or a hammer . . . and yet looking at the painted walls and the beautifully carved table, Joe knew that this *was* the work of his father. Every line and brush stroke seemed to have his name embedded in it.

This must have been built for Debbie and Richie. Angela hadn't even been born yet. But he and Heather had never brought the kids up here. How did his dad know they would? The thought of his father sitting up here alone day after day, creating these wonderful gifts for his grandchildren, was too much for Joe and he turned and stepped quickly back outside, wiping his face with the back of his hand.

Walking down to the car, he tried to get his emotions back under control. In a meadow off to the left he could see hundreds of tiny purple and white wildflowers nodding in the gentle evening breeze. What was it that Jesus had said in the Sermon on the Mount? Something about the lilies of the field being arrayed more gloriously than Solomon in his finery. He thought to his recent study of the sixth chapter of Matthew. *Therefore take no thought, saying, What shall we eat? or, What shall we drink? or, Wherewithall shall we be clothed? . . . But seek ye first the kingdom of God.* Was that why the Lord had brought them here, so that they could stop worrying about clothes and houses, cars and money, and instead focus on what was really important?

As Joe stepped from the packed pine needles of the forest floor out onto the dirt road, something on the ground caught his attention. Kneeling by the front bumper of the car, he ran his finger along a pawprint embedded in the dirt. Having spotted the one, the rest suddenly became obvious, leading away from the cabin, across the road, and disappearing in the direction of the trees near the south end of the lake. Stepping off the distance between each set of prints, he whistled softly, and uneasily scanned the steadily darkening woods around him.

It was a silly thing to worry about. The prints were deep, obviously made after a long rain, while the packed dirt of the road was still muddy enough to take and hold an impression. It was June, a dry time of year in California, and it could easily have been a month or more since the last big storm. Still, he was suddenly anxious to get Debbie and Heather up into the cabin before the evening light disappeared completely. And it might not be such a bad idea to have Angela and Richie close the shutters to the windows of their downstairs rooms at night.

They were solitary animals, inclined to avoid people as much as people avoided them. And yet on more than one occasion over the last few years they had been known to attack humans. Especially if the human in question was alone and small. And based on the length of the creature's stride while walking—the tracks were deep and clear, not smeared as would have been the case if it had been running across the road—it was obviously a very large, very powerful mountain lion.

CHAPTER 10

The combined aromas of pine logs blazing noisily in the fireplace and stew bubbling on the stove slowly overpowered the smell of Murphy's Oil Soap on the cool night air. After hours of sweeping, mopping, and dusting, even Debbie was too tired to complain anymore. Standing in the doorway, watching the moon's orange reflection dance on the rippling black surface of the lake, Joe wondered if his father had felt the same sense of fulfillment that he did now, living the way their pioneer forefathers had done more than a hundred years ago. Okay, so they probably hadn't scooped their stew out of a can, but it still felt good.

"Okay guys, let's get washed up and eat." Joe wiped his hands on his dirt-smeared blue jeans, and closing the door securely behind him, walked back inside.

"Er da bafoom?" Angela, who had been setting the table, looked curiously around the large open first floor as if she had a missed a door somewhere.

"There is no bathroom here, sweetie. We wash at the kitchen sink." Joe pumped the cast-iron handle up and down and a stream of water poured out of the faucet and splashed down into the copper sink. It was comfortably warm, having been heated by the stove.

Angela seemed to think this over for a minute before nodding her approval. But then another realization seemed to dawn on her and her small eyes opened wide with alarm. "No go poddy sank," she said, eliciting a tired laugh from Richie and a groan from Debbie, both of whom had already made the same discovery their younger sister was now making.

"No, we do *not* go potty in the sink," Joe agreed. "We do that outside in the outhouse."

"Side?" Angela looked shocked. "Angewa no poddy side. Is noddy."

"Here, let me take you." Realizing that it would be easier to show her than to continue trying to explain, Joe picked up a flashlight and opened the front door. With Angela tagging curiously along behind him, Joe walked down the front steps and crossed to the narrow path that led around the side of the cabin and to the garishly painted building next to the tool shed. The crescent moon cut into the top of the door identified this as the outhouse, as if the smell that was already beginning to emanate from between the weathered boards, and the buzz of flies, who had somehow discovered that this building was back in use, didn't make that obvious enough.

Swinging open the door, Joe played the beam of the flashlight across the wooden bench with its single toilet seat and the fresh roll of toilet paper hanging from a long nail on the wall. "Well this is it kid." Joe handed the flashlight to his daughter. "I'll wait outside the door while you do what you need to do, and then we'll go get some chow. Okay?"

Wrinkling her nose at the unpleasant odor, Angela stepped warily through the door and aimed the light down into the darkness beneath the seat. "No," she screamed, running back out the door, shaking her head wildly. "Angewa no go poddy ina hoe."

Joe covered his mouth with one hand trying to muffle his laughter at the unmollified look of horror on his daughter's face. He could remember only too well how worried he had been as a boy that he might fall into that deep black pit. The thought had kept his trips to the outhouse as brief as possible. Now, however, he needed to convince Angela that it wasn't really as bad as it looked, and his giggles weren't helping matters at all.

"It's okay," he said, trying to sound reasonable. "It's just like a toilet, except without the water."

"No." Angela folded her tiny arms firmly across her chest, refusing to budge an inch toward the black hole inside the smelly building.

"Look, it's easy." Joe perched lightly, the rear of his jeans resting on the seat that had been polished by thousands of derrieres over the years, and held out his hands to either side. "See, nothing to it."

"Um, um." Angela turned her back on him as if embarrassed by seeing her father in such a compromising position.

Frustrated with his lack of success, Joe marched back out to stand in front of her. "It's either in here," he pointed toward the outhouse, "or out there." He turned and pointed toward the trees.

Angela, her knees now squeezed together in obvious discomfort, looked from the dark building to the dark woods and back again. For a moment Joe thought that she was actually going to head toward the trees, and he couldn't completely blame her. But finally she pointed her flashlight up into his face and asked earnestly, "You ode and?"

"Of course, I'll hold your hand." Taking her fingers in his, he walked her through the door and up to the bench. "I'll just look the other way while you go."

"Out." Angela ordered.

"But I thought you wanted me to hold your hand."

"Fru a doer."

"Sure. What was I thinking?" Leaving the door cracked just enough so that he could fit his arm through it, Joe knelt in the darkness and held Angela's hand as she went to the bathroom.

* * *

"Bwess Mama, an Bwess Addy, an Ebby, and Wutchy. Name a Jezuz, men." Angela climbed into bed, snuggled happily into the goose-down mattress and ran her fingers along the silky fabric of the canopy.

"Now remember," Joe said in a mock serious tone, waving one finger at her, "no matter how handsome this prince who comes to visit you every night might be, you tell him that you are my little girl and you are not allowed to ride off to some beautiful castle on any white stallion and get married until you are at least eleven. Is that clear?"

"Uhm, hmm, hmm," Angela giggled sleepily.

"Then give me a kiss." He bent over and kissed her good night, but as he started to stand, she pulled him back down and blinked her eyelashes against his cheek.

"Wow, butterfly kisses in the morning and at night. How did I manage to rank that?"

"Duhkee, Addy." Angela whispered even as her eyes began to close. "You're welcome, baby."

He stopped in Richie's room to talk for a few minutes. But his son was either already fast asleep or pretending to be, and Joe had to satisfy himself with pulling the thick quilt up over Richie's shoulders and kissing him softly on the cheek. He hoped that spending some quality time together would help them patch up their differences, and maybe get his son to open up to him.

Turning out each of the lamps, he climbed the stairs and paused briefly outside the door to Debbie's room. A light was still shining beneath the crack of her door, but he hesitated to intrude. It seemed like everything he said lately set her off, as if even his voice were offensive. And yet, wasn't learning how to talk to each other one of the reasons they had come here?

"Debbie?" he knocked gently, and then again a little louder. "Debbie, are you still up?"

"What?" Debbie's irritated-sounding voice answered.

Joe swung the door open a few inches. "Can I come in?"

"It's your house." Debbie slid a pair of headphones from her ears and quickly hid something under the blankets.

"There's no cell phone service anywhere around here," Joe said, seeing the thin black antenna sticking out from under the quilt.

"You don't have to tell *me*." Debbie said sharply. "I've tried it everywhere. Leave it to you to bring us somewhere even AT&T can't reach."

"Why does everything we say have to turn into an argument?" Joe sat on the foot of her bed.

"Maybe if you listened to what *I* want every once in a while instead of making me do everything *you* think is best, it wouldn't."

"What *do* you want?"

"What do I want?" Debbie asked warily, as if sensing a trap.

"Yes. What do you want that I haven't given you?"

"Okay fine. For one thing I don't want to be here. I want to be back home with my friends. And I want to be treated like an adult. You can't just keep yanking me around like a dog on a leash. I'm eighteen. If I'm old enough to vote legally, don't you think I'm old enough to start making my own decisions?"

"I do." Joe nodded.

"Then you should let me."

"Do you know what *I* want for you?" Joe asked.

"What?" Debbie pouted a little as if she had known all along that this was the direction their conversation would eventually take.

"I want you to be happy."

"And . . ."

"That's it. I just want you to be happy."

"Well you've got a pretty strange way of showing it. Is stranding me in the middle of Hole-in-the-Wall Mountain your way of trying to make me happy?"

"It is."

"Look Dad, I appreciate what you are trying to do here." Debbie took Joe's hand. "Richie's going through a pretty tough time right now, and I don't know if Mom's having a nervous breakdown or just really depressed or what, but she's been pretty out of it. And obviously Angela thinks this whole outdoors thing is wonderful. So bringing them up here might be the best thing in the world. Who knows, maybe after a weekend of roughing it everything'll be different. But *I* am doing just fine at home. I don't need this."

"Are you happy?" Joe asked.

"Yes. I—"

"No, don't answer so quickly." Joe reversed their grip, suddenly holding his daughter's hand in his. "I'm not talking about the "ha-ha" kind of happiness that stays while you're goofing around with your friends and then leaves. I'm talking about the kind of happiness that fills your soul, the kind that stays with you even when things are not going so good. Are you feeling the kind of happiness that your Heavenly Father wants you to feel, Debbie?"

Debbie exhaled slowly and fiddled with the dials on her CD player. "Look Dad, I know you believe in God and all that, and maybe I do too. But I'm just not sure anymore. I don't feel like I used to. Things aren't black and white like they teach you in Primary."

"You know there's a way to get answers to your questions. It's called prayer."

"Has it helped you?" Debbie asked, suddenly angry again. "Dad, you are one of the best people I know. Look at you. I go crazy and knock your keys in the lake, and you're up here trying to make sure I'm happy. Why would God treat you this way? Has he answered *that* prayer, because I know you've asked, I've heard you at night when you think nobody's listening."

"I . . . " Joe looked away, afraid to meet his daughter's eyes. How did he answer her? Yes he had prayed, and no he had not yet received an answer. But could he tell her that? Would she sense his frustration and disappointment? His eyes stopped on a small gilded picture frame standing on the night table next to Debbie's bed. He recognized it instantly. It had belonged to his grandmother. But what was it doing here? The last time he had seen it was on the fireplace mantel at his father's house.

"That picture belonged to your great-grandmother," he said, nodding toward the nightstand. Debbie picked it up and examined it briefly.

"I remember seeing it at Gram and Gramp's house," she said.

"Do you know why Great-Grandma Stewart found that particular picture so inspiring?"

"Because it's Jesus, I guess."

"Yes, it's the Savior, but what is He doing?"

Debbie held the picture up to the wavering flame of the kerosene lamp. "Knocking on a door. But I don't understand what that has to do with—"

"Why do you imagine He's knocking? Why not just open it up and go on in?"

"Look Dad, I got this lesson in Primary when I was like five." Debbie dropped the picture into her lap—eyes glinting with either anger or tears. "The teacher stood up in front of all us wide-eyed kids and showed how there was no knob on the outside of the door. And then she makes the *big promise*. 'All you have to do is open the door to your heart and let Christ come in.'"

Joe nodded excitedly. "Exactly. The Savior is always there. He wants to help us, to answer our prayers, ease our burdens, lessen our sorrows. But we have to let Him in. It isn't always easy, and can sometimes even be—"

"Just stop, okay." The tears were now flowing freely down Debbie's face. She folded her arms fiercely—almost protectively—across her chest, seemingly unaware that she was clutching her grandmother's picture.

"I fell for that once. I remember sitting there in class, while everyone was eating their graham crackers, going, 'Yeah that's really great. You just have to let Jesus in and everything will be fine.' But you know what the teacher forgot to mention? She must have just overlooked the fact that when you open up your heart, there are a lot of other things waiting to come in too. And some of them—maybe most of them—are things that start eating you up once they get inside."

"Debbie." Joe reached out to his daughter trying to comfort her, but she jerked back out of his reach. He wished desperately that Heather was there to help him. Scraped knees, broken arms—those were things he understood and could do something about. But he had no idea how to cure whatever was hurting his oldest daughter. "I don't understand."

"That's it exactly. You don't understand, and you never will." Drops of salty water slipped from Debbie's cheeks and splattered darkly against the brown paper backing of the picture. "Everyone says, 'Just open the door and let the Savior in.' But did you ever stop to think how it might feel to know that if you opened the door that He would be so disgusted by what was inside that He would just turn around and leave?"

Before Joe could answer, Debbie was up from the bed, swiping away the tears with the back of her hand and pushing him toward the door. "Get out. Just get out and leave me alone."

* * *

"Aughh," Joe grunted in pain as bacon grease spattered out of the frying pan and stung his forearms like tiny white-hot needles. Throwing the lid back over the pan, he madly pumped water out of the sink while slapping at the burning drops on his skin.

"Did you rinse the frying pan with water before you used it?" Debbie asked.

"Of course I did. I wouldn't cook breakfast in a dirty pan," Joe said, patting at the tiny red spots with a wet paper towel.

"Next time dry the pan before you use it." Debbie smiled halfheartedly as Joe recognized his mistake.

"Okay, so Tia I'm not." Apparently Debbie was willing to put aside what had gone on between them the night before. And for the moment Joe would as well. But there was something festering inside her, something too painful to let out, and he hoped that if he watched closely he could find the right time and place to help her face it.

"Why don't Richie and I take Angela down to the lake while you try not to burn the pancakes?" Debbie pointed back toward the wood stove.

"Yeah okay, that would be—oh shoot, the pancakes!" Joe tried to scrape the smoking circles of batter off the griddle while Debbie, Richie, and Angela headed out the front door.

* * *

"Debbie, Richie, Angela, come and get it while it's hot and only slightly caught," Joe called out the front door, trying to wave the worst of the smoke out of the cabin. He would have to close the air vents on the stove further next time so that it didn't get so hot.

"Sweetheart, would you like to come in and have some break-fast?" Joe called to Heather, who was sitting on the wooden swing that Joe and Richie had carried out to the front porch from the tool shed that morning. Heather, who seemed to be getting worse, continued to stare out over the lake as if she hadn't heard him.

"Come on sweetheart." As he reached down to pull her out of the swing, his shoulder muscles flared with pain. It felt as though he were coming down with something. He had been fighting a headache all morning, and despite the incredibly soft down mattress he had slept on, his back felt as if . . .

"Oh no." Running back into the cabin, Joe climbed the stairs two at a time and searched through his toiletries. That's why he had felt like he was forgetting something; the small brown bottle was nowhere to be seen. The antibiotics had done such an amazing job that first day, that he had completely forgotten about the Lyme disease. He would have to go heavy on the aspirin and hope that things didn't get any worse. If it got too bad, they would just have to cut the trip short and hike out earlier than they'd planned.

Walking down the stairs, he heard the excited voices of the chil-dren coming back from the lake. Richie came through the door first, carrying Angela on his shoulders. She was too tall for the doorway, and they nearly fell as she ducked to miss hitting the jamb. Behind them, Debbie walked through the door with a bemused smile. A long black-and-white feather was tucked into the back of her french-braided hair.

"Gode man make Ebby inwun prisess," Angela blurted as Richie set her down at the table.

"An Indian princess huh?" Joe smiled. He would have to find out who the gold man was later. That was a new character, but he was sure that they could tie him into their running fairy tale. "Now sit down before everything gets cold."

"Looks like you kind of burned the pancakes." Richie jabbed his fork at one of the crispy black disks.

"Not burned, just caught a little. Besides, outdoor living makes you work up an appetite. They'll taste great." Richie rolled his eyes at his dad's expression for "lightly" burnt food. Searching out a couple of the lighter ones, he laid them onto Angela's plate and began to cut them up for her. "So, would you like syrup or butter?" he repeated a joke his dad had always teased him with.

"Boaf." Angela laughed, and for the first time Joe noticed that she was playing with some kind of wooden toy.

"Hey, what have you got there, kiddo?" he asked reaching across the table.

"Es a dokey," Angela answered, but Joe barely heard her. He was staring with rapt fascinationat at the figurine Angela handed him. It was beautiful, a lovely young woman with long curled hair sitting astride a donkey. But it wasn't the beauty of the carving alone that held his attention. It was a memory. He had seen this exact carving somewhere before. It hadn't been completed at the time, but it was unquestionably the same piece. The old fisherman he had met at the reservoir had been working on it.

"Where did you get this?" he breathed.

"Da gode man give a to me."

"The gold man?" Joe asked, suddenly holding the statuette far too tightly.

"She means the prospector. You know, down by the lake." Debbie slid the feather out of her hair. "The same old guy who gave me this."

"The prospector?" Suddenly Joe seemed incapable of breathing.

"Is everything all right, Dad?" Debbie dropped the feather on the table as if it had suddenly grown hot.

"He said you knew him. He even called you by name so we figured it was all right, you know, to talk to him," Richie added, his eyes wide with worry.

"Where?"

"The north side of the lake. You can see the smoke from his . . . " But Joe was already out of his chair and sprinting through the door before Richie had even finished speaking.

* * *

"I know you." Joe skidded to a stop in front of the old man, sending a spray of pine needles into the campfire where they instantly burst into flame. He wasn't wearing the same clothes. His khaki shirt and fishing hat had been exchanged for a long-sleeved flannel, plaid with assorted patches, and a grease-stained fedora, kind of like the one Indiana Jones had worn. His beard was a little longer and his knuckles were grimed with dirt, but it was definitely the same man. He was just picking the last few scraps of meat from a set of shiny white fish bones.

"You do." Joe couldn't tell if it was an affirmation or a question.

"Yes, you're the guy from the reservoir. The one who said I should bring my family here."

"I said that." Again the inflection was impossible to read.

"Well not in so many words. But I was praying and you showed up talking about getting away and taking my family fishing and . . . and you carved this." Joe held out the small figurine.

"Yes I did, Joe. Your daughter seemed to like it, so I gave it to her. I hope you don't mind."

"Mind? No I don't mind but how did you . . . I mean . . . and that's another thing. How do you know my name?"

"Well like you said, we must have met before." A loud braying, like the world's most annoying laugh, made Joe jump nearly into the fire, and for the first time he noticed the donkey tied to the tree. It was munching on a green fern near the base of a pine, its long ears occasionally twitching at the gnats that circled its head.

"Well yes. But I don't remember telling you my name. And how did you find me here?"

"Find you? I didn't find you. *You* found *me*. I was just sitting here finishing my breakfast before I set to work panning my . . . Oh, but would you listen to me blathering on. I have the manners of a donkey. No offense, Pete." He waved at the donkey, who seemed almost to nod before returning to its fern. "Sit down, Joe, and grab a plate. That last trout is looking awful lonely."

"No, I couldn't," Joe protested, his mind still reeling. And yet the smell of fresh fish, battered and frying in butter, made his stomach rumble in a way that he hadn't remembered it doing in years.

"Come on, pull up a log and sit a spell." The prospector slipped a long-bladed knife under the fish and expertly slid it onto a battered tin plate. He handed it to Joe along with a fork that looked like it had come from an old Boy Scout mess kit, and Joe took it gratefully.

"Nice family you've got there." The old man set his plate on a hot stone near the fire, leaned back, and belched softly into his hand.

Joe peeled back the crisp skin of the trout and bit into a forkful of the tender meat. It tasted every bit as good as it had smelled.

"You know what your problem is though?"

"My *problem?*" Joe asked around another bite of fish.

"You're too used to giving orders all the time. Believe me, I know. We leaders of industry get used to having everything go our way, and when it doesn't we have trouble coping."

"*We?*" Joe couldn't envision the man sitting across from him as a leader of anything, except maybe his donkey Pete.

"Oh, I see," the man's face split into a wry grin. And he waved at the gold pan and sluice box leaning up against the tree behind him. "You think that I'm just some crazy old prospector wandering aimlessly through the forest."

"No, I didn't say—"

"Would it surprise you to learn that at one time I was one of the wealthiest men in the East?" Before Joe could answer, the old man stood and gestured toward Joe to follow him. "Come on, I want to show you something."

Looking down at his plate, Joe was amazed to find it empty except for bones, the head, and a little skin. He must have been hungrier than he thought. When he looked up again, he could see that the prospector was nearly a hundred yards off and disappearing into the trees. He moved quickly for someone his age, and Joe nearly had to run to catch up to him. They were heading away from the lake, roughly paralleling the stream that fed into it.

"'Nother couple of months and the gooseberries'll be ripe. Perfect for pies and such." The old man waved at a stand of low bushes.

"Yeah, I guess they will." Joe glanced down at the small green berries, and nearly ran into the man, who had stopped abruptly.

"You see that?" Joe's gaze followed the prospector's pointing finger, and he gasped in surprise. On a tree a few feet away was a blaze. Two bare marks, one above the other carved into the thick bark.

"Just like in my dream," Joe whispered.

"What's that?"

"Oh, um, nothing." This was getting too weird. First the inexplicable appearance of this man he had seen at the reservoir. And now reality and his dreams seemed to be intermingling with a frightening ease. There had to be dozens of explanations for this, but for the life of him he couldn't think of one.

"Pay attention," the man commanded, and something about the deep timbre of his voice sounded very familiar. "That tree marks the beginning of a very long and at times difficult trail." Looking down at the forest floor, Joe could see a faint trail disappearing up over a small rise.

"If a man were to become lost, not through any fault of his own say, but because of the weather, faulty directions from a friend, or because he had his eyes set on other things, do you think he would follow this trail?"

"I guess so."

"Would you?"

"I don't need to. I know my way out of here."

"Do you?" the resonant voice took on a knowing, almost amused tone.

"Sure, I've explored every mile of this property. I know every stream, every valley, every . . ." And yet as he looked around, things seemed to have been subtly altered. The sun was rising from a different direction than he expected, the stream sounded further away and behind him instead of off to his right. He looked for the stand of gooseberries that he had just passed, but except for a scraggly red manzanita, there were no other bushes in sight. "Look, I don't know how you—" he began, but when he turned back, the prospector was gone.

Now the transformation into his dream was nearly complete. He was lost and his family was back at the house. And somewhere out in the woods was a crazy man who seemed capable of almost anything. Sweat began to drip down Joe's face as though he had been running for miles, although he had yet to even move. He turned slowly around again, trying to get his bearings. The sun was rising off to his left, which meant that he must be facing south toward the lake, and yet the stream sounded as though it were behind him, which made no sense. He should have been able to see the mountains through the trees; California forests were more spread out than those in the East. And yet in every direction he turned he could only make out more trees.

"Okay, take it easy now," he tried to calm himself. "You're not that far from the cabin. If you shout the kids will be able to hear you." And yet the memory of shouting for Angela in his dream was too clear. His recollection of drawing her into danger too vivid. Turning back to the tree again, he eyed the blaze and the trail that it marked. The scar was old, no longer bright white but faded to gray. It wasn't here when he had been a boy, but it must have been marked by his father before he died. Surely it would lead back to the cabin eventually. So thinking, he began to follow the trail, first walking from blaze to blaze, then, jogging, and eventually, losing any semblance of self-control, running all out, his breaths coming in short, ragged gasps.

He lost all sense of how long he followed the winding trail, over hills that gave him no better view than he'd had before and across streams that should have provided him with landmarks, but didn't. Running until he had to stop to keep from passing out, and then, after catching his breath, racing further along. It wasn't until he tripped over a rock, his hand plunging into the middle of a fire ring, that he discovered he was back where he had met the prospector.

"Oh!" Joe pulled his hand from the ashes, already beginning to feel the seared flesh before he realized that the ashes were cold. Turning, Joe searched for some sign of the prospector, ready to scream at the man for somehow getting him lost. But the old man and his donkey were gone, no trace remaining that either of them had ever been there in the first place. The plates, equipment, fish bones, everything was gone. Searching the ground, he saw that the only footprints were his, and he was not surprised to find that there was also no sign of the trail that had led him here.

He dropped to the ground, burying his face in his hands, and tried to keep from going completely bananas. He had gotten lost. It could happen to anyone—even someone who knew these woods as well as he did. He had gotten lost and panicked. After everything he had been through in the last week, it wasn't even all that unexpected. And the uncanny resemblance between the old man here in the woods and the man at the reservoir? That's all it had been—a coincidence. A couple of old coots who spent too much time out in the sun and started spouting nonsense. It was really very logical when you thought it all out.

But what about his family? They would be frantic by now. He must have been gone for hours. As he stood up, something caught his eye. A small rock resting on top of a slightly larger rock held down a single sheet of white paper. He unfolded it as he jogged back toward the cabin. But something was wrong. The sun, which should have been high in the sky by now, was still barely above the eastern mountain peaks. And through the cabin doorway he could see that his family was still sitting at the table just as he had left them.

Debbie looked up from her bacon and asked, "So was everything okay, Dad? Do you know that guy?"

"Yeah it's . . . fine. Everything's okay." Realizing that he was still clutching the small figurine, he handed it back to Angela and finally read the note he'd found under the rock.

> *Joe,*
> *Sorry I had to eat and run. But some lessons are better learned than explained. It's easy to fool yourself into thinking that you can always find your own way. We get so busy trying to control our own destiny, that we sometimes forget that another has been there before us. He has traveled every footstep that you and I will ever know and the wonderful thing is, He has marked the*

trail for us. Sometimes we get a little lost, a little confused. But just because we don't know where the trail leads doesn't mean that we shouldn't follow it. Have faith that whoever marked the trail knew that it would lead you home, whether it was your father or your brother.

P.S.— Don't forget—know your enemy and protect that which you deem most valuable. Oh, and also, nice shirt.

Reading the last line again, Joe felt a terrible pounding in his head and he suddenly found it hard to keep his balance. That was why the voice had sounded so familiar. *The homeless guy in the parking garage.*

* * *

"Come on guys, we have to get back up to the cabin and get dinner started," Joe called to Richie and Angela. They had been practicing skipping stones into the lake, but he wanted to get back to the cabin to check on Heather. Although Debbie was keeping on eye her, Heather's behavior was becoming more and more erratic by the day. Most of the time she was nearly comatose, but every once in a while, she began to shout meaningless phrases or would suddenly burst into tears.

"Come on, just one more try?" Richie asked, already searching for another flat stone.

"Mo twy." Angela mimicked, and tried to pick up a rock nearly the size of her head.

"Here, let's try this one." Joe searched through the stones at the side of the lake until he found a chip of granite. Rough on one side, but smooth enough to polish a knife with on the other.

"Watch." Richie drew back his arm and brought it quickly forward, flicking his wrist just as his father had taught him to do. The flash of white shot toward the water, angled shallow so that instead of knifing into the water it ricocheted off the surface and skipped six times before sinking.

"Six times, did you see that, Dad? Six!" Richie raised his hands into the air, and for Joe it was like seeing his son for the first time in months, maybe years. Could it have been this easy? Would their new improved relationship last after they went home?

"Frow wok, Addy." Angela held out the rock Joe had picked, waiting for him to help throw it. Taking her hand gently in his, he guided her arm and tried to help her flick her wrist. The rock flew clumsily out of her hand, but fortunately it was flat enough and met the water the right way, causing it to bounce once, briefly, before dropping into the lake.

"Ray, ray!" Angela shouted. "Hate times, hate times!" For a moment, Joe thought that Richie would argue. His six bounces was the night's record. But then Richie smiled and held his sister's hand up into the air.

"The new rock-skipping champion," he shouted, his voice echoing off the mountains across the lake. "With eight skips, Angela Stewart!"

Taking both of the children in his arms, Joe walked them back up to the steps of the cabin, before guiding them toward the big pump in the front yard. "You guys wash up and then use that bucket to fill the storage tank outside the kitchen window. I want to get some water warming by dinner. I'm going to go cut some wood."

He walked around the side of the cabin, took the ax from the shed, and was starting toward the woodpile when he saw the dusty prints on the outside of Angela's window. They were there at Richie's window too, more than five and a half feet above the ground. Following them around the side of the house, he saw that the big cat had jumped up onto the porch and peered through the front window before disappearing back into the trees.

Unlike the prints he had seen in the road, these were new. They had swept the porch the night before, and the shutters had been closed until then. These had to have been made either after they went to bed or this morning. He had decided not to close the kid's shutters last night, and the idea of a pair of hungry golden eyes peering in at his children made his throat tighten to the size of a straw.

Mountain lions were not ordinarily drawn to humans like bears and raccoons were. At the first scent they would head in the opposite direction. There were exceptions of course. He remembered reading about a woman who had been killed by a mountain lion while running on the trails near her home. But even then, it had probably been more a matter of chance—being in the wrong place at the wrong time. This was different. The cat that left these tracks was actively stalking his family. It was an active danger, and for whatever reason it saw them as prey. He would close the shutters tonight, but that wasn't all.

Going back to the shed, he searched high in the beams at the back of the building where a child would never be able to reach, until he found a long leather case. His dad had never been a hunter, but he had always kept a rifle nearby, just to be safe. Next to the case, Joe found a hank of cloth wrapped around two boxes of shells. Pocketing the shells, he carried the rifle back to the house.

He was not about to let anything threaten his family.

CHAPTER 11

Joe slipped out the front door, careful not to let the latch click as he pulled it shut behind him. The predawn air bit his skin and he stopped to button the cuffs of his long-sleeved shirt. He would light the wood stove when he returned, warming the cabin for the rest of the family when they awoke, but for now he left it cold. Wild animals were sly, and he didn't want to offer any more clues to his presence than necessary. He quickly scanned the front porch for new prints. There weren't any, but that didn't mean that the cat wasn't still there, just that it hadn't come onto the porch.

Having already loaded several shells into the rifle and checked to make sure that he could switch the safety off without looking, he stepped down from the front porch, careful to avoid the second step, the squeaky one, and started off into the woods. Straight ahead, gauzy tendrils of mist hovered just above the lake's surface. To the left was the road and the trees across from it. About a half mile in that direction, the ground dropped into a valley where the lake fed several smaller pools. To the right, north of the lake, where the old man's campsite had been, the forest was thick and deep for several miles until it reached the base of Irakwa Peak.

Behind the cabin the woods were broken up by a series of steep granite cliffs and jagged rocks that could be dangerous to someone unfamiliar with the area. He had warned the kids to stay away from there unless he was with them, and had decided to avoid it as well this morning. In the semi-dark it would be easy to fall and become injured. Telling himself that he was choosing the south side of the lake because that was where the first set of prints led, not because it was opposite of where he had seen the prospector, Joe set off across the road and into the shadowy trees beyond.

* * *

Resting the rifle across his knees, Joe leaned back against the thick gnarled bark of a tree trunk. The deep cracks in the bark gave off a faint scent like butterscotch. He knew his father had told him what type of tree this was, but he couldn't quite remember it. At the pool below the knoll he was resting on, three white-tail doe and a fawn nibbled grass. Every few seconds one of the doe would raise her head—nose into the air, neck cocked slightly—using both smell and sound to sense for danger. The rest of the deer watched her tensely as they continued to feed, until she decided that the coast was clear and returned to the sweet grass near the water's edge.

He had thought this would be the perfect place to spot the mountain lion. In the hour and a half he'd been here, he had seen several deer, a skunk, and scores of squirrels and chipmunks, one of which had become the last meal of a large brown owl before the bird flew back into a tree a few hundred feet to Joe's left. But with the exception of the owl, there had been no other carnivores. He had just about decided to move on to another spot when all of the deer stopped eating in unison. Frozen in place like statues, legs poised to leap back into the cover of the trees in an instant, it was obvious that they sensed something was coming.

Joe carefully raised the rifle and peered through the scope. All of the deer were staring in the direction of a small deadfall just beyond several saplings at the south end of the pool. Training the scope on the pile of brush and branches, Joe searched for any sign of movement as his finger slipped toward the safety. He caught a brief flash of motion behind one of the logs and heard the deer leaping back into the woods. Silently he pressed the safety to the off position and tried to steady his aim. His hands were shaking, and it was hard to keep the crosshairs trained on one spot. Taking slow half-breaths, Joe willed his muscles into steadiness. It worked for a second, but then the trembling returned again.

Another flash of movement appeared near the end of the deadfall, and he moved his aim ever so slightly. Through the magnification of the scope, he could make out the big blackened limb on the ground that had probably been the result of a lighting strike, and the other bits of wood and brush that had blown up against it over the years. Suddenly a head appeared above the limb, and Joe nearly pulled the trigger before realizing it was only a fox. He watched the fox nose the air before prancing across the meadow, red tail dancing in the air behind it. Furtively glancing around once more, the fox quickly dropped its muzzle to the water, lapped up several mouthfuls, and then streaked back into the woods. It was not until the fox had been gone for several seconds that Joe realized his finger was still locked on the trigger.

Relaxing his arm muscles, he lowered the rifle slowly back to his lap and sighed with relief. It felt as though he hadn't taken a breath since the fox had first appeared. Laughing silently at himself, he reengaged the safety and flexed his fingers. He needed to relax a little. For all he knew the cat was probably miles away. It had come up to the cabin under the cover of darkness to see what all the ruckus had been about, simple feline curiosity, and had probably high-tailed it out of there once it realized that humans were back in the neighborhood. He was just beginning to stand up when he saw the yellow eyes watching him from slightly above him and less than a hundred feet to his right. The long body was crouched, the tail switching slowly from one side to the other.

At first, all Joe could do was stand frozen eye to eye with the mountain lion, mesmerized by the big cat's muscles, clearly pronounced beneath its tawny coat; the slow twitch, twitch, twitch, of the tail setting his pulse rate like a metronome. It was the thought of his children that forced his arms into motion and pumped adrenaline to his heart in a massive rush that sent it racing. His quivering left hand raised the front of the barrel while he numbly punched at the safety with his right index finger. He didn't have time to lift the stock to his shoulder, the cat could be on him before he ever got off a shot. Instead, he pressed the rifle back against the front of his right thigh, adjusted his aim slightly and began to squeeze the trigger. In that instant, all of the normal forest noises seemed to cease and a deathly silence fell over the two of the them.

"Hey, you take that boy of yours fishing yet?" Joe started at the unexpected voice in his ear. The barrel of the rifle jerked upward as he pulled the trigger, sending the bullet harmlessly into the air, and in an instant the cat was gone, bounding into the trees before Joe could even think about getting off another shot.

"Be careful with that thing, you're liable to shoot something." The prospector reached out to the rifle and set the safety.

"That was the idea," Joe growled, turning on him. "And I *would* have if it wasn't for you."

"Oh, you had your eye on something then?" The man removed his hat and scratched the crown of his head as he studied the now-empty space where the mountain lion had been only seconds earlier. "Hoping to bag one of them big old elms I guess?"

"Never mind." Joe ejected the remaining shells from his rifle and dropped them into his shirt pocket. He had the feeling that he was through hunting for the day. "And by the way, I don't appreciate you getting me lost out in the middle of the woods and then leaving."

"Lost?" The prospector shoved the misshapen fedora back onto his head. "I didn't know you were lost. Why I'd never a gone back to clean out my camp if I'd a known you were gonna get lost. I figured a guy like you who knew every valley and—"

"Yeah, yeah, very amusing. So where were you when I got back? You have a pretty amazing way of just disappearing."

"Had work to do. Gold doesn't pan itself you know."

"I wish you could give my kids a few tips on cleaning their rooms that well." Joe set the rifle against a tree and folded his arms across his chest. "You know, you've never told me your name, although obviously you know mine."

"Yup, kids are funny that way." The prospector said, ignoring Joe's question completely. "They index their baseball cards, by team, name, and year. Store 'em carefully in those fancy little plastic doohickeys. But you can't get them to hang up their clothes for the life of ya." He pressed his hat back down onto his head and stoked his beard a moment before continuing. "But not your boy. I'll bet he's a good kid. Always does what he's told, shows respect for his parents. Probably the ideal son."

"Not likely," Joe said.

"No?" The prospector's eyes opened wide with surprise as he leaned back against a tree trunk, one booted foot set out in front of him, the other cocked back against the tree.

"No. And the thing is I don't understand what's changed. He used to be such a good kid. It's only in the past year or so that he's started acting up. I thought that we had taught him better than that. But lately he's been hanging out with a bad crowd, getting involved with things I'd never even heard of at his age." Joe lowered himself to one knee and picked up a pineapple-sized pinecone.

"And he hasn't told you why, in any of those long heart-to-hearts you have with him?"

"That's just it," Joe said, yanking pieces off the cone in frustration, "we don't have any conversations at all. Every time I try to talk with him he just shuts down. All of his answers are one syllable."

"You know, I've found that boys are kind of like donkeys. Just about the most stubborn creatures on God's green earth. Doesn't matter which direction you tell 'em to go, they'll up and head in the other direction just to spite you."

Joe nodded, smiling in spite of himself. "You seem to know an awful lot about boys for someone who only had daughters."

"Did I say that?"

"Well you said you had six daughters, so I just assumed . . ."

"Well I did have six daughters, Keren-happuch was the baby, we called her Keren for short of course. But I had fourteen boys too. And each of them was more stubborn than the last." The prospector shook a calloused finger in the air as if remembering how he had scolded them.

"Fourteen?" Joe asked, astonished. "You had twenty children?"

"Yup, with a little help from my wife." The prospector beamed, his bearded face splitting into a grin. "But the thing about boys and donkeys," he said, turning serious again, "is that you just gotta know how to work with them. You've got to be patient, let 'em think that they're going where *they* want to, then you nudge 'em a little this way and a little that way till they're headed back in the right direction.

"But you've got to think like a donkey, or a boy in this case. Although with my sixth son there wasn't much of a—but that's another story entirely. You take that boy of yours fishing. Don't push him into talking right away. Let him come around to it himself. And when he does, *listen*. And I mean listen *hard*. Boys and donkeys don't always come right out and say what they mean, but a smart father can sift through the testosterone. Set aside the talk that's just designed to show his dad that he's ready to be a man, and what you have left will tell you how to help guide him. You get my meaning?"

"I think so." Joe stood, tossing the stripped pinecone aside, and picked up his rifle. "By the way, where is your donkey?"

"Pete? He won't come within a mile of a mountain lion. They scare him to death."

"A mountain lion huh?" Joe smirked. "I should have figured." He took a few steps toward the cabin before stopping and turning back.

"Hey, I never did get your name—" But there was no one there.

* * *

By the time they actually got out onto the lake, the sun was not only up, but fast making its way overhead. As Joe stepped off from the shore, lifting and pushing the end of the canoe opposite the one Richie was sitting in, the coolness of the lake water felt good on his feet and ankles. He thought that when they returned everyone would be ready for a swim. From the dock, Debbie and Angela waved and wished them bon voyage. Angela was still a little unhappy at being left on land, but Debbie had promised to play *Candy Land* with her.

It had taken a while to get the canoe down from the rafters, and even longer to find the life jackets and paddles, which were tucked under the tool shed in a storage area Joe had nearly forgotten about. Then they had sorted through the fishing rods and gear, making sure both the poles had enough line, and by that time they needed to do something about breakfast. Hopefully the fish were sleeping in today.

"Okay now, take the paddle in both hands. No, no, on the other side." Joe guided Richie, and soon the dark green wooden canoe was slicing smoothly through the water's still surface.

"Let's take it over to the other side. I seem to remember that right along the rocks were some good spots."

"All right." Richie said, concentrating on keeping his paddle moving smoothly in and out of the water.

As he paddled, first on the right of the canoe and then the left, keeping the craft headed roughly in the direction of the granite cliffs on the other side of the lake, Joe had a chance to take a close look at his son. Richie had his mother's eyes, crinkling up in good humor even when he wasn't smiling, so that he perpetually looked like he was up to something. Over the last year, his shoulders had broadened and his biceps and chest muscles had filled out. Joe wondered how long he would still be able to beat his son in an arm-wrestling contest.

The dark bruise by his left eye was nearly gone, and Joe noticed for the first time how much Richie looked like his grandfather. The girls probably swooned over him at school, if girls swooned anymore. Why was it that he hadn't noticed these things before? He saw his son every day, and yet in his mind he still envisioned him as the scrawny twelve-year-old who had nearly spilled the water tray on the bishop the first time he passed the sacrament.

"Okay, this is good." Joe back paddled and turned the canoe sideways so that it paralleled the rocks. He lowered the cinder block that served as the anchor over the side. It wouldn't reach the bottom, but its weight would keep the boat from drifting much and generally stabilize things.

"Do you want me to tie on your lure?" Joe asked, plucking a couple of spinners from the tackle box.

"No it's okay, I can do it."

Joe picked a leader out of the tackle box and watched Richie do the same out of the corner of his eye. Richie tied it to his line using the same fisherman's knot, six wraps and a loop down through the opening at the bottom, that he had learned from Joe, who had learned it from his father, and so on. Joe wouldn't have been surprised to learn that Noah had taught it to his own kids while they were on the ark. Joe tried to do the same, but the trembling he had felt in his hands that morning was worse, and he kept missing the loop.

"Are you okay, Dad?" Richie asked, as Joe once again failed to thread the line through his knot.

"Yeah. Maybe I ought to switch to decaf," Joe joked, trying to hide his embarrassment.

"Here, let me help you." Richie took Joe's line and quickly attached a leader and lure. He watched his father carefully as Joe swung back his pole and prepared to cast.

"May the best fisherman win," Joe said, pretending everything was fine. He cast his lure toward the edge of the rocks, waiting for a few seconds to let it sink, and began to reel it in.

An hour later they had each caught several good-sized fish, lost at least one lure each, and tangled lines numerous times. As Joe had guessed, the day was a hot one and they were each starting to sweat as the sun reached closer to its zenith. They hadn't said more than a dozen words between them in the last thirty minutes, but that was okay. The silence had been a companionable one, and both had cheered the other when one hooked a fighter.

"So you about ready to call it a morning?" Joe asked, watching a fingerling trout barely as big as his lure chase the glittering gold fleck of metal, before darting back into the darkness as he pulled his line out of the water.

"Let's try over by that log," Richie said, pointing to a seventy- or eighty-foot pine that at some point over the last few years had lost its footing and toppled down into the lake.

"Looks good." After affixing the lure to his pole, Joe laid it in the bottom of the boat and began to raise the anchor. As Joe rowed, Richie bobbed the end of his rod in and out of the water, watching the circle of ripples it made each time it hit.

"My dad and I came fishing out here a lot when I was your age." Joe said, keeping his eyes fixed on the tip of the fallen tree and he slowly rowed toward it.

"Oh yeah?" Richie's voice was noncommittal.

"Yeah. We didn't always see eye to eye on things, but we both liked to fish."

Richie nodded slowly, lowering his spinner into the water and reeling it back in. "What kind of things didn't you agree on?" he asked, an edge of wariness in his voice, as though he feared a verbal trap.

"Oh you know the usual. Girls—I liked blondes, he liked brunettes. Money—he thought I was extravagant I thought he was a penny-pincher. Careers—he didn't trust all this computer business, and wanted me to become a machinist like he and his father were. Of course he might have been right on that count." They both laughed, neither seemingly anxious to get back to fishing. A soft breeze blew across the water, gently rocking the canoe.

"Did Grandpa get mad at you much when you were a kid?"

"Seems like I was always doing something that set him off. Taking his tools without asking or skipping out on my chores. He would get angry all right. But nothing like your grandma. When she cut a switch from the apple tree, I knew it was time to vamoose for a while." Joe could tell that there was something on his son's mind, but he remembered the prospector's words and let Richie navigate his own course.

"Did you ever do, you know, do anything that you later wished that you hadn't?"

"Yeah, I guess I did." The breeze was now pushing the canoe away from shore, but Joe made no move to begin paddling, instead letting the canoe drift. "I think that everyone has, except for maybe the Savior."

"So what did you do about it?"

"Well, I tried to make it right. Make up for what I'd done wrong."

"But what if you couldn't fix it? What if what you had done was . . ." Richie seemed to struggle for the right words, ". . . past that?"

Joe thought about it for a minute. "I'm not sure anything is irreparable. But if there really was nothing that you could do about it, then I imagine you'd just have to go on with your life, trying to do enough good things to offset the bad, and committing to never do it again."

"Yeah, but what if what you had done was still hurting someone else? What if you had started out trying to help that person, but . . ." Like the baby trout, Richie pushed forward, only to shy away again at the last minute.

"Richie, why don't you just tell me what's going on? Even if you can't do anything about it, maybe *I* can." Joe reached across the boat toward his son, but Richie jerked back as if Joe's words had burned him.

"No." He shook his head violently and turned away wiping at his eyes. "That would make it even worse."

It was one of the hardest things Joe had ever done, but he picked up the paddle and began rowing back toward the fallen tree without pressing his son further. On the other side of the canoe, Richie, looking miserable, sniffed against the back of his hand and fiddled with the lure on the end of his line.

"Thanks for listening, Dad."

"You're welcome, Richie, and if you ever feel like you want to talk some more, I'm right here. Sometimes what looks hopeless to one person, isn't quite so bad when they've got someone else on their side."

Richie nodded. "Okay, I'll think about it."

* * *

"Where is that filleting knife?" Joe checked each of the kitchen drawers for a second time, but still came up empty. He knew that his father kept a good sharp knife specifically for gutting and filleting the fish they caught, but he couldn't find it anywhere. Angela, declaring that cutting fishies' heads off was *gross*, had gone into her room to play tea party with a collection of friends she had found around the house. Debbie was down at the lake swimming, and Heather was upstairs taking a nap. Richie, after putting away the fishing gear, was sitting on the couch engrossed in *The Red Badge of Courage*.

"You haven't seen a sharp knife around here anywhere, have you? About nine inches long with a thin curved blade?" Joe called out over his shoulder as he checked under the sink.

"Nope, sorry," Richie answered, barely looking up from his book.

"I just hate to use a regular knife and ruin these beautiful fish." Joe glanced up at the cupboards. He had checked there already, but maybe it was at the back of one of the top shelves, out of sight. Opening the dish cupboard, he reached up and ran his hands along the top shelf. Other than a few cobwebs and a broken saucer that was apparently still waiting for someone to glue it back together, he came up empty. The next cupboard was no better. On the last one, he was just finishing sweeping his hand along another dusty shelf, when his fingers brushed against something and knocked it to the floor.

Thinking that it was probably a piece of garbage, a candy-bar wrapper or a piece of paper, he leaned over to pick it up off the floor and then stopped. At first he couldn't believe what he was looking at. He had seen it once before, but he thought it had been in a dream. Tweezing the plastic baggie between two fingers as if it was infected with a deadly disease, Joe held it in front of his face and stared at the pills inside of it. The white plastic tape had been cut, but it was definitely the bag he had seen on Richie's dresser.

"Richie," Joe tried to keep his voice under control, but he could hear it wavering on the edge of hysteria. "What is this?"

"What's wha—" Richie looked up from his book and stopped. His eyes grew wide at the sight of what his father was holding. "I don't . . . I mean they're not mine. Somebody must have left them here."

"Don't you lie to me." Joe's voice seemed to shake the timbers of the cabin. "How dare you bring drugs into my house? You couldn't even go on a family vacation without bringing this . . . this filth?" Joe knew that he was losing control, he could see what he was doing to his son, but he couldn't seem to help himself. His hand shook as he crushed the pills in his fist, sending a shower of powder to the floor.

"What if your little sister had gotten into these? What if your mother had found them? You are a disgrace."

Richie rocked backwards as if he had been slapped in the face. His eyes widened, and his book dropped to the floor. For a second, he looked as if he were going to say something—his mouth worked open and closed silently—but then he jumped from the couch and ran out the front door.

Instantly, Joe regretted what he had said. Was this what Richie had been trying to tell him? It must have been. But instead of trying to help his son, he had attacked him. Racing to the front porch, he screamed out his son's name. "Richie, come back. Wait. I'm sorry." But Richie was gone.

At the lake, Debbie was just coming out of the water. She picked up a towel, toed her feet into a pair of flip flops, and started toward her father. "Dad, what is it?"

"Richie. Where did he go? Did you see him?" Debbie pointed to the north end of the lake and Joe set off running in that direction.

* * *

Hours later, exhausted, all of his muscles trembling, Joe collapsed onto the ground near a small brook and splashed some of the cool water across his face. He must have covered eight to ten miles easily, calling out Richie's name every minute or so, and still he hadn't covered a tenth of the territory his son might have ended up in. It was getting on toward evening, the sun beginning to cast long shadows from the tall trees around him. If he didn't find Richie in the next hour, he would have to go home alone. He couldn't even imagine the looks on the rest of the family's faces if he told them that Richie was out in the woods alone overnight.

Burying his face in his hands, he called out with all of his energy. "Father, please help me find my son. How could I have said those things to him? How could I have let him down when he needed me most? Please help me find him so I can say I'm sorry."

Standing, he took a deep breath and looked around him. Again, he was reminded of what the prospector had said. *You have to think like a boy.* When he had been upset with his father, and there had been plenty of those times, where had he gone? His eyes followed the brook, took in the trees, and then stopped on the snowpacked mountain beyond them. Irakwa Peak. He would hike as high and far away as he could get, until his lungs burned and he had to rest. It was the place he had always gone to work things out. Up the side of the mountain is where he would find his son. Setting off at a steady jog, he crossed the creek and started in the direction of the sinking sun.

The climb was steeper than he remembered it being. Sweat poured off his face and soaked the back of his shirt as he left the forest behind and made his way up the steep ravines and crevices. As he climbed, he began to recognize some of the easier routes from his years of exploring as a boy, and soon the old routine of searching out hand and foot holds, moving at a steady even pace, came back to him. He tried to ignore the shaking in his arms and legs and the way the setting rays of the sun stung his eyes. The rock was warm beneath his hands and feet now, but he knew from experience that once the sun set it would quickly cool down.

It was a little less than an hour later, as he pulled himself up over a narrow ledge, that he heard the sound. Resting against the rock wall, he tried to hear over the pounding of his own heart. It was coming from the left, the sound of crying, but not the kind of crying he was used to hearing from his children when they were hurt, or scared, or sick, or angry. These were sobs, pulled deep from the soul. Filled with a pain that children should never know.

Crossing the ledge, Joe found his son sitting on a small grassy ravine, his face buried in the side of a great cedar that had somehow managed to find enough soil to take root, and ran to him. Wrapping him in his arms, he pulled Richie's hot, wet face to his chest, and held him as if he would never let go. "I'm so sorry. I should have listened, I love you, I love you, I love you."

Richie's arms wrapped around Joe's neck in return, and for a long while, the two of them held each other, tears dripping down both of their faces, incapable of any words, while around them the creatures of the forest began to settle in for the night. Finally, Richie pulled his face away from his father's chest.

"I'm sorry, Dad. It's all my fault."

"No, it's okay. We'll work this out. I promise, everything is going to be all right."

"I should never have bought them in the first place." Richie's body shook in Joe's arms. "But she really seemed to need them."

She? She really seemed to need them? Suddenly Joe thought he understood. Richie's words from that morning made sense. *What if you had started out trying to help that person, but . . .* Richie hadn't been surprised that Joe had found the drugs. He had been surprised that they were in the kitchen. *Because he hadn't bought them for himself, he had bought them for Debbie,* Joe assumed. That was why she had been acting so strangely lately.

"It's okay, Richie. We'll work this out. We can help her." He ran his hands across his son's hair over and over. That was the problem. The thing that had been causing Richie so much pain, making him so secretive. He couldn't tell anyone without feeling like he had betrayed his sister.

"Don't tell her I told you," Richie pleaded. "She'll be mad. Please Dad, don't tell Mom I told you."

CHAPTER 12

"Get a good grip with both hands, and swing your right foot across to the crevice. Feel it? Good. Now just step down with your left." As Joe watched Richie traverse the last difficult part of the climb back down Irakwa Peak, the final rays of sun were just disappearing from the sky. Standing in the shadow of the great mountain, it was night already.

Rather than going directly through the deepest part of the woods, Joe led Richie around their edge. It would take a little longer to get back that way, but it would be easier to see where they were going by the moon and stars that before long would be the only lights in the sky. And Joe thought that with all they had to talk through, a little extra time might be a good thing.

For a half mile or so, the two of them walked side by side in companionable silence, both letting their minds work around the edges of the secret that had stood between them for so long. Each gnawing a little here and a little there, like the first few nibbles of an early summer apple, checking to make sure that it was not too sour before taking a bite.

For Joe, understanding that Heather had been taking painkillers was like waking up in the middle of the night and seeing a familiar object, a lamp or a chair, transformed by the darkness into something strange and a little frightening. You knew that it was only a lamp, but the decorative switch looked so much like a beak. And why had you never noticed how the shade, tilted just so, could have been a head? He knew that something had been wrong with his wife, had felt it with every fiber of his being. But drugs? He couldn't have been any more shocked if she had been arrested for shoplifting. Yet it all made sense. Her inability to communicate, sleeping so much, the mood swings . . . The clues had been there all along, he had just missed them. He even thought that Officer Holstein had noticed, the night someone had thrown a brick through their window. The red-faced police officer had started to say something to Joe about Heather as they stood in front of the house, and then backed off at the last minute.

In his son's demeanor, he thought he could see worry combined with a strong sense of relief. Was he afraid that his father and mother might divorce over something like this? Divorce was the rule rather than the exception in the area where they lived.

"Now that I know, I can help her." Joe took a first tentative stab at opening a dialogue.

"Can you?" Richie shot a quick glance at his father, out of the corner of his eye, as he leaned over to pick up a long branch, just the right size to make into a walking staff.

"I think so." Joe thought about the pills that he had crushed in his hand. He had tossed them into the woods at some point in his search that afternoon. "Were those the only drugs?"

"Yeah." Neither of them knew what Heather would do when she discovered that the pills were gone, but they both picked up their pace a little.

"Why did . . ." *you buy her drugs in the first place,* he almost asked, before deciding to approach the subject from a different direction. "Tell me everything, from the beginning."

Richie was silent for so long that Joe was afraid he might have scared him off again. While it was true that his fifteen-year-old son looked like someone had just lifted a hundred-pound rock from his shoulders, there were still a lot of painful memories stored inside his young mind. Joe wouldn't hurt his son any further for the world. But he thought that those memories might be like thorns. Until they were pulled out, they would just continue to fester, poisoning everything around them. And if Joe was going to help his wife, he needed to know the truth.

"I . . . thought . . . I was . . . helping her." The words came slowly at first. It seemed that after hiding them for so long, Richie had trouble convincing himself that it was okay to let them go. He kept his eyes glued to the walking staff as he snapped the twigs from its length. At last though, the words began to come more naturally.

"It was back when the doctors first discovered her cancer. When they started the chemo, before they knew they were going to have to operate. She was so sick all the time. She was tough, you know, on the outside. She didn't want anyone to know how trashed she felt. But I used to go into her room and just talk to her. Tell her about my day at school and stuff. I guess that kind of helped her or something." Richie shrugged, but Joe could tell from the gruffness in his voice that he was trying to keep from crying again.

"Anyway, it kind of got to be a thing with the two of us. At first it was just me telling her about all the things that were going on at school. I felt really dumb talking about my problems—girls, and mean teachers, things like that—when compared to hers they were nothing. But she wouldn't let me just skim over stuff. She had this way of getting me to open up. I think it helped her, but it *really* helped me. There was this girl at school I liked. But she kept totally blowing me off. Mom said that I should just stop worrying about her and talk to other girls. And she was right. In like, two days she was all talking to me and wanting to hang out and stuff.

"So, I was thinking that if it helped me so much to talk about my problems, maybe it would help Mom too." Richie was quiet again for a few moments, but Joe waited. He sensed that they were getting close to the heart of Richie's story.

"At first, she wouldn't talk about it. But one thing I learned from her is how to ask a question and then just wait. When she first opened up, it was like she was scared that telling me about her pain and fear was going to hurt *me*. But it didn't, not at all. It was like I was taking some of the weight from her shoulders, and it felt so good to know that even if it wasn't much, I was at least doing something to help her, after all she'd done for me. Do you know what I mean, Dad? Did the two of you ever talk like that?"

Now it was Joe's turn to be silent, thinking about how impressed he had been with Heather's resiliency. While *he* had been trying not to fall apart, Heather had supported him, retaining her sense of humor even when she was so sick she could barely sit up. He had just taken for granted that Heather was a rock, never bothering to dig through the surface to see what lay beneath her tough veneer. They had talked of course. But had he asked the right questions? And when she didn't give him the whole answer, had he possessed the patience to *just wait*? When the weight of carrying all the pain and fear had finally grown too heavy, where had he been? At the office? In a meeting? On a trip? Who had she turned to? Now he knew.

"Not enough."

"Oh. I'm sorry. I didn't mean . . . " Richie mumbled, embarrassment clear in his voice.

"No, it's okay. Maybe we're both realizing we made some mistakes." In the moonlight, they were just two disembodied shadows, but he felt closer to his son than he had in years.

"Yeah," the silhouette that was Richie nodded. "Well, once she realized it was safe to talk to me, she started opening up a little more and a little more. At first it was just small stuff. How the smell of chicken made her want to puke, or how she was losing weight and she hated that none of her clothes seemed to fit right. But I think I was the only one that she felt like she didn't have to hide things from, so pretty soon she was telling me everything.

"Everybody knew the chemo made Mom really sick. But what they didn't know, and she made me promise not to tell, was how she felt like the cancer was slowly taking away everything that made her who she was. When she lost her hair, she just joked about looking like Charlie Brown, and wore a lot of hats and scarves and stuff. But she told me that when she looked in the mirror she felt like she was staring into the eyes of a stranger. And she couldn't cook any more because the sight of raw meat made her really sick. You remember how she used to be really busy with all kinds of activities? You know, going to Angela's school, volunteering with the reading program at the library, helping me and Debbie with our homework?"

Joe nodded, but he realized with a sick feeling in his stomach that the only reason he remembered those activities at all was because Richie had mentioned them. He hadn't known that his own wife was taking illegal drugs, but how many of the good things that she did had he been unaware of as well?

"Well, after she got sick, she had to start dropping those. Either because of the treatments or because she was just too weak. And every time she lost another one, she said it was like losing another piece of herself." Richie broke the last twig from his walking staff, examined it, and then abruptly tossed it into the trees.

"Mostly I just listened. I mean, what else could I do? I'm a kid, right? It's not like I could tell my Mom how to live her life or anything. I'm trying hard enough just to keep from screwing up my own. But when they had to up the treatments, it was really bad. Sometimes when I came into her room, she was in so much pain she couldn't even talk. I would just sit there and hold her hand. Or sometimes we'd just listen to music. She said it helped her imagine that she was in a happier place. And I kept wishing that there was some way I could help. Some way I could make her feel better, you know?

"So a couple of days later, I was telling this girl about Mom. I figured that she didn't know any of you guys, so it wasn't like really breaking my promise. And she goes, 'I know where you might be able to get something that would help her.' Well at first I didn't know what she was talking about. I thought she meant something like those magnetic bracelets you see golfers wearing or, I don't know, one of those adjustable beds or something. But then, when I realized she was talking about drugs, I just about blew up. I was like, 'You want me to bring my mom a bag of dope?'

"But the thing that finally made me think it was okay was that it wasn't any of the stuff you hear about, like coke, or marijuana, or ecstasy. It was just painkillers. Not really drugs, but medicine. She said that the doctors are really stingy about giving out painkillers. That's why having babies is so painful when it doesn't have to be. She told me that you couldn't get hooked on that kind of stuff, because it was just a heavier dose of what your body already made. Now I know that she didn't have any more clue about that kind of stuff than I did, but at the time it sounded so good. It was like I could finally do something for Mom. Not like those little macaroni necklaces you make in kindergarten, but something that could really make a difference." Richie gave a tired, sad-sounding kind of laugh.

"You should have seen her when I brought them home. I don't know what I was expecting. I guess I kind of thought that she'd throw her arms around my neck and thank me. Like when Prince Charming saves the princess from the evil dragon. But instead it was like one of those TV commercials, where the parents tell their kids not to do drugs, except much more intense. I thought for a minute she was gonna tear my head off she was so mad, but then she gave me this really big hug, and said that she knew I was just trying to help. But she made me swear up and down that I would never buy drugs again and not hang around with the kind of kids that did. She threw the pills in the trash, and I thought that was the end of it."

They were nearing the north end of the lake now, and Joe thought he could just make out the lights of the cabin between the thinning trees. Reaching out through the darkness, he found Richie's hand and held it like he had when his son was small and he used to help him cross the street. Richie hesitated at first, but then returned his father's grip for a brief moment.

"But it wasn't." Joe already knew the answer.

"No. I didn't find out until later that she had taken it back out of the trash. She said that she was afraid someone might find it and get the wrong idea. She was going to throw it out in a dumpster or something. I'm not sure why she didn't, maybe she just forgot about it, or maybe, even back then, there was a part of her that thought she might need it. I don't think she actually took the first one until they told her the cancer was back and they were going to have to do the operation. I thought about it a lot later on, and I think that moms are a lot stronger than most people give them credit for. She toughed out the treatments, and the sickness, the weight loss, the pain, everything. And she never touched those drugs, even though she must have really wanted to.

"I think what finally cracked her was the operation." Richie's voice cracked a little, but Joe nodded—completing his son's thought.

"It was like they wanted to take away another part of her, only this time with a knife. They wanted to steal a big chunk of her and she didn't have anything left."

"Yeah," Richie said. "I think that's what finally did it. And even then, she must have only been taking one of those pills every few days. There were only thirty in the first place and it was almost two months after the operation when she came back."

Now the lights of the cabin were in clear view, reflecting off the hidden darkness of the lakelike pixies. Richie rushed through the rest of his story, obviously wanting to finish before they came within hearing distance of the cabin.

"She was really bad when she finally came into my room. We hadn't been having our talks nearly as often, but I figured that was because she wasn't sick all the time anymore. I noticed that she seemed to be sleeping a lot, but everyone said she was just getting her rest back after everything her body had gone through. When she walked in, she was shaking and talking funny. She kept scratching her arms and kind of shuffling her feet around like Angela does when she has to go to the bathroom. I didn't know at the time that it was withdrawal symptoms, what the kids call DTs. I just thought she looked sick.

"For a little while she just asked me about school and stuff, but I knew there was something else. So finally I asked her and then just waited. She started to cry, and she looked so terrible, man, I would have done anything to help. I was sure she was going to tell me the cancer was back, and I started shaking too. I remember feeling relieved when she told me what was really wrong. And I know this really stinks but there was a part of me that actually felt kind of glad. Glad that I could fix what was wrong with her.

"But I was stupid. Everyone warns you about drugs. How they seem like they're helping for a while, but then they really start hurting you. Well I didn't think about that at all. All I could think about was how I was doing something for my mom. Something she couldn't do for herself. I think maybe neither one of us realized what we were getting into. Then it just turned into this kind of giant black whirlpool. By the time I saw what the drugs were doing to her, she was way too hooked to stop. And she would bawl every time she came back to ask for more. She used to say, 'What kind of terrible mother would do this to her child?' And then we'd both start crying. We were both so messed up that I was surprised everyone in the house didn't know what was going on. I kept waiting for someone to just grab me by the neck and shake me and go, 'What have you done to your own mother?' But no one ever did."

"I'm sorry. I should have seen. I thought I was being a good father, a good husband, but I must have been blind." Joe and Richie had stopped by the edge of the lake. Joe thought he could see Angela looking out one of the windows. She wouldn't be able to see them in the darkness, but the light from inside the cabin silhouetted her perfectly. "She managed to quit though, didn't she?" he asked, remembering how Heather had pulled out of the depression just in time for him to hit her with the news of his job.

"Yeah she did." Richie spoke quickly now, also looking toward the face in the window. "Like I said, moms are tougher than you'd think. By that time I'd quit waiting for her to come and ask for more. It was too hard on both of us. I just picked up another bag every two weeks. I was like a regular customer to this guy at school. But one day when I gave them to her, she got this look in her eye and she just said, 'No more.' And she quit. I don't know how she did it. She was real, real sick for a few days. But she never touched that bag. I knew where she hid it and I checked." He rubbed his palms against his eyes and turned away from the cabin.

"But then I screwed up again. Just when everything was starting to get back to normal. I really had no idea that we were breaking into somebody's house. I just thought we were cutting school. But when they said they were calling Mom down at the jail, I knew. I just knew that God was going to punish me. But I had no idea that He'd take away your job and everything. If I'd have known that it would push Mom back onto the drugs . . . Only this time it's much worse, she's been taking so many and . . . if I'd just known. But I screwed up and it's all my fault. It's all my—"

"No." Joe put his hand gently over his son's mouth, unwilling to hear him blame himself again, and with his other hand pulled Richie toward him in a hug.

"It's not your fault. It's our problem now and we'll find a way to fix it together. As a family."

* * *

"Dad, Richie, thank goodness you guys are back. I was scared to death." Debbie crossed to the door in three long strides, throwing her arms around her father and brother. Under the flicker of a kerosene lamp, the three of them embraced. It was a feeling Joe relished, unsure of what was ahead, but knowing they could face anything together.

"Something's wrong with Mom. You need to go check on her,

Dad. She won't let anyone in, but it sounds like she's really sick. She was throwing stuff around in the kitchen, and then she went upstairs and locked the door. I'm really worried about her."

"It's all right. She is sick, but we're going to take care of her," Joe said, trying to sound confident. But inside he was scared. Heather was going through withdrawal symptoms. He knew that much, but he had no idea how to help her get through them. She needed to be in a hospital, but even if he started hiking out tonight, they would never get her there in time. Somehow they were going to have to deal with this on their own.

"I'll take care of everything down here," Debbie said, seeming to sense Joe's indecision. "You just go take care of Mom."

Hurrying up the stairs, he knocked softly on the door. When there was no response, he pulled out his pocket knife and opened a blade that would be thin enough to jimmy the lock.

* * *

As the moon rose higher into the night sky, casting a bluish-white glow on everything in the room, Joe again soaked a cloth in the bowl of cool water by the side of the bed and ran it across Heather's parched lips. Her cheeks were so hot he was surprised steam didn't rise when he touched the cloth to her face. Moaning, Heather thrashed beneath the blankets that he had pulled up to her chin, knocking them onto the floor. The tip of her tongue darted quickly out to lick the moisture from her lips, as her eyes opened briefly, rolled back to the whites, and then closed again.

Lifting the blankets from the floor, Joe tucked them back up around his wife. Although her face and body were flushed with heat, goose bumps quickly covered her arms and legs and she began to shiver uncontrollably if he didn't keep her covered.

He was scared. Maybe more scared than he had ever been in his life. He hadn't thought to bring a thermometer, but he guessed that Heather was running a fever of at least 104. She hadn't been able to keep any kind of liquid down and she had thrown up until there was nothing left to regurgitate, thin strands of drool hanging from her lips as she retched so violently that he felt sure she must be damaging her insides. At least she was finally managing to get some rest.

What he did know, was that if Heather's condition didn't show any sign of changing in the next few hours, he was going to have to get her some help. He hadn't noticed the weight she'd lost over the last month until he slid off her jeans and pulled a nightgown over her head. She had always been trim, but now he didn't even need to unzip her pants to get them down over her hips.

"Father, please help Heather to fight this terrible addiction. Help her body to overcome the effects of withdrawal, and help her to keep down some—"

"Dad?" Debbie had slipped the door open so quietly that he hadn't heard her. "I chipped some ice from one of the blocks. I thought she might be able to keep that down." She carried a metal bowl and a stack of clean towels into the room.

Joe stood up hastily from Heather's bedside and took the towels from his daughter. "Thank you. That was very thoughtful, but you kids should be in bed."

"Richie and Angela are down. But I thought you might need some help." Debbie knelt by her mother's side and gently slipped a shard of ice between Heather's lips.

"No, I'm fine. You just go get some rest." Joe wasn't sure whether he was trying to protect his wife from being seen in this condition or his daughter from having to see it.

"Have you looked in the mirror lately?" Debbie watched the ice melt on her mother's lips and pressed another chip to her mouth. "You're the one who needs to get some rest. You always think that you have to do everything alone—be the white knight who swoops down to rescue us. But who helps you Dad?"

"You shouldn't have to . . ." his words ground to a halt as he realized how completely exhausted he was.

"It's okay, Dad. I'm a big girl. Maybe I'm not even all that surprised. I knew something was wrong with Mom. And then with Richie weirding out, I should have put two and two together. Now sit down and let someone help you for a while." She waved toward the chair by the window, and at last Joe dropped gratefully into it. Almost immediately he fell into a deep, and thankfully dreamless, sleep.

* * *

The sky outside was balancing on the thin purple edge that divides the black of night from the crimson of dawn when Joe awoke. Rising from the chair, he tried to stretch the muscles in his stiff back. He was going to have to hike out to the highway soon, while he still could. The Lyme disease was strengthening. His spine, shoulders, and hips all ached, and the trembling he had noticed in his hands yesterday had spread to his arms.

Heather was lying peacefully in bed, her chest softly rising and falling. Her arms and legs were covered with angry red marks where she had scratched herself until he had to physically restrain her. Kneeling on the floor beside her, head resting on the edge of the quilt, Debbie was asleep as well.

Joe leaned on the windowsill, pressing his head against the cool glass, and searched for any sign of the prospector. He hadn't come across him since their encounter with the mountain lion, which left Joe both relieved and a little uneasy. Could he count on the old man for help if it came to that? He wasn't sure, and he hoped he didn't have to find out.

"I guess we're all pretty screwed up, huh?" Debbie's voice was so soft that Joe might have thought he'd imagined it if not for the fact that he could see she was now awake, brushing her fingers lightly over Heather's damp hair.

"What do you mean?" Joe walked from the window to kneel by his daughter's side. Debbie dipped the washcloth into the nearly empty bowl of water and moistened her mother's cracked lips, averting her eyes from Joe's.

"It's just that if God really does exist, I'm not surprised that He wouldn't answer our prayers. You and Angela are probably the only ones He'd even listen to."

"Is that what you think? That Heavenly Father doesn't love you enough to answer your prayers?"

Debbie pressed the cloth between her fingers, working it like a baker with a wad of bread dough as she shook her head. "He couldn't."

Laying one hand on Debbie's shoulder, Joe turned her so that she was facing him. "He's your Father and He loves you as much as I do."

Still looking down, Debbie kneaded the cloth even more furiously with her trembling fingers. "You don't love me, Daddy. Not the *real* me. You just love who you think I am. If you knew what I really am, the terrible things I've done, you wouldn't love me either."

"Debbie." Joe cupped his daughter's face in his hands, raising her chin until her eyes finally met his. How could she think that he would ever—*could* ever—stop loving her? "Sweetheart, there is nothing that you could do that would ever decrease my love for you even a fraction."

"I had sex with Mike. Before he left for college," Debbie spit the words out. Her face flushed with color, but her eyes clouded as though she were pronouncing her own death sentence. "I don't know why I did it. Maybe I thought it would keep him from forgetting me when he was at college, but that's no excuse." Joe waited, sensing that Debbie had more that she needed to say.

"When I was little I was always your princess. Always going to church, getting good grades and all. Trying to make you and Mom happy. Wanting you to be proud of me. And I guess that when Angela came along, I realized that I wasn't going to be your princess anymore. I wasn't ever going to be like her. You know how even when she does something wrong, you just can't stay mad at her because you know that she is so innocent?" Joe nodded. He did know what she meant.

"Well I knew that I was never going to be like that. And a part of me was like, 'Why did you bother being good all those years?' I wondered if maybe I'd missed out on something. And then Mike and I were in his car, and I didn't mean to let things get that far. I was just trying not to be such a Molly. But when it was over, I knew I hadn't missed out on anything after all. I felt so dirty. And I realized that all I had done was prove that I was right. I wasn't like Angela. All those years of going to seminary, and keeping the commandments and all didn't matter. I was just like everybody else." She tried to turn away, but before she could, Joe pulled her into his arms.

Holding her and rocking her like he had when she was a baby, he whispered to her. "It's all right. You will always be my princess, and I will always love you. And your Heavenly Father will always love you. And you will never be like anybody else."

Debbie pulled back from Joe's embrace, her tear-filled eyes searching his with something like wonder. "Really? You still love me?"

"Always—" Joe began. But before he could say more, the stillness of the morning was rent by a blood-curdling scream.

"Ahhhh! Get it off me!" Heather lurched from the bed, her normally placid green eyes now bloodshot and opened wide with terror. Gouging at her face with her fingernails, as if trying to tear off some kind of unseen parasite, she ran headfirst into the door, rebounded off of it and crumpled to the floor. Still screaming, she threw up the few spoonfuls of water she had been able to keep down.

Joe scooped her from the floor, her body like a furnace against his, and turned her so that she wouldn't choke on her own meager bile. He could feel her bones protruding through the paltry amount of flesh still on her body. How long could she survive like this? He had to get something to stay in her stomach, her body was literally consuming itself. It wouldn't be long until her organs began to shut down. Laying her gently onto the bed, he pressed his lips against her fevered cheek and began to whisper to her.

"Please, you have to be okay. You have to. We need you. *I* need you. Things will be so much different, I promise."

"Dad?" Richie was standing in the doorway. Heather's screams must have awakened him. "How is she?"

"Not so good. But she's going to be all right. Why don't you just go back to bed?"

"Why don't you bring her downstairs, Dad? It's warmer there. I lit the fire. And it doesn't smell so bad." Richie wrinkled his nose at a smell which Joe had grown accustomed to hours before.

"He's right, Dad. It would probably do her some good to get out of here for a while." Debbie began to collect the dirty towels from the floor. Her eyes were still damp, but her voice sounded better—stronger.

"I don't know." Joe said, looking at Heather's emaciated body, her scratched face and arms.

"It's okay, Dad. We're a family. We have to help each other." Dropping the towels in the hallway outside the door, Debbie walked to her father's side and rested a hand on his shoulder.

Joe nodded. Wrapping the blankets tightly around Heather's body, to help hold her in place in case she started to struggle as he carried her down the stairs, he lifted her into his arms, again marveling at how little she weighed.

Following Debbie, he carried his wife down the stairs and into the living room. Richie was standing in front of the stove stirring something that smelled like Campbell's Chicken Noodle Soup. Angela was rocking in one of the chairs near the fire, a blanket covering her head and shoulders like a shawl.

As he lay Heather's limp body down onto the couch, Richie began pouring the steaming soup into a bowl. "I thought that maybe chicken soup would help." Richie tried to smile. "They say it's good for colds and stuff like that."

"It couldn't hurt." Joe enjoyed the feeling of the roaring fire against his back as he readjusted his wife's blankets. And the kids were right on both counts. It *was* nice to have some company and it *did* smell a lot better down here.

Taking the bowl of soup from his son, he spooned up a little of the broth and blew it cool. Maybe the warmth would help her keep it down. After all, ten thousand Jewish grandmothers couldn't be wrong. But as he lowered the spoon toward her lips, her teeth snapped violently together, and her entire body began to shudder beneath the blankets.

"What's wrong with her?" Richie jerked back away from his mother's side, knocking the bowl of soup from Joe's hands onto the floor. On the couch, Heather's arms and legs flapped around so violently that Joe could barely hold her down. Although he would have sworn that her mouth was too dry to produce any moisture, a foam of spittle formed at the corners of her lips.

A thousand bits of advice came into Joe's mind. *Put a spoon between her teeth, don't touch her, hold her down, don't let her swallow her tongue.* But the only one that he knew was sound advice for sure, *dial 9-1-1*, did him no good. Pressing his body against hers to keep her from tumbling off the couch, he answered the only way he could. "Pray for her kids. Pray for her quickly."

CHAPTER 13

"Dad, you've got to do something for her." Richie looked up from the spot where he was kneeling beside his mother. "She's so hot."

"Yeah, okay, just let me think for a minute." Joe wiped at the sweat that was streaming down his forehead. The fire's heat, which had felt nice only a few minutes ago, was now stifling. There was a dull throbbing behind his eyes, and it seemed nearly impossible to concentrate on a single coherent thought. He needed to start hiking to the freeway. He could make it in six, maybe seven hours. He would have Debbie . . . he would have her . . . have her . . . what?

Taking the tender flesh of his lower lip between his thumb and forefinger, he pinched until his eyes began to water. He couldn't have his mind wandering right now, he needed to focus. Although he was utterly exhausted, there was no time to rest. "All right kids, what we're going to do is—"

"Could you give Mom a blessing?" For a moment, Richie's question fell blankly on Joe's fuzzy brain. All he could picture was the family sitting around the dinner table praying over the food.

"Richie, Mom needs medical attention. She needs doctors not religion." Debbie spoke softly, almost with pity, but Richie shrunk back from her words anyway.

"Yeah, I guess you're right. It was a dumb—"

"A blessing, yes." Why hadn't he thought of it before? He had been so focused on Heather's physical needs, the hospital that was out of reach, that he had completely forgotten the spiritual help that was accessible anywhere, anytime. "Richie, that is a great idea."

If Richie had been hurt by Debbie's words, *she* seemed positively singed by Joe's. "Dad, we don't have time for that stuff. The time it would take to give her a blessing means it will be that much longer until you can get an ambulance up here or a helicopter."

But Joe was already moving to the end of the couch where Heather's head lay, placing his shaking hands on top of her matted hair and burning brow. He didn't have any consecrated oil to anoint her with, that had been a mistake, but he could still call on the powers of heaven to bless his wife. Heather had been the one who insisted that he give the kids a father's blessing every year at the start of the school year, the first one to suggest to Joe that he bless a family member who was sick. She might be lost inside a struggling body right now, but he knew that Heather's spirit possessed the faith to help heal her body.

Closing his eyes, he asked a silent prayer of help. If he ever needed to focus, the time was now. He had to use all of his strength and faith to seek the power of God that could do for his wife what he could not. He opened his mouth, attempted to speak the words, and came up empty. It was as if making the connection, reaching the understanding of what he needed to do, had sucked up the last of his strength. In his mind he pictured a nine-volt battery with a wire running from each terminal to a small light bulb. The battery gave a last blue spark and the light went dead.

"Debbie, Richie, I need your help." He barely had the strength to open his eyes, and he wasn't sure if he had even spoken the words until the children came to his side.

"What is it, Dad?" Debbie asked.

"I can't . . . I can't do this alone." Dragging out each of the words was like pulling lead weights from his throat. "Each of you take your mother's hands and pray with all your strength." Richie instantly took Heather's right hand in his left, and grabbed Debbie's hand with his right, but Debbie looked as if someone had asked her to take hold of a live scorpion.

"Dad, I can't. I don't . . . He wouldn't listen to me. I'm not . . . " Tears began to roll down Debbie's cheeks. Joe thought it strange that he couldn't remember the last time he had seen her cry.

"Please . . . I need you . . . Mom needs you."

"I wouldn't be any help. Why would God listen to me?" She looked from Joe's pleading, careworn face to Richie's bowed head, ran one hand tenderly across Heather's cheek, and then nodded. "I'll try, but I don't think it will do any good." Taking her mother's hand, Debbie dropped to her knees and buried her face against Heather's nightgown.

Help me, help her, Joe whispered in his mind. But still the words wouldn't come. He didn't know what or why, but something was wrong. Some piece of wiring needed to complete the circuit was broken or missing. Was it Debbie? Was it because of her lack of faith that he was unable to use his priesthood power? "I can't—" he began to say, conceding that, for whatever the reason, he would not be able to give his wife the priesthood blessing she so needed, when suddenly he felt as if every hair on his body was standing straight out on end.

It was as though his tiny battery had suddenly been connected to a generator. Not the kind you ran in your garage either; the kind that could light up entire cities, maybe even states. He had heard people compare faith to power, but this was the first time he actually understood how the faith of a mustard seed could move a mountain. What was flowing through his nerve endings right now, almost crackling with power to spare, could move a whole range of mountains. Opening his eyes, he saw that Angela had completed the loop, stepping between her older brother and sister, taking their hands in her own tiny fingers. Her face, eyes closed, mouth slightly upturned at the corners, held the same expression of peace that he had seen the night before. On either side of her, he could see that tears were pouring from the closed eyes of Richie and Debbie.

"Try now," he heard a tiny voice whisper clearly inside his head. And when he tried, he found that he had no problem speaking.

"Heather Stewart, in the name of Jesus Christ I lay my hands upon your head to give you a blessing . . ." Later, he would not be able to remember the words which he spoke. What he would be able to remember was the unmistakable surety that the blessing, which he gave, came from his Heavenly Father. The knowledge that the power of faith, the power of God, was doing what no mortal medicine could do. Strengthening muscles, rehydrating tissues, reaching down to the marrow of his wife's bones, to each individual cell in her body, and healing them. If he never felt the power of God operating through man again, this one instance would forever be enough to convince him of the existence, the reality, the all-encompassing love of God.

When he closed the prayer, and removed his hands from his wife's head, the energy left him. The power of his family's faith had poured vigor into his muscles like a tidal wave. It fled from him just as rapidly and his legs first trembled and then gave out completely.

He felt his knees buckle, felt his body drop to the floor like a rag doll, sleep claiming him even before his head hit the rug. But it was with the knowledge that everything was going to be all right.

* * *

Danger was coming. No longer slinking through the shadows, creeping silently up on its prey. Now it was racing toward his family, claws extended, teeth bared. It sensed his presence, recognized the threat he presented, and was making an all-out attack. It was what the old man had warned him of in his dream, and later in person. He had to protect what he held dear. If nothing else, this trip had made it perfectly clear to him that his family was what he held dear. His job, his health, his reputation, the goodwill of the people who knew him—they were all important. But when compared to his family, they were nothing, less than nothing.

But how could he protect them? Even in his sleep, in this state of half-waking, he knew that his body was quickly failing. The disease doing battle with his immune system was attacking his muscles to the point that, in another couple of days, he would be unable to even stand. He knew that the power of God could heal him, just as he knew that it had healed his wife. But he also knew that it was not to be. If this was some kind of test, it was a test that he needed to pass with his body in its current state. He had been robbed of everything that the world viewed as important for a reason. Stripped down to his soul, his faith, his essence, he was forced to focus on the only things that mattered in this life—the only things he could take with him when it was over. And with those he would either stand or fall.

Joe awoke to the sound of the front door swinging closed. His initial thought, as he looked dreamily around the first floor of the cabin from the armchair in which he had been sleeping, was that the room was unnaturally quiet. None of the children were anywhere in sight, and the sofa Heather had been resting on was empty. Rising from the chair, his muscles stiff from sleeping in an upright position, he limped to the window. It took him a moment to reconcile the position of the sun with his impression of how long he had been asleep. He would have guessed only two or three hours had passed since he carried Heather down from the bedroom. That would have made it eight or nine in the morning at the latest. But the sun had passed nearly halfway from its zenith to the point where it would disappear behind the mountains to the west.

On the lake, several hundred feet from the dock, he could make out the orange life jackets of Debbie and Richie. They were paddling the canoe roughly parallel to the shoreline, seemingly lost in some conversation. A few hundred feet from the porch, Angela was serving tea to the friends she had collected since their arrival. Debbie and Richie must have carried the table and chairs from her room out to the meadow. Joe thought that they fit in quite well with the wildflowers that surrounded her. A flash of pink distracted his attention from the peaceful scene of his children at play, and as he turned to see what it was, a bolt of apprehension ran through his body.

Heather had somehow managed to get up from the couch and walk out the front door. It must have been the sound of her leaving that had interrupted his sleep. The hem of her nightgown tugged at the grass and brush as she tottered toward Angela. He could just make out the dusty prints of her bare feet in the dirt at the base of the front steps. Her back was toward him, so he couldn't see the expression on her face, but she was carrying what looked like a length of firewood. As he watched, she raised it slowly in her trembling right hand like a club.

"Angela, come here baby." Heather's voice, weak and hoarse, barely rose above the sound of the wind washing through the trees down by the lake. Angela looked up from her play, and a huge smile lit up her face.

"Ommy!" As Angela stood up from one of the four mushroom-shaped chairs, Heather raised the club a little further, her body swaying visibly even from this distance. Her head turned ever so slightly to the left, and as Joe followed her gaze, he saw something that turned his entire body to ice.

The mountain lion's muscular body lay flattened against a patch of dead grass at the edge of the meadow, its dusty coat rendered all but invisible by the surrounding brush and dead pine needles. Its golden eyes were fixed intently on Angela. As she rose from her chair it flexed its powerful rear legs as if preparing to spring.

"Go away. Leave her alone." Heather's words, little more than a whisper, confused Angela. The little girl paused a few feet from the table, unsure of whether to continue toward her mother or stay where she had been playing. But the mountain lion seemed for the first time to register the presence of another person. Taking in the stick Heather held feebly above her head, it let out a low deep growl and bared its razor-sharp incisors. It was going to attack them both.

Joe stumbled from the window to the door, his palm slipping on the knob before he could get it open. In his mind, he pictured the big cat loping easily across the meadow, muscles bunching as it leaped onto his wife. He was already too late. It would sink its teeth into Heather's throat before he could even get off the porch, and Angela would be its next victim. He imagined that he heard Heather scream as he finally managed to twist the knob. But when he stepped through the doorway, the mountain lion had fled, and Heather—Angela wrapped in her arms—slumped slowly to the grass.

* * *

In the last hour, the sky had gone from dazzling blue to a bruised purplish haze. The sun's slanting rays still cut through the low cloud cover that had blown in, but the heavens were quickly darkening and the afternoon's gentle breeze now wailed through the tops of the trees as if bemoaning the sudden change.

"I don't think this is a good idea." Heather lay resting on the couch, a hand-knitted afghan wrapped around her shoulders, and a cup of soup warming her thin fingers. She watched Joe warily as he wiped down the barrel of the rifle and began loading it with shells. Seated around the room, the children watched him as well. All except Angela, whose voice occasionally carried a snatch of some song or the other from her room where she was playing.

"It will be fine." Joe loaded the last shell, checked to make sure that they were all seated properly, and took his jacket from the peg by the front door.

"It's getting late. Why don't you just try in the morning?" Heather added. Joe turned away from the worried look in Heather's deep green eyes. He would like nothing better than to stay and marvel at her amazing recovery, basking in the warmth of his newly reunited family. The thought of leaving them, even for a moment, was nearly unbearable. But he had to go out, now, tonight. Every fiber of his being told him that tomorrow would be too late. They were hurtling toward some terrible conflux of circumstances that brooked no turning back.

He opened the door, and the wind whipped through the cabin, plastering his hair against his skull and whipping the flames in the fireplace to a frenzy. Turning back to look at his wife and children, he was tempted to wait just a little while longer, but now that he had identified the danger threatening them he had to face it. "I'll be back."

Buttoning his denim jacket up to his neck, Joe turned up his collar against the cold and planted the stock of the rifle against his shoulder. He fingered the safety to the off position, and headed around to the back of the cabin. One of the first things that they taught in hunter safety classes was to keep your safety on and your gun pointed toward the ground. But he was going to disregard that today. He had no doubt in his mind that the big cat would come, and when it did it would be fast. He couldn't afford to waste a second raising the rifle to fire or releasing the safety.

He thought he might know where to find the mountain lion's lair. It would be through the woods behind the cabin, hidden somewhere in the maze of steep granite cliffs that made the area so treacherous. It would be dangerous, tracking the beast to its own domain, but wasn't that really why he had been led here? It all came down to protecting those he loved. If he wasn't willing to risk a little danger to do that, what kind of father did it make him?

Walking through the forest, sheltered from most of the storm but hearing the trees groan as the wind howled through their tops, he felt as if he were making his way into the belly of some gargantuan creature that was just beginning to awaken. Occasional shafts of light made their way down to him, but even those seemed to have their vitality drained away and did little to light the space around them.

As he neared the edge of the sheltering trees, the force of the wind pushing against him increased. When he finally reached the bare granite plateau, the buffeting was so great that he had to lean into it to stay upright. Which way now? The flat rock extended twenty or thirty feet before shattering into dozens of steep crevices. As a boy, he had spent days exploring out here, imagining that he was an outlaw, a spelunker, a miner, or any of the hundred other fantasies that this wilderness could inspire. It was easy to get lost in the network of interconnecting passages that, as often as not, dead-ended in impassable drop-offs.

"So you're off to slay the dragon, are you?" Joe found that the deep voice behind him, now shouting to be heard above the wind, came as very little surprise. Somehow he had known that the prospector would find him.

"Isn't this what you wanted me to do all along?" He too had to raise his voice above the tumult as he turned and faced the old man and his donkey.

"What? To break your neck, or shoot yourself in the foot?"

"To protect my family. You told me that. Don't you remember? Protect that which you deem most valuable."

"And is that what you are doing?" Joe found the old man's unreadable face maddening. His implacable features revealed nothing of the man's inner thoughts, while his words seemed only to run in circles.

"Of course I am. Can't you see that?" Joe held the rifle out before him as proof of his intentions. "There's a wild animal out there that is stalking my children, and yes I am protecting them."

The prospector took the gun from Joe, tested the tension on the trigger, sighted down the scope, and squeezed off a shot. A few yards away, a small chip of rock leapt into the air as the explosion rang out through the valley below. The wind quickly whipped away the smell of cordite. Handing it back to Joe, stock first, he scowled and shook his head. "What will this weapon protect them from?"

Joe was dumbfounded. Had this man not listened to anything he had just said? "From being attacked, mauled, and killed for starters."

"There are worse things than pain. Worse even than death."

"What do you know about it?" Joe was incensed. "If you had just watched your youngest daughter innocently playing less than a hundred yards away from death, you might feel a little bit differently."

"I lost half my children in a single freak storm. I think I might have an idea of your pain." The old man's dark eyes glared at Joe with a power that he had never noticed before. Above the two men a single streak of lightning illuminated the dark gray sky, and almost simultaneously thunder rattled the ground on which they stood.

"I'm sorry. I didn't know."

"There are many things you don't know, Joe Stewart." The old man no longer seemed to be shouting, and yet his voice carried easily above the roar of the impending storm. "That is why you are here."

"At the cabin?"

"On this earth. You are here to experience, to learn. Somehow your generation has come up with this crazy notion that God is supposed to keep you from experiencing pain. You think that adversity is a punishment, instead of realizing that it is an opportunity. You are so busy trying not to get hurt that you miss the chance to grow— so busy chasing imaginary dangers that you are blinded to those right in front of you." The prospector's voice now seemed to drown out even the sound of the distant thunder.

"What should I do then?"

"That is perhaps the one thing I cannot tell you. The pathway has been marked, but only you can decide whether you will follow it and where it will take you." As the old man took the bridle of his donkey in hand, the first drops of rain began to fall from the sky, marking the dusty rock with round dark spatters.

"Then at least tell me this," Joe took the man's arm entreating him not to leave, "who are you?"

The man's eyes softened a little as he lifted Joe's hand from his arm and pressed it tenderly to his whiskered cheek, almost as a grandparent would to his grandchild. "I am a man who cannot number the clouds in the sky or stay the bottles of heaven, yet I am wise with years. In my life I lost much, yet gained even more. If I have suffered, it was only that I could learn endurance. If I was brought low, that I might gain humility. I was sent to help you find your way. But ultimately there is only one that can be your guide, and of Him I am scarcely worthy to kneel at His feet and wash them with my tears.

"Now I must leave you, Joe. But I know that I leave you in good hands. Remember, be constantly vigilant in—"

"Protecting that which I deem most valuable." Joe completed the sentence that he had heard over and over, and yet still was not sure he understood. The old man nodded briefly, tipped his weather-beaten hat, and as he began to lead his pack-loaded donkey toward the woods, the heavens opened up in earnest.

* * *

Joe slogged through the thick reddish-brown stream that had been the pathway leading to the front of the cabin, kicked his boots against the steps to knock off some of the mud, and walked wearily up to the porch. As he leaned down to untie his shoelaces, rainwater poured from his hair. Setting his dripping rifle against the wall, he pulled off each of his boots, set them side-by-side next to the mat, and wrung out each of his socks. For a second, he wasn't sure he was going to be able to straighten up. The muscles in his back felt as though they had been placed on a medieval rack and stretched beyond any hope of repair. But finally, with what felt like an actual tearing of the sinews, he stood, picked up the rifle, and shuffled into the cabin.

Most of the lights were out, and the last log in the fireplace was a blackened stump with only a few glowing embers to show that it was still hot. He was not surprised, since it was nearly eleven. After the prospector had left, he had gone ahead with the hunt, searching up one crevice and down another. He hadn't held out much hope of finding the cat in the pouring rain and the cold that only grew heavier as the night went on, but it was the only way he could think of to take the old man's advice. And he had failed. Somewhere out there the big cat was still lurking, and he had done nothing to make his family any safer.

"Oh, sweetheart, come here and get dry." Heather rose from the dark couch like a wraith and wiped his face with a towel.

"Dad, are you okay?" Debbie and Richie, who had been wrapped in quilts by the fire, were right behind her. In minutes, Joe was sitting on a chair by the fire, a plate of ham and beans on his lap and his wet shirt and jacket replaced by a terry-cloth robe.

"Did you get the mountain lion?" Richie perched on the arm of the couch next to his father.

"No, I didn't even see him." Joe shoveled a mouthful of beans into his mouth, but it seemed that the hunt, or perhaps the old man's parting words, had rendered everything tasteless, and he set the plate aside. Debbie took the plate from him and wiped a bead of water from his forehead.

"It's all right, Dad. Maybe this is one of those times you're always talking about, when men's ways are not God's ways." He couldn't tell if the gleam in his oldest daughter's eyes was the reflection of the dying embers in the fireplace or the possible rebirth of something more.

"Where's Angela?" His wet jeans seemed to weigh a hundred pounds as he pushed himself up out of the couch.

"She is asleep in bed where we should all be as well." Heather took Joe's hand and led him toward the stairs. "Now, good night children."

* * *

"You have failed." If words could be said to carry their own odor, the words that floated out of the darkness reeked of corruption and death. Or perhaps it was only the breath of their owner, but since Joe could see neither face nor body, but only a pair of glowing red eyes, it was all the same. From outside the window, lightning shredded the night, illuminating the bedroom, but the foot of the bed where the voice had originated stood empty.

"I warned you once. And now you have failed to protect those you hold dear and they are in my hands." The low laughter that filled the room was thick and greasy—the laughter of a monster.

"Noooo," Joe moaned softly, his body shivering uncontrollably beneath the quilt and blankets. The voice in the darkness was the sum of all his fears. It embodied the dangers that every parent imagines when their children are late coming home or unaccounted for. The car accident, the seductive stranger, the allure of the quick thrill, the innumerable threats that mothers and fathers hope to protect their sons and daughters from, but that ultimately only leave them feeling helpless and afraid.

"How could you ever have hoped to stand up against me, Joe Stewart? Don't you know that *I* am he who marks the trail? It is *my* blade that slashes out the path you will ultimately follow. *My* whims decide who will die and who will live. Tonight my eye has found those you love, but I could look elsewhere. I give you one last chance. See how you have lost everything? *He* has not saved you. Worship me now—curse God! Bow down at my feet and beg for my mercy and perhaps I will spare your family."

"No, go away, leave me alone." Joe's weak voice trembled along with his body.

"Worship me. Pray at my feet." The voice was all powerful, all consuming.

"No!" Joe screamed, waking himself from the horrible dream. As his eyes flew open, another flash of lightning lit the room and he saw that a figure stood at the foot of his bed. Outside, the wind crashed the shutters closed against the window, throwing the room into complete darkness.

"Go away!" Joe cried. "Leave me alone. I won't worship you. Leave me alone, leave me alone!" Throwing his hands over his face, he lay trembling in his bed until at last he dared open his eyes. The shutters were once more open, and the figure, whether real or imagined, was gone. Sighing with relief, he buried his face in his pillow and returned to his fevered dreams.

* * *

"Dad, Dad."

"Wha . . . ?" Joe struggled to open his eyes, and when he managed to, the morning sunlight spearing through the window nearly blinded him.

". . . gone." Richie was yanking on his arm, trying to pull him out of bed.

"Richie, what is it?" Heather sat up next to Joe, a blanket pulled up to her chest, her sleep-filled eyes confused.

"She's gone. I looked everywhere, but she's gone."

"Who?" Suddenly Joe was wide awake, his heart hammering against his ribs.

"Angela, Dad. She's gone."

CHAPTER 14

When he was nine years old, Joe's father and grandfather had joined in the search for a missing little girl who had wandered away from a campsite some thirty or forty miles from the Stewart cabin. Sitting in his grandfather's pickup truck that afternoon, he had watched as the rescuers calmly examined photographs of the girl and referred to various maps of the area. He remembered feeling comforted by the sight of so many people confidently planning the girl's safe return. Positive that they would find her, he had been shocked by the sight of the girl's father later that day. He was a broad-shouldered man in his mid-forties. A bright red beard hid the lower half of his solid, ruddy face. He was racing from one member of the team to the next as they returned from the search empty handed, hoping for some clue of his daughter's whereabouts. As the night wore on, his wide shoulders seemed to slump further and further down.

But it was the man's eyes that Joe would always remember. They held a panicky look of desperation, filling with hope when word would come out that someone thought they had seen something, only to cloud over with despair when it turned out to be a false alarm. As a child himself, Joe had been unable to understand what could cause a bear of a man to get that look in his eyes. But he had wondered about that man, especially when he heard that the girl's tiny lifeless body had been found, caught in the branches at the edge of a fast moving river. Now he understood.

At first, no one could fathom that she was really gone. They checked the obvious places—under each of the beds, in the pantry, behind the couch. Even cupboards that were too small for her to possibly squeeze into were checked and rechecked. Debbie and Richie spread out to either side of the cabin, shouting their sister's name until they were hoarse. With a growing sense of dread, Joe ran down to the dock, deathly afraid that he would find his daughter's bright blue eyes staring up at him from the depths of the lake's cold clear water. But it wasn't until Heather, obviously still weak, started around the back of the cabin to check the tool shed, that they found the first clue to Angela's disappearance.

"Joe, come here." Heather's voice was nearly frantic as she knelt by the side of the cabin.

The footprints were faint, but unmistakable in the thick mud created by the night's relentless rains. Angela had a pair of fuzzy Winnie the Pooh slippers that she loved, each with a silhouette of the chubby-faced bear imprinted on the bottom. Everyone had rushed out the door in such a hurry that they had missed the small Pooh tracks leading from the front steps and around the side of the cabin. Judging from the amount of water puddled in the imprints, the rain must have stopped falling shortly after she went out.

"Why would she come out here?" Heather asked. But Joe was already back on his feet following their daughter's trail. The prints continued around the side of the cabin to the outhouse. But instead of going directly up to the door, they stopped, went left a few steps, crossed back to the right, turned, and seemed to shuffle a little. At some point in the middle of the night she had come out here to go to the bathroom. That she had hesitated before entering the outhouse was no surprise. After four days of using it, she was still deathly afraid of the dark, foul-smelling little "uggy ouse." She refused to go in without first finding an adult and asking, "You ode and?"

Somehow though, she had found the nerve to go in. He could just see the faint outline of a muddy footprint that the rain had been unable to completely wash away from the step in front of the outhouse door. He swung the door open, even though it was obvious that she was no longer there. The tracks of her small slippers continued to tell the story. He could see where they came back out. But somehow she had gotten turned around, perhaps a lightning strike or the crash of thunder had startled her, or maybe she had just become disoriented by the darkness. Instead of retracing the tracks that led back to the front of the cabin, she had turned right, past the tool shed, and toward the woods beyond it.

Why had she come out here alone? She was terrified of lightning and thunder, and Joe couldn't imagine how frightening the wind must have sounded to a small child, blowing against and through the weathered boards of the old wooden structure. She must have lain in her bed, trying to convince herself that she could wait until the morning, until the need grew too great—until her fear of wetting the bed outgrew her fear of the "uggy ouse" and the storm. But why hadn't she come upstairs to ask one of them to take her? It didn't make sense. She would never have come out in the dark alone unless it was a last resort, unless . . .

"No, please God, no." Suddenly the dime dropped and realization hit him with a guilt like nothing he had ever experienced in his life. When he had awoken from his nightmare, just before the shutters slammed shut, he had seen a figure standing at the foot of his bed. In his fear, he had cried out for it to go away. But it couldn't have been . . . even in the terror that had filled him, surely he would have recognized his own daughter. Still his memory persisted in throwing the image up before his eyes. The figure was no longer imposing, but small, standing not much higher than the bed itself. The arms stretching out to take his family from him now seemed to be pleading for his help. Could he have sent his own daughter, shivering and terrified, out into the storm alone? Was her father's voice, screaming at her to go away and leave him alone, the last thing she had heard before disappearing into the forest?

"Look. It's a piece of her pajamas." Near the woods, Heather pulled a scrap of pink flannel from the pointed branch of a manzanita. Looking toward where his wife stood, Joe caught sight of another set of tracks. They were smaller than the slipper prints but just as familiar. And the story they told was just as clear; following the slipper prints past where his wife was holding the piece of pink fabric and into the woods, they tracked his daughter's prints step for step.

* * *

"Dad, let me come with you." Richie placed one hand on his father's shoulder as if trying to hold him back from charging into the woods alone.

"No. It's too dangerous." Joe adjusted the rifle's shoulder strap, concentrating on keeping his hands from shaking as he pulled the nylon webbing through the metal buckle. "Stay here with Debbie and your mother. You need to keep an eye out in case Angela comes back." The words sounded good, comforting, as though Angela might just stroll up the road at any minute. But really, how long could a six-year-old survive a storm like last night's without succumbing to hypothermia? It might already be too late. Shrugging off his son's hand, he turned and started toward the woods.

"Joe, wait." Heather was watching him carefully, tracing the length of his body with her eyes. Was the trembling that he felt in his limbs visible to her? "I think you should take Richie with you. Debbie and I will keep watch here, but it might be dangerous out there, and if anything happened to you we would have two lost people to search for."

"I . . ." Joe hesitated. This was *his* problem. He put his little girl into harm's way, and the idea of endangering any of his other children just made matters worse. Still, Heather was right, it was stupid to go out alone. The look in his wife's eyes finally settled it for him. It was the look of determination that he hadn't seen in her eyes in months, maybe years. She wasn't going to let this go without a fight, and he didn't have time for that. "All right, come on. But be careful."

"You be careful too." Heather stepped up next to Joe and kissed him gently on the cheek, whispering as he turned to leave, "Find my baby."

Joe fought the urge to run haphazardly through the woods calling his daughter's name. Even with his muscles aching, he longed for action—running, screaming, shooting, anything that would bring him closer to finding his daughter—but now was not the time to lose his head. Every second was precious, and heading in the wrong direction at the start might mean hours of backtracking. "Let's spread out about twenty feet apart," he said, waving Richie off to his left. "Look for footprints or any sign that your sister was here. We'll take turns calling her name every minute."

Richie nodded and moved off to one side, his eyes scouring the ground for any signs. Although the rain had stopped several hours before, the tree branches were still heavy with moisture, and soon both Joe and Richie were soaked. The thick bed of pine needles made footprints nearly impossible to spot and, after thirty minutes Joe felt no closer to finding his daughter than he had when they started out. "See anything?" he called to Richie, although it was obvious that he hadn't.

"No." Richie mumbled, leaning against a tree to catch his breath. His gaze roved across the hundreds of acres of forest surrounding them. "She could be anywhere, Dad."

Joining his son at the tree, Joe tried to rub some of the stiffness out of his joints. "Why don't we stop for a minute and say a prayer." They should have done it earlier, at the start of the search, but better late than never. As the two of them knelt side by side on the spongy, damp ground, Joe took his son's hand and asked, "Would you offer it?"

"Yeah, okay." Richie bowed his head, seemed to search for the right words, and then began. "Heavenly Father, please help us find Angela. And please help her to be okay when we get there. I know I haven't been the best person lately, so maybe my prayers don't count for that much, but Angela is about the most perfect person I know. When the rest of us get mad and argue sometimes, she always makes us smile and stop fighting. And even if I can't always understand what she says in her prayers, she has so much love and faith that I can always feel the Spirit. So please help us find her, because she's little and she really needs Your help. And so do we." He finished the prayer to reverent amens.

"Was that okay?" he asked Joe, when he had finished praying.

"That was just perfect," Joe said, wrapping one arm around Richie's shoulders and allowing his son to help pull him to his feet. "And I think your prayers count for a lot."

Twenty minutes later they stepped out of the trees and onto the granite cliff top. The last clouds had disappeared from the sky, leaving it a brilliant blue, but the air still carried the chill of the night before. The smooth stone surface was slick with puddled water.

"Angela!" Joe's shout echoed off the rocks below, seeming to bounce back in hundreds of disjointed fragments, but there was no returning call. Walking up to the edge of the cliff, he stared down at the jagged rocks below, unable to keep his mind from imagining what had happened if Angela had made it this far.

"Dad, what's that?" Richie was pointing to a fissure a few yards to their right and twenty or thirty feet below them. Something bright red and yellow stood out against the gray face of the rock.

Scrambling down to the outcropping, Joe pried one of Angela's Pooh slippers from the crack. It felt cold and wet in his hand, but it smelled like his daughter, and suddenly he felt his control slipping away from him. Would he find Angela lying somewhere like this tiny slipper, crumpled in a heap on the cold, unforgiving stone? Or had the mountain lion caught up with her first? What had she felt wandering alone, lost in this alien landscape, while the storm raged around her? It wasn't fair. She hadn't done anything wrong, so why was she being punished for *his* sins?

"Come on," he said, tugging at his son's elbow. "We've got to find her, *now*."

They abandoned all pretense of order, launching themselves down the ravines with reckless abandon. Stopping briefly to shout out her name, and then racing onward when the only answer was silence. Although the cliffs weren't as expansive as the woods, they were far more difficult to search. Hidden caves appeared only when seen from the right angle, and the many dead ends forced them into continual backtracking.

They had just reached another impassable precipice, when Joe stepped on a loose rock and his right leg suddenly collapsed, dropping him dangerously close to the edge of the cliff. As he fell, the rifle's shoulder strap entangled his arm and the scope gouged a deep furrow in the side of his temple. For a moment he could only lie at the edge of the cliff waiting for the dizziness to go away.

"Dad. Are you okay?" Richie's voice sounded faint and far away.

"I think so. I just—" Joe began to slowly sit up when he noticed something move on a ledge across the precipice. As he rubbed his eye, his palm came away smeared with blood, but he barely noticed it. Anger raged through his body as he pulled the rifle from his shoulder, and fit the scope to his eye.

"Is that the—?"

"Shh." Joe hushed his son and tried to steady the barrel of the rifle. The mountain lion's head and shoulder were clearly visible over the edge of the cliff on which it was resting. The distance was less than one hundred feet, an easy shot. And yet he found that he couldn't stop his hand from trembling, even when he rested it against a small rock outcropping. It was as though his arm muscles were no longer under his command, twitching and jerking uncontrollably.

"If you've hurt my baby," he growled, his voice filled with frustration as he again tried to steady the gun. For a split second the crosshairs centered on the cat's head, but before he could squeeze off a shot the barrel again jerked upward. Slamming his fist to the ground, he laid the rifle on the rocks next to him and buried his face in his arms.

"Let me try, Dad." Richie was on the ground beside him reaching for the gun. Joe's first impulse was to stop him. Richie would miss and the cat would be gone. But could he do any better with his arms shaking like an invalid?

"All right, Richie. See what you can do." Taking the rifle, Richie set the stock against his shoulder, pressed his eye to the scope, and zeroed in on the spot above the ledge.

"Easy does it now. Take a deep breath, hold it, release halfway, and then gently squeeze the trigger." Joe watched his son as he steadied his breathing and began to tighten his finger. *Kill it*, he thought. *Stop it so that it can't threaten us any more. Because it is the . . .*

"Know your enemy." It was as if the prospector had been right there with them, kneeling on the rocks. But they were alone. What did it mean, *Know your enemy?* It was obvious, wasn't it? His enemy was right there, only a stone's throw away, and he was protecting his family from it. That was his job. To take care of his family. And yet what had the prospector said? *There are worse things than death.* But if he couldn't protect his family from being hurt or killed, what could he protect them from? Still the words repeated over and over in his head, *know your enemy, know your enemy, know your enemy,* as he watched his son squeeze the trigger. He *did* know his enemy, and it wasn't the cat at all, it was the voice that had come to him in the night. The voice that had commanded him to curse God and worship *it* instead.

"No." Joe managed to bring his hand down on the barrel of the gun just as Richie pulled the trigger. It wasn't much, but it was enough to send the bullet ricocheting harmlessly off the rocks five or ten feet below the ledge. At the sound of the shot, the mountain lion sprang to its feet and bounded out of sight.

"Why did—" Richie began, but his words caught in his throat at the sight of what had been hidden behind the cat.

"Addy!" Angela's voice was tired and weak, and even from this distance they could see that her body was twisted unnaturally, but she was alive.

* * *

"Hang on sweetheart, we're coming!" Joe called out encouragement to Angela as he carefully lowered Richie six feet down to a small outcropping. After exploring several possible routes, he had finally realized that there was no easy way to get to his daughter. In the dark she had fallen down one of the sheer walls. It was a miracle that the drop was only twenty feet and not a hundred or more.

When Richie had gained a solid footing, he cradled his hands together, forming a basket that Joe could step down into. Pressing their bodies against the rock face, they edged along the lip of rock that eventually opened out onto the ledge where Angela had landed.

"Addy, Wutchy, oo finda me." Although Angela's face was streaked with dirt and tears, her bright blue eyes glowed with excitement at seeing them. But a moment later, she gasped in pain and lay her head back down, eyes pooled with tears. Joe found himself incapable of speech. His first impression upon seeing his daughter was that she had somehow put her pajamas on wrong. Although she was laying flat on her back, her legs were cruelly contorted sidewise and one of them was bent nearly up to her back. It took him a moment to realize that she must have broken her hip or possibly her pelvis in the fall.

"Ohh," Richie groaned softly, his face as gray as the rock on which he was standing, and dropped to the ledge.

"Wutchy K?" Angela reached one bruised hand out toward her brother.

"Yeah, Richie's all right, baby." Joe sat down on the ledge and cradled his daughter's head in his lap. Removing his jacket, he laid it gently across her body, and wiped at the blood that was seeping from a cut beneath the blonde curls on the side of her head. Her face felt like ice beneath his hand, and he could see that her slipperless foot was nearly blue.

"I faw dowin, Addy." Angela glanced down at her twisted legs and moaned softly.

"I know you did, sweetheart. But we're going to get you home and take care of you." Angela smiled at first, but then her face clouded over.

"I cat ge up." She started to wriggle the toes on the foot she could see and then cried out in pain.

"It's all right, baby. Don't try to move." Without taking his eyes from his daughter, Joe reached back and found his son's hand.

"Richie, are you all right?"

"I think so," Richie said, but his voice shook. "Dad she's . . . "

"Shh." Joe gave his hand a slight squeeze. "She's going to be fine. Now I need you to go back to the cabin as quick as you can and bring me some rope, the oars from the canoe, as many blankets as you can carry, and the first-aid kit. Can you do that?"

"Yeah, but how—"

"Just go, quickly." Behind him, Joe heard Richie's feet scrape against the rock as he slid back along the ledge. As he listened to the sounds of Richie climbing, Joe did everything he could to make Angela comfortable. Removing his socks, he slid them over her cold hands, and pulling his shirt off he wrapped it carefully around her exposed foot.

"Why kyin Addy?" Angela asked, raising one sock-covered hand to the tears slipping down her father's face as he lay next to her tiny shivering body, trying to share his body's heat with hers.

"I'm just happy to find you," he whispered, and cradled her face against his chest.

* * *

"Okay, now very gently pull up on the rope." Joe raised the makeshift stretcher until it left his fingertips, grateful that Angela had passed out while he was strapping her onto the blankets. She had been tougher than he could ever have imagined, grimly biting back the tears as he carefully lifted her small body. But when he had to straighten her leg to lay her down, the sound of her cries had nearly killed him. It was only the knowledge that she would die if they didn't move her that kept him going.

On the other end, Richie and Debbie strained against the rope while Heather tried to keep the stretcher steady so that Angela's head would not bang against the rocks.

"That's it. Just a little more." Joe watched the tiny bundle that was his daughter sway slowly back and forth on the rope, only relaxing when the stretcher disappeared from his view into the hands of his family.

By the time Joe made it to the top of the cliff, Angela was awake again. Heather had bandaged her obvious cuts and given her as many baby aspirin as she dared. And although she was obviously in terrible pain, Angela was busy telling Heather, Debbie, and Richie about the kitty cat that had slept with her all night.

"I bet him un e rrrrred."

"You pet him?" Debbie asked incredulous.

Angela nodded. "E ent rrrrrrrr." Blissfully unaware of the look on her mother's face, she showed just how the mountain lion had purred when she petted him. But the bubbly sound her chest made every time she breathed worried Joe, and he could see that Heather had noticed it as well.

"Well, you just lay your head back and rest, sweetheart. We're going to carry you back to the cabin as carefully as we can."

"Urts, Addy." Angela's eyes teared up at the mention of moving her, and in her father's socks, her small hands bunched up into fists.

"I know it does, honey." Joe tried to give her a comforting smile, but he seemed incapable of making the corners of his lips rise. "But you try as hard as you can not to cry, and we'll try as hard as we can not to hurt you."

"Awight, Addy. I pwomiz." Angela smiled obediently. In his heart Joe promised himself that he would not hurt her. But by the time they finally made it the mile and a half back to the cabin, they had both broken their promises.

* * *

Laying his hands on his daughter's head, Joe struggled with the words that came into his mind. This wasn't like when he had struggled to give Heather a blessing. He felt the Spirit strongly and knew the words he needed to speak. These just weren't the words he wanted. He had felt God's power move through him to cure his wife, and he wanted desperately to do the same for his daughter. He would give anything to speak the same words he had spoken only the day before. Trading his own life for the power to breathe healing back into Angela would be a bargain. But even if he spoke the exact same words now, they would be powerless. A lie.

"Angela, I bless you that the Lord's will be done." The words were bitter worms in his mouth. The Lord's will. Who knew the Lord's will? Who could guess why He saved one person and not another? Still Joe did what he could, what the Spirit that whispered to him allowed. He blessed her with comfort, that she would be able to rest. That her pain would ease and that she would find her burdens bearable. I bless you with your Heavenly Father's love, and with all the love that your family has to give you, in the name of Jesus Christ, amen."

As he concluded his prayer, he opened his eyes and met his wife's questioning gaze. Reading the question she dared not ask, he shook his head. "It's in God's hands now. We can only pray that He will choose to save her." Standing next to the beautiful little bed their grandfather had crafted, Richie and Debbie wiped the tears from their eyes and the four of them looked down at Angela who was lying peacefully on her frilly pink pillow.

"Duhkee," she whispered with a smile and then drifted off to sleep.

After they had left the bedroom, Joe took Heather's hands in his.

"I have to leave now."

"I know." She nodded. "Will you take Richie with you?"

"No." He shook his head. "Not this time."

"Why not?"

There were many answers he could have given. He was the only one with any hope of finding his way out. If something happened to him out there Richie might not even be able to find his way back to the cabin. The family needed to stay together. But the truth was far more simple. "I don't know. I just know that I have to do this alone, and Richie needs to stay here."

"All right." Perhaps Heather had felt this as well, perhaps she just saw the same determination in his eyes that he had seen in hers. Angela didn't have long. They all felt it. And the only hope of saving her was for Joe to bring back help tonight. "Can you make it?"

"I have to." There wasn't anything more to say. They didn't need to ask what would happen if he didn't. Who would find him and when? What would happen to Angela? They were questions that answered themselves.

Hugging each member of his family as if they would never see each other again, he shouldered the small pack that contained enough water and food to get him out to the highway, and walked out the door.

CHAPTER 15

The noon sun sent heat ripples off the top of the black Lincoln Navigator as Joe walked past it, turning the lake and mountains beyond into a rippling surreal landscape. The car itself might as well have been a piece of modern art too, Joe thought, for all the good it could do him. There it sat, nearly three quarters full of gas, capable of getting his daughter back to civilization in the time it would take him to cover seven or eight miles. But without the keys it was of no more use in getting them help than the maroon outhouse, and he turned his head away as he passed it, trying not to think about how dumb it had been not to bring a spare set of keys.

By the time he reached the gate, sweat streamed down his face and his T-shirt stuck to his back. The cool of the night before was only a memory, and his head pounded with the rhythm of his steps. As he swung back the big metal bar, a sparrow swooped down from a nearby pine to land on the gatepost, chirped inquisitively, and when he ignored it, flew away in search of something else to satisfy its curiosity. He left the gate open—the ambulance driver wouldn't want to slow down on the way in—and tried to keep his aching legs and arms pumping along at a steady mile-eating pace.

Would his father ever have gotten his family into a situation like this? The question was absurd. This was the man who had replaced the fan belt on their '66 station wagon with a pair of nylon pantyhose when it snapped in the middle of the Nevada desert, and then somehow made it last seventy-five miles to the next town. His father could repair a broken toilet with a hanger and a pair of pliers, and could calculate in his head the board feet necessary to add a bedroom onto their house. He would have found some way to jump-start the car, or more likely would never have found himself keyless in the first place. Dad was a firm believer in the magnetic spare key holder tucked under the back bumper.

"Why'd you do it, Dad?" Somewhere in the distance a wood-pecker stopped its rapid-fire tapping at the sound of a human voice out here in the middle of nowhere. "Why did you build those extra rooms onto the back of the cabin and decorate them the way you did? You didn't build that little fairyland for Debbie. She was almost too old for it even back then. But you weren't building for back then, were you? The books you left for Richie weren't for a three-year-old, they were for a young teenager whose father might not have read him some of the classics you read to me.

"Somehow you knew that we would be up here now. You knew that Richie would treasure that room you built for him, just like you knew that Debbie would need that picture of the Savior. And you knew that somewhere down the line we would have a special little girl who would learn everything she needed to know about the grandfa-ther she never met from the wonderland he built for her. Were you one of the friends that joined her for tea every day?" There was no answer, but he didn't need one. His father's words were in the gentle creaking of the tall pines, in the chirping of the birds, and the chat-tering of the chipmunks and squirrels.

When he'd realized that his father had been preparing the cabin for their return, Joe had surreptitiously searched each of the rooms for a note—some letter tucked away for the moment when his only child would bring his family to the cabin he had loved. He had been a little disappointed when it hadn't turned up. But now he understood that his father's last message of love had been the cabin itself.

"I guess that makes you some kind of prophet." Talking to himself seemed okay out here. Isolated among thousands of acres of uninhab-ited forest, it felt natural—as though he were speaking to someone who chose to remain just out of sight. "Heather and I had never talked about having any more children, and I couldn't have guessed even a month ago that Debbie would experience a real crisis of faith.

"No, not a prophet. A builder. That's what parents do. They work and sweat and save so that they can build something for their children and grandchildren. When you rock a helpless infant in your arms for the first time, you have no idea what the future holds for the child. You have to take it on faith that you'll be able to provide for needs that you can't even imagine at the time.

"But what have I built for my own children? Everything I've sweat and saved for is gone. I can't even afford the cost of Debbie's textbooks, and by the time I get back home, I might not have a home to return to. Does that make me a failure?" If there was an answer in the sounds of the forest, he couldn't understand it. He was left to ponder his thoughts alone, but his journey seemed just a little more bearable. If he closed his eyes, and listened closely, he thought he could hear the soft tread of someone walking beside him and the faint tuneless whistle that had always marked his father's approach as they roamed the woods together.

* * *

"Have . . . to . . . rest . . . a minute." Joe dropped onto the side of the road and leaned back against a tree. Shaking first one and then the other of his water bottles, he found that they were both empty. He thought that he had remembered to fill them at the last creek he crossed. Could he really have emptied them both so quickly? Perhaps he had forgotten. He placed the back of his hand against his forehead and thought it might feel feverish. But then again, his whole body felt feverish so how could he really tell for sure?

"Too far to . . . go back . . . anyway," he huffed. He couldn't recall whether it had been a mile ago or three, but both distances made doubling back out of the question. He would just have to tank up again at the next sign of water. Until then, he had to content himself with squeezing every drop of moisture out of the last of the grapes he had in his pack. He considered one of the peanut-butter-and-jelly sandwiches Heather had packed for him, but finally decided against it. His stomach had started feeling a little queasy some time ago. It might have been the creek water, but he thought it more likely to be just another of the symptoms of this disease that seemed determined to tear his body apart.

"Okay, back on your feet, Dad. We sit here any longer and you might fall asleep." Joe tried to get his legs under him and found that he couldn't do it without turning around and using the tree for support. Favoring his right leg as he moved down the road made his left leg ache even worse, but he couldn't help it. A few hours into his hike something felt like it had come loose in his right hip and now it ached with every step. If he didn't pay close attention, he found himself beginning to walk off the side of the road.

"You know, Dad, I met a guy up here that I think you'd like. To be honest I'm not entirely sure that I didn't just hallucinate him. Although I seem to remember him giving something to one of the children, Angela I think. Anyway, he was a pretty nice old guy. I think you'd like him. Did I say that already? He gave me some pretty good advice. Talked about being patient with the kids, and recognizing that I couldn't control everything. But here's the strange part . . ." Joe paused as the road he was on came to an end, forming a "T" with a gravel lane.

"Don't exactly remember this stretch." Joe stood at the junction of the two roads peering first to the left and then the right, searching for something familiar—some kind of landmark that might give him a clue. Those two trees that leaned against each other, seeming to almost kiss, looked like something he might have seen before. But could he be sure? The rain had washed away any tire tracks he might have left coming in, and neither direction looked like it had seen more traffic than the other.

"What do you think, Dad, right?" If his father had any ideas he wasn't sharing them, so Joe shrugged and went in the direction of the two trees. If it started to look wrong, he could always turn back.

"So anyway, I was telling you about this guy. See, I think that he believes he's actually Job. The one in the Bible. When he told me about half of his children dying, I got to thinking. And then before I went to bed last night, I looked it up. He told me his daughter's name was Keren-something, 'happy' or 'hiccup'. At first I thought he was saying Karen—like Karen Carpenter the singer. But in the last chapter of the book of Job it says that he had three more daughters. Really beautiful I guess. But the youngest one was named Keren, just like he said.

"So what do you think? Could someone who was dead actually come back just to give advice to a guy like me? I know it seems prideful, assuming that someone right out of the Bible would come back to Earth just to visit you. Can you imagine if I told the high priests back at church that I ate fish with Job? You know, when most people read the book of Job, they think of him as this person who suffered a lot without complaining. But maybe the real message of the story is what he was trying to tell me. That we can't control what happens to us, but we *can* control what we do about it—what we learn from it."

Joe stopped at a small concrete bridge, probably built by the CCC during the great depression. There was water flowing under it, not much, but enough to fill his bottles. But the steep bank going down to it looked daunting. He could get down, sliding on the seat of his pants if he had to, but could he make it back up? Which was the greater risk, the embankment or thirst?

"Alright, I'm going to try to make it down there to get a drink. Think I might pass out soon if I don't. But first I want to ask you a question. This might seem a little loony, but I'm not feeling the best right now so bear with me. Is there any chance that after you died you might have met this Job, the actual one from the Bible? I remember that you always liked reading the book of Job. So if you met him, and you knew that he was a pretty sharp guy, and you knew that all this was going to happen to me, is it possible that *you* asked him to come down and give me a hand?"

After thinking it over for a few minutes Joe decided that it *was* possible. "Listen Dad, if he's around, you might want to go get him. Because I'm pretty heavy and I think you might need a little help to pull me back up out of that creek."

* * *

"I found him . . . by . . . by the . . . fountain . . ." Joe stumbled over the words to "A Poor Wayfaring Man of Grief," the lyrics of the hymn barely audible, the tune nonexistent. "No, I did . . . that . . . part . . . already . . . by the . . . the . . . the highway." *Of course, by the highway side. How could I have forgotten that?* Joe laughed, weakly, bending over at the waist and clutching his thighs, but his laugh turned into a coughing spell that he wasn't sure he would be able to stop. He emptied the remaining drops from his water bottle into his mouth, gagged, and spit the liquid back out onto the road. It was the last of his water, and he wouldn't have the strength to get more, but at least his coughing had stopped. The bottle dropped from his hand and rolled slowly to the side of the road. No point in trying to pick it up. It would take more energy than it was worth, more strength than he could muster.

In the sky, the moon and a few of the brightest stars were beginning to appear as the last rays of sunlight disappeared behind the mountains. How had it grown so dark so quickly? He had left at noon, or was it one? Either way, he should have been able to cover the twenty-five miles back to the freeway in six hours or seven at the most. And now it was . . . He stared dumbly at the spot where his watch had been. That it was gone didn't really bother him—he didn't imagine anyone would be asking him for the time in the next few hours—but that he couldn't remember taking it off . . .

"Keep . . . keep . . . moving," he commanded his legs, but for a moment he wasn't sure that they would obey. Finally his left leg dragged forward. Two inches . . . six . . . ten, and then reluctantly his right did the same. He had to keep moving. If he stopped now, Angela would never make it. And how would his family find their way out? He *had* to keep moving.

What song had he been singing? His father had suggested it, or maybe it had been the prospector . . . not the prospector, Job, he corrected himself. Job seemed to be especially fond of the old favorites, the ones that missionaries always requested for their farewells. "Onward Christian Soldiers" or "Hail, Hail, the Gang's All Here." No that wasn't right. Whatever it was, Joe didn't think he had the strength left to sing anyway.

"Guys, I . . . think . . . I'm . . . l, l, . . . lo . . . " But his lips would no longer form the words, so he continued speaking mutely, inside his head. Not that there was really anyone there to listen anyway. The conversations had just been his way of taking his mind off of the pain. Something to make the hours and miles pass more quickly. *I think I'm lost. Should have hit the highway hours ago. Thought I was going to make it when I reached the blacktop, but still haven't heard a single car. Must have made a bad turn. Don't think I can make it much . . . No!*

He stared down at his legs again, realizing that they had stopped moving. How long had he been standing motionless at the edge of the road, while his mind was elsewhere?

"Mo . . . ove." The word came out in a hoarse strangled whisper that Joe could barely recognize as his own voice, but this time his legs refused to budge. "Come on, move," he cried, striking at his legs, demanding that his body obey him. First one and then the other of his legs wobbled, jerked, and finally collapsed, dropping him into the brush at the side of the road.

Panicked, he grabbed the branches of a small bush and dragged himself back onto the road. He would crawl if he had to, pulling himself along the asphalt a foot or an inch at a time, whatever it took. But despite his resolve, his arms gave out after less than ten feet, and as his chin dropped to the pavement, he was forced to realize, at last, that he had failed.

Disintegration. Piece by piece over the last ten days, the mortar that held together the bricks that made up Joe Stewart had been chipped away until there was nothing left. He found himself trapped in the dark morass, a place where doubt is king and self-loathing the currency in-kind. It was the place reserved for those who feel that they have broken the sacred trust of caring for their families—and there was no way out.

"Joe." It was the voice of the prospector.

Go away.

"Joe."

Too late, can't make it. Where were you when I needed you?

"Here, all along."

Joe forced his eyes open, and as he expected, the road was empty. He was alone. *No. You're just in my head.*

"Yes."

Going crazy.

"No."

I failed.

"No."

She's going to die because I failed.

"You still don't understand, do you Joe? You can't do this alone. You succeed or fail together, as a family. And your family succeeded. Just as I knew you would. Just as your father knew you would."

But we didn't save her.

"That was not your purpose."

Then what was *our purpose? Why did you bring us here?*

"What do you deem most valuable, Joe Stewart?"

My family, of course.

"Do you?"

Yes. I mean No. I mean . . . I don't know what I think anymore. He could feel his brain shutting down completely—his focus disappearing into a long black tunnel—but he had to at least finish this conversation first.

"You shared it with each one of them when they needed it most, while at the same time clinging to it when many would have cast it aside. You've been protecting it all along without even realizing it."

I . . . it . . . The answer was near, Joe could feel it buzzing around in his head like an evasive fly, but before he could grab hold of it, it disappeared into the darkness that finally enfolded him.

"My son, peace be unto thy soul; thine adversity and thine afflictions shall be but a small moment." The voice that spoke to him was neither the voice of the prospector nor the voice of his father, but a quiet whisper. And yet it was filled with such love, such peace, and such comfort that his spirit was at last able to rest, and he lay his fevered brow onto the roadway, not yet cooled by the night air, and closed his eyes.

* * *

Hands, grabbing, pulling. "Dad." *Someone's calling me?*

The feel of his body being pulled from the road. His legs refusing to help as he was dragged toward a light. "Joe. Wake up. He's burning up. Drink this." *Heather?*

He was in his car. But that was not possible. The keys were . . . were there, dangling from the ignition. How could that be? They were at the bottom of the lake, irrecoverable. Heather was pressing something into his mouth. He didn't think he would be able to swallow, but cool water washed the pills down his throat.

"Just relax, we're almost back to the freeway." The car began to move and Joe weakly turned his head. Heather was driving. Angela, her eyes closed, lay across the middle seat, her chest weakly rising and falling. Debbie and Richie leaned forward from the back.

"Are you okay, Dad? Can you hear us?" they asked. He tried to answer *yes*, but fell back asleep instead.

The car had stopped and Heather was speaking into his cell phone. *There's no service up here,* he began to tell her, but then heard the fuzzy sound of someone's voice coming from the speaker. That would mean they were . . . Through the windshield he saw the green street sign that marked the exit from highway 163. They'd made it back to civilization.

"A helicopter? That would be perfect. But please hurry. He is very sick and I don't know how long *she* can hang on." Heather disconnected the line and realized that Joe was awake. "How are you feeling?"

"Water," he croaked. Heather pressed a cup into his hands and helped steady it as he let the liquid trickle slowly down his throat. His body responded to the aspirin and water immediately. "How?"

Heather smiled softly, her eyes glowing in the light of the dashboard instruments. "You can thank the kids."

"No, it was Mom too," Debbie said from the backseat, "If she hadn't thought of the cabinets, it never would have worked."

"It was Debbie's idea to pray," Richie said, and Joe craned his neck around to look at his daughter.

"No, it was your idea, Dad. I just remembered what you said." Debbie seemed almost embarrassed. "I was up in my room, worrying about you and Angela, and I saw Grandma's picture. You know, that one where Jesus is knocking on the door?" Joe nodded.

"I remembered what you said about how the Savior wanted to help us, but we had to let Him in. So I went downstairs and got Mom and Richie. I felt kind of dumb, asking everyone to pray after the things I've said lately. But I thought that if I ever needed the Lord's help it was then. And I would never have forgiven myself if I hadn't allowed Him to help me just because I wouldn't open the door."

"It was a beautiful prayer," Heather said. "I was so proud of her. I wish you could have heard it."

"So when we finished praying, I still didn't know what to do," Debbie continued. "But Richie suddenly jumped up and ran out to get one of the fishing poles."

"I know it sounds kind of dumb," Richie said, "but when Debbie was praying, I kept getting this image in my mind of the car keys. I knew they were lost for good, but for some reason I just kept seeing myself in the canoe with a fishing pole reeling them in. I don't know what I thought I could hook them with, maybe just a lure or something. But I knew I had to try. Then Mom thought of the cabinets."

"When I realized what Richie was trying to do, I thought about how hard it would be to hook the key ring. After all it's not like the keys were going to jump up and hook themselves. I thought that what we really needed was a magnet of some kind, and suddenly I remembered the catches on the cabinet doors. They are all magnets. I actually dropped a spoon once and it stuck right to the catch. So I thought that maybe if we unscrewed a few of them from the wood and tied them all together . . ."

"And it worked, Dad." Richie was nearly bouncing in the back seat. "I dropped the line from the canoe and just kept bobbing it up and down off the bottom, until I felt a tug."

"You guys are . . . I didn't think anyone would find me." But how had they found him? "All the turnoffs, how did you know where to go?" Joe asked.

"It was all right here." Heather tapped the squiggly green line on the car's GPS screen. "It recorded every turn when you drove in, and we just followed it back out."

"How do I thank you all?" Joe wiped at his eyes, trying to find the words that would express how he felt.

"No, we need to thank you, Dad." Debbie spoke quietly. "You were the one who kept saying that Heavenly Father had a plan. Even when we didn't believe, you never lost your faith."

"When I thought I had lost you all . . ." Joe let his words fade away.

"No yost. Finded." Angela's eyes were open, and everyone in the car turned to look at her.

"Sweetheart, you're awake." Joe reached back to take his daughter's hand, still cold despite the warmth of the car.

"Oo . . . finded . . . fambly . . . Addy." Her voice was weak, and she had to inhale between each word, but Joe thought he understood.

"No honey, you found me. I was lost and—"

"No." Angela interrupted him, her voice soft but her face fierce with determination. She bit her lip, closed her eyes, and her tiny blood-streaked brow furrowed. Suddenly it was as if the top of the car was no longer there, the starry night clearly visible. For a moment the heavens seemed to shiver and fade, and then they were replaced by the image of Joe standing alone, surrounded by a thick dark fog. He looked around him, seemed to shout something, and then extended his hand into the fog.

The fog cleared just enough to show Heather, taking her husband's hand. Then she too reached into the darkness and took Debbie's hand. As Debbie's fingers closed around Richie's, the family began to move together, forming a circle. Finally Richie took Angela's hand, pulling her out of the mist. As the circle closed, a ring of white fire seemed to glow from the family, burning back the darkness until it became obvious that another circle of people surrounded them. Joe recognized his father and mother, and his grandparents. Heather's mother, who had died when Heather was still a little girl, suddenly appeared holding the hand of her father. And beyond them yet another circle of faces appeared from the mist.

As if it were a great wave, the white fire jumped from one circle to the next, devouring the darkness as it went and revealing thousands of people, millions. Some of the faces were familiar to him, remembered from pictures in old albums or just bearing familial resemblances. But many of them were unknown. Still, Joe thought he understood that he was seeing the lineage of the Stewart family linking back all the way to Adam and Eve. He realized that all of the people were singing. He couldn't understand the words, but from the looks on their faces it seemed to be a song of great joy.

And at the center of the circle, Angela was squirming, nearly dancing with happiness as she looked at all the people surrounding her. Her mouth was opening and closing, singing the words to the unknown hymn of joy, and her face shown brighter than even the fire.

"Finded." Angela's voice was barely audible, and as the image disappeared and the top of the car returned, Joe realized how much of her strength it had taken to show them what she had.

"I understand now."

"Duhkee . . . finta . . . fambly."

"Shh." Joe pressed his fingers to her lips. "Just rest."

"Cad go dow."

"No not yet. But soon. We can go just as soon as the helicopter gets here. It'll be a fun ride."

Angela shook her head slightly, the motion barely perceptible. "Finta . . . fambly. Cad . . . go . . . now." And suddenly Joe understood.

"No you can't go. I can't lose you again. *We* can't lose you, we need you. Just hang on a few more minutes, baby."

Angela held out her hand to him and Joe squeezed back between the bucket seats to reach her side. "Ot yost. Ony aitin." She concentrated and formed the word again carefully. "Wait-ing."

She took his face in her tiny cool hands as he shook his head back and forth, tears welling from his eyes, and pulled him close.

"Patafwy . . . kiz . . . Addy?" her voice was barely a whisper now.

He pressed his face against hers, the tears from his rough, whiskered face dripping onto her soft pink cheek, and brushed his eyelashes open and closed against her skin.

"Duhkee . . . patafwy . . . kiz." He felt the soft brush of her lashes against his cheek. Blink. Blink. Blink. And then her bright blue eyes closed for good.

EPILOGUE

And so it was that Joe and his family returned to the valley of chips and disks. And there he laid to rest his youngest daughter. One who had brought much joy and light to the earth in the brief time she was there. The stone that marked her resting place was small and plain, he being a man of humble means. The inscription upon it read simply, "Our Angel." The only decoration, an unadorned, but strangely beautiful engraving of a lovely woman astride a donkey. Those unfamiliar with the family might have mistaken the woman for the Virgin Mary.

And when they saw that he was a blameless man, wrongly accused by those around him, those who had turned against him repented of the things they had spoken and returned to his house to comfort him. But those who had never doubted him remained at his side in good times and bad.

So the Lord blessed the latter end of Joe more than his beginning. Not in earthly treasures, for Joe had learned that those came and went as the sands of the sea blow in the ocean breezes, but in that which he deemed most valuable, his love of God. For he had learned that with *that,* true bonds form between a family that cannot be hewn by trials, nor by the storms of adversity, nor by the sword of death itself.

And he lived many years in a house, not so grand as that which he had owned before, but adequate for the needs of his family. And he and his wife watched their children grow and find spouses, and have children of their own. And they often traveled to the cabin in the mountains, now expanded even more to fit the needs of their families. And as they watched the children splash in the lake and explore the woods, they agreed that no grandchildren were as smart and beautiful as theirs.

And although the daughter he had lost could never be replaced, he thought of her often and felt her presence close to him many times. He knew that she was safe and watched over, for in the hour that she passed from him, with tears still clouding his vision, he had looked into the night. And there he had seen two men standing beside a donkey. And on the donkey rode a woman so fair and beautiful that words could not possibly describe her, and around her shown a light so bright that it put the stars in the firmament to shame. And in that moment, he knew that he could not ask for two more capable guides to return his daughter home.

So being full of years Joe died, and as he passed from this world to the next he saw a house with welcoming light streaming out of its windows. From the open front door came the comforting smells of freshly baked bread and hot buttered corn. And standing on the front porch, waiting to welcome him home was his Angel. And as he hurried forward to feel her arms around his neck and her kiss on his cheek, he repeated the four words he had whispered so long ago, "Thy will be done."

ABOUT THE AUTHOR

Author of the best-selling, high-tech thriller *Cutting Edge*, Jeffrey S. Savage enjoys writing novels that keep readers on the edge of their seats. (He loves it when readers tell him they were up until the wee hours because they had to know how a story would end.)

Jeffrey was born in Oakland, California, and spent most of his youth in the greater Bay Area. He served a mission for The Church of Jesus Christ of Latter-day Saints in the Utah Salt Lake North Mission. He met his wife, Jennifer, in an institute class and they were married four months later in the Oakland Temple. They currently reside in Spanish Fork, Utah, where he serves in the Sunday School presidency, and teaches the youth as often as they will let him. Jeffrey and Jennifer have four wonderful children, with whom they enjoy games, reading, computers, and outdoor activities.